Victim Rights
a ryan dooley mystery

Norah McClintock

Red Deer P R E S S

Published by Red Deer Press
A Fitzhenry & Whiteside Company
195 Allstate Parkway, Markham
ON, L3R 4T8
www.reddeerpress.com

Edited for the Press by Peter Carver
Cover and text design by Jacquie Morris & Delta Embree, Liverpool, Nova Scotia, Canada
Printed and bound in Canada

We acknowledge with thanks the Canada Council for the Arts, and the Ontario Arts Council for their
support of our publishing program. We acknowledge the financial support of the Government of Canada
through the Book Publishing Industry Development Program (BPIDP) for our publishing activities.

 Canada Council for the Arts   **Conseil des Arts du Canada**   **ONTARIO ARTS COUNCIL CONSEIL DES ARTS DE L'ONTARIO**

Library and Archives Canada Cataloguing in Publication
McClintock, Norah
Victim rights / Norah McClintock.
(A Ryan Dooley mystery)
ISBN 978-0-88995-447-2
I. Title. II. Series: McClintock, Norah. Ryan Dooley mystery.
PS8575.C62V52 2010   jC813'.54   C2010-904509-2

Publisher Cataloging-in-Publication Data (U.S)
McClintock, Norah.
Victim rights : a Ryan Dooley mystery /Norah McClintock.
[340] p. : cm.
ISBN: 978-0-88995-447-2 (pbk.)
1. Mystery and detective stories. I. Title. II. Ryan Dooley mystery.
[Fic] dc22   PZ7.M34656Vi 2010

 **Mixed Sources**
Product group from well-managed
forests, controlled sources and
recycled wood or fiber
www.fsc.org Cert no. SW-COC-002358
© 1996 Forest Stewardship Council

 **ANCIENT FOREST ™ FRIENDLY**

To Peter Carver and Richard Dionne,

for making it possible

So far, so good. Dooley made it back to his uncle's house without running into anyone he knew and, as far as he could tell, without anyone taking special notice of him. With the exception of the light on his uncle's front porch, the house was dark, which meant that his uncle had made an early night of it, either because he was tired or because Jeannie was over. As Dooley walked up the driveway, he pondered his options.

His sweatshirt was the worst. He had actually felt blood splatter on it. He'd peeled it off before he got back to the street, rolled it up, and dropped it in under a couple of rank-smelling garbage bags in one of a row of garbage bins behind an apartment building he'd passed. No way would the cops ever think to look there. Garbage pickup was first thing Monday morning. The sweatshirt would be on its way to a landfill site in Michigan by Monday night at the latest.

But what about the rest of his clothes? He'd seen his share of crime-scene shows on TV. He'd also heard his uncle grouse that they should be billed as fantasy, they were that unrealistic. Some of the things they did on those shows were made up. Some of it was stuff some brainiac had thought up and experimented with but hadn't been adopted by any crime lab his uncle had ever heard of—and his uncle stayed on top of things, even though he was retired. Some of the things they did on those shows took minutes, whereas in real life, his uncle said, it could take months—if you were lucky. But he'd also heard his uncle and his cop friends tell their war stories: how they'd nailed some guy because he'd decided to hang onto some piece-of-shit jacket or a pair of crappy boots that had turned up trace evidence—blood, spit, semen, you name it. How some other mope had put his clothes through the wash, thinking that would do the trick. Well, guess what, Charlie? It doesn't. How maybe some of the knuckleheads and psychos that got themselves into trouble would benefit from checking out some of those shows, but thank Christ they didn't, or at least were impervious to learning anything from them if they did because, really, who needed the job to get any more com-plicated than it already was?

Dooley was pretty sure, although not positive, that he didn't have to worry about the cops. He was pretty sure the guy wasn't going to lay a complaint. No, Dooley's biggest worry was keep-ing his uncle from getting suspicious.

He used his key to slip in through the back door and went straight down to the basement where he stripped off his clothes, removed his sneakers, and shoved everything, even the shoes, into the washing machine. He set the water on extra hot, mea-sured detergent and bleach (for the unbleachables) into the right slots, and pushed ON. While the tub filled, he fished out and put on a pair of shorts and a t-shirt from the pile of clothes he'd brought down two days ago but had never got around to washing. What the hell—he opened the washer lid and threw in the rest of the dirty clothes pile. Then he went upstairs.

He walked straight through the kitchen, even though he was starving (go figure) and continued on up to his room. He clocked his uncle's room on the way. The door was closed, which meant that Jeannie was in there. If he'd come through the front door instead of the back, he probably would have seen her purse on the table next to the stairs. The lights were off, too, so, hopefully, they were both asleep. Either that or ... well, he didn't want to think about it. He ducked into his room, grabbed a clean T-shirt and pajama bottoms, and went to the bathroom to shower. He was back in his room, hair still damp, when his uncle knocked on his door. Shit.

"Yeah?" Dooley said.

His uncle looked relaxed when he stepped into the room. Only Jeannie had that effect on him.

"Is that the washing machine I hear?" he said.

Jesus. The guy must have been some ace cop way back whenever. Dooley couldn't hear a thing. The washing machine was at the back of the basement two floors down. His uncle's room was at the front of the house.

"Did it wake you up?" Dooley said.

His uncle ignored the question.

"I nag you every week, *every week*, Ryan, to do your laundry, and now, all of a sudden, you get the urge to do it at—" His eyes flicked to the clock-radio on Dooley's bedside table. "—at one in the morning?"

"Some guy came up to me on the way home. He was totally wasted. He hit on me for some money. Halfway through his spiel, he puked all over me—and I mean *all* over me. I couldn't wait to get home, strip down, and shower."

His uncle stared at him. Dooley met his eyes full on.

"I know what you're thinking," he said. "You're thinking if I don't stay clean, that guy could be me in twenty years."

"If you don't stay clean," his uncle said, "you'll be in prison or dead and it won't take twenty years."

Right.

"Get some sleep," his uncle said.

Easier said than done. Dooley kept replaying the night. Jesus, what had he done? More to the point, *why* had he done it? And what would happen next? That was the part he always hated, the part that had him looking to sniff, smoke, inject, or otherwise pump himself full of whatever it would take to put himself up there in the stars, far, far from all the bullshit down here on earth.

◆ ◆ ◆

At first, when Dooley ran through the sequence of events, he would say that it had started the day that Nevin, of all people, walked up to the counter of the video store where Dooley worked and, to Dooley's complete surprise, started to talk to him instead of doing what he usually did, which was either ignore him or, more often, regard him with a detached superiority. But as time went on, he realized that, no, it had started earlier than that, namely, two days before Beth and her entire home form were scheduled to go up north to Camp Whatchamacallit, some phonied-up native name, in so-called cottage country where the so-called cottages were all million-dollar-plus homes with hot tubs and entertainment centers and well-stocked docks. That was when he'd found out that Beth's class had been paired with the home form of another private school—a boys' school—and that it just happened to be Nevin's school and Nevin's home form. The whole bunch of them would be together for a week doing manual labor for the first and probably last time in their lives. He was surprised when she told him—why did it have to be Nevin, of all people? He hated Nevin, hated everything about him. His surprise turned to a prickly sense of betrayal when it came out that she'd known about the pairing from the get-go, but had "forgotten" to tell him. "It's no big deal," she said.

Maybe it wouldn't have been, if everything had been as smooth and easy between them as it had been even a month earlier. But it wasn't. Dooley had seen less and less of her lately, and it wasn't his choice. She was busy all the time. She was studying harder than ever.

"Study with me," he'd say. And she would roll her eyes and tell him, no, she *really* had to study, she needed to get a scholarship, she was tired of her mother always holding it over her head how much money she was spending to give her the best education money could buy. She was in some kind of study group, she said, with kids whose parents weren't loaded. It was only a couple more weeks, she said, then it would be summer and they'd be able to see each other every night after she finished work—well, assuming Dooley wasn't on shift, which he would be probably four or five nights a week, night being prime movie rental time.

For the past few months, he'd seen her twice a week if he was lucky. And when they were together, it wasn't the way it had been at the beginning. She was tired a lot, which meant he was out of luck most of the time. She complained about how hard she was studying but got angry and said he didn't understand when he told her, "So, take a break."

And now, here she was, going away for a week to build a house, which, she said, would look good on her applications and, besides, it was just one of the things they did at her school—and at Nevin's. They gave back to the community.

So, what shouldn't have been a big deal turned into a winner-take-all hand. She said, "You're going to see me off at the bus, right?"

Wrong, he decided.

"I can't. I have to work." Then, to make it stick, he traded shifts with Linelle. While Beth and her classmates and Nevin and his classmates were getting on the bus and riding up north, Dooley spent the whole day wishing all his customers would drop dead and thinking, too late, that probably all he had accomplished was to piss Beth off or even make her cry, so that now she was ripe for the picking by Nevin or one of the other rich boys she was going to be spending the week with.

Way to go, Dooley.

Before she left, she told him that she would call him every day. In point of fact, she didn't call until Monday, after she had been up there two days, after he'd put his fist through the dry wall in his room and then moved a poster to cover the damage so that his uncle wouldn't start in on him. When he answered his phone and heard her voice, his heart pounded so loudly that he could hardly hear what she was saying, which turned out to be, "You're right. I should have told you. I'm sorry."

Well, okay.

She was having a great time, which, he hated to admit even to himself, irked him.

"You can't believe what I'm learning," she said. "They started me off hammering nails. I must have bent dozens of them before I learned the right technique. Then, yesterday they showed me how to use an electric drill. It was amazing!" Her voice quivered with the excitement of a lottery winner. "The people we're working with are so nice. Some of them are the families who are going to be living in the houses. I'm having the best time, Dooley."

That *really* irked him. And, if he was honest, he knew exactly why. She was up there having the time of her life, without him.

He told her, "That's great." He said, yeah, he was doing okay and, no, just the same old same old. And that was that.

As soon as the call was over, he wished it were just starting, not only because he wanted to hear her voice—although that was part of it—but also because if he had another chance, he'd play it differently. He'd ask her all about what she was learning and who she was learning it with. He'd make sure he sounded as if he really cared what she was up to, as if he were genuinely happy that she was enjoying herself. He'd tell her how much he missed her and, with luck, he'd hear her say how much she missed him, too.

He thought about calling her back, but he didn't have the number and she hadn't taken her cell phone. It was a rule for the trip, one that had caused a huge protest, according to Beth, among both students, who lived to text each other 24/7, and parents, who were used to being able to get hold of their offspring whenever they wanted. Beth had said that on the latter basis alone, she was more than happy to leave her phone at home, since she and her mother were going through a rocky period, due, in large part, to Beth's relationship with Dooley.

She didn't call again until Thursday night. The original plan was that she would be coming home the next day, but that had changed.

"One of the boys here has invited a bunch of us to his country place," she said.

What boy? What country place?

"His name is Parker," she said. "His dad made a fortune during that whole dot-com craze—and I do mean a fortune, Dooley. He was smart. He got out before the bubble burst." What was she even talking about? "I haven't seen the place, but I've heard about it. It's supposed to look like a castle—a huge castle—and it's right on the water, except, of course, it's too cold to go swimming now. But there's a pool. Actually, there are two pools. One indoor. One outdoor."

Because, *of course*, that's exactly what you need when you build a castle on a lake.

"I'll be back Saturday afternoon," she said. "I have to go. My break is over."

She was off the line with his barely having gotten a word in but having framed a clear picture of the guy, Parker, who, he decided, he didn't like, not one bit. And that was before he knew the half of it.

◆ ONE ◆

Fuck!

Dooley saw black and white with flashes of red. He snapped his cell phone shut and spun around, his arm arcing first backward and then forward, and let fly—just as his uncle stepped into the kitchen, sweat-drenched after a mid-Sunday-afternoon run. By then, the phone was sailing across the kitchen, on its way to a rendezvous with the ceramic backsplash that ran from the countertop to the bottom of the cupboards along the wall where the sink and stove were, ETA 0.05 seconds, give or take a nanosecond.

Zlat! Dooley's uncle's hand shot out and fielded the phone.

"What the hell's the matter with you?" he said, pissed off. "You have any idea how much that tile cost? You know what would happen if you cracked one?" Dooley had a pretty good idea, based on the two questions his uncle had just asked. "You want to know what my chances would be of matching that tile? Zilch—that's what."

He was good and mad, looking at Dooley like he was wondering what this hothead was even doing in his kitchen—a solid question, given that he wasn't really Dooley's uncle, and one that remained, as yet, unanswered. He flipped the phone back to Dooley.

"What flew up your nose, anyway?"

"Nothing," Dooley said. It had started off as a miserable

day, and it hadn't gotten any better. He wanted—*needed*—to throw something. Break something. Smash something to tiny little pieces.

His uncle crossed to the fridge, pulled out a cold beer— his after-workout ritual—and popped it right there in front of Dooley. Dooley never knew if he did it on purpose, his way of torturing him, or if he was completely oblivious to the way the *shhhtt!* of the cap coming off and the beading of the water drop-lets on the outside of the bottle made Dooley thirstier than he had ever been—another question as yet unanswered. His uncle upended the bottle and swallowed down half the contents. It must have been a hell of a run, Dooley thought. Or maybe he was reliving the previous day at the store, maybe remembering some woman who had bitched at him over missing buttons or stains that hadn't come out. His uncle was in the dry-cleaning business.

"You talk to Beth yet?" his uncle said. "Did she have a good time?"

Dooley looked sharply at him, surprised that he had remem-bered about Beth's trip and, at the same time, not surprised. His uncle used to be a cop, after all, and cops, the ones that are any good, notice stuff and remember stuff.

His uncle studied him a moment and set down his beer.

"Problem?"

Dooley shook his head. He shoved his phone into his jeans pocket.

"I gotta go."

"Go where?"

"To work."

"I thought you were off today."

"Linelle had something she had to do. I said I'd cover for her."

His uncle peered at him for a moment, wary now. It seemed to Dooley that he'd been that way for months. "Look, Ryan, if there's anything you want to talk about ..."

"I'm gonna be late."

First thing when Dooley walked through the door to the video store where he worked part-time, Kevin, the shift manager, was in his face, waving the weekly schedule in one hand and a sheet of paper in the other.

"Did you do this?" he said, spraying Dooley with droplets of spit. He shoved the schedule in Dooley's face.

Dooley wiped his face with his hand. "Do what?"

"This," Kevin said. He jabbed the Saturday night column.

Dooley peered at it. His name had been crossed out and Linelle's name had been scrawled in above it.

"Yeah." He circled around Kevin.

"I'm not finished talking to you yet," Kevin said.

Dooley's instinct was to keep moving to the back of the store, to the small windowless closet that Kevin referred to as the staff room, and change into his red polo shirt with the name tag attached to it. But Kevin had leapfrogged in front of him.

"Who authorized this change?" he demanded.

"I told you two weeks ago that I needed next Saturday night off," Dooley said. Next Saturday was the six-month anniversary of his first official date with Beth. He'd figured she'd like it if he remembered it and planned something special. But now, having spent all night trying—and failing—to get her on the phone, he wasn't so sure.

"Told me?" Kevin's face had turned almost as red as his shirt. "You *told* me?"

"Yeah. But you went ahead and scheduled me in anyway. Linelle offered to cover the shift for me."

"You need to get permission for that."

"Since when?"

"Since when?" Kevin shook his head. "Even Linelle knows the drill, for crying out loud." He waved the schedule in front of Dooley again. "What do you see next to your name in to-day's box?" Then, before Dooley could answer, "My initials. Because Linelle—*Linelle*, Dooley—came to me, *as per procedure*, and got my approval for you to cover her shift for her today. And you know why? Because *Linelle* took the time to read the memo posted in the staff room." Kevin shoved the other piece of paper in Dooley's face. Dooley only had enough time to read the words "memo" and "scheduling" before Kevin whipped the paper away again and started reading aloud from it, the gist of it being that from now on, all shift changes had to be approved by a shift manager in advance and that no employee was permitted to work more than forty hours a week, a dodge, Dooley bet, to avoid having to pay overtime.

Dooley made a note to talk to Linelle. Jesus, she never played by the rules. In fact, she considered it a point of pride to dodge as many rules as possible. If you couldn't count on Linelle to ball up a memo and shoot baskets with it, who could you count on?

"I didn't see that," he said, aware of how lame he sounded and resenting Kevin for making him feel that way.

"Ignorance is no excuse."

Ignorance? Dooley felt like popping him one. A year ago, he probably would have. But now? Well, now he knew that, sure, it would make him feel pretty good and, sure, it would guarantee that he wouldn't have to work next Saturday, but that would be because he'd been fired. So instead, he sucked it up and said, "It won't happen again."

"It won't happen, period," Kevin said. "Policy is policy. You're scheduled to work. You didn't get the change approved. You're just going to have to live with it."

"Or," Dooley said, working to keep any sense of menace out of his voice, "you could approve the switch."

"What kind of precedent would that set?" Kevin said.

Prick.

"Maybe the precedent that every now and then you're not such a tight-assed little bureaucrat."

Kevin stared at him, open-mouthed. Then he pulled himself up straight so that the top of his head reached Dooley's shoulder.

Up front, the electronic bell over the door sounded. For once, Kevin didn't check to see if a potential shoplifter was entering the store.

"I do not approve the switch," he said. "You work the shift or you're fired. You got that? And don't even think about calling in sick. You're here Saturday night or you're through. It's right here in the memo. No deviance from the policy will be tolerated. It's signed by the Ops Manager. The Ops Manager, Dooley. And it applies to everyone. You mess with it, and Mr. Fielding won't be able to bail you out."

Mr. Fielding, the area manager, had hired Dooley, even though—or maybe because—Dooley had been straight with him about his record. Whenever Mr. Fielding came into the store, he always stopped and chatted with Dooley. Kevin hovered around when that happened, trying to find out what Mr. Fielding was laughing at, probably worried, Dooley thought, that Dooley was telling stories about him.

"You got me, Dooley?" Kevin said.

One more kick from an already bullshit day.

"Whatever," Dooley said. Under his breath, he muttered, "Asshole."

"I heard that." Kevin scowled at Dooley. "Don't mess with my schedule again." He wheeled around and headed for the front counter.

Dooley slammed into the "staff room," changed into his shirt and stupid name tag, and went back into the store again, where he nearly collided with Alicia. She grinned when she saw him. Alicia was the only person Dooley knew who was always overjoyed to see him. He couldn't help himself. He smiled.

"How's it going, Alicia?" He glanced behind her to her brother Warren. "Man, you looked wiped." Warren's round face looked wan, and his eyes, behind thick lenses, were glassy.

"I haven't been to bed yet. I worked last night, and then some guy called in sick this morning, so they asked me to stay. I did a double."

"Worked? You got a job?"

"At the hospital. As a cleaner. A couple of evenings a week, nights on Fridays and Saturdays, plus filling in if they need someone last minute."

"A *cleaner*?" Dooley said.

"It's what they had. And it's union. It pays nearly twice what you make here."

Dooley whistled.

"You saving for a car or something?" he said.

Warren turned to his sister. "Why don't you go and look around, Leesh? I'll be there as soon as I finish talking to Dooley."

"To Ryan," Alicia said. She was one of the few people who

called him by his given name. She said she liked it better than Dooley.

"We got a new penguin movie in," Dooley said. "This one's a cartoon. Check it out, Alicia. It's on the top shelf."

She beamed at him and headed for the kids' section. Alicia was a year older than Warren. She had Down's. Warren was protective of her. He watched her go. He also scanned the kids' section to see if there was anyone there who might conceivably give her a hard time. There wasn't. When she was safely out of earshot, he dropped his voice.

"My mom sends her to this special camp every summer. Up until this year, she's been able to get a grant to do it. But with all the cutbacks that have been going on ..." He shook his head. "I figure I should have enough by the end of June so that she can still go. It's a whole month, Dooley. She loves it. She looks forward to it all year."

The first time Dooley had met Warren, a guy was getting ready to use him as a punching bag out behind the school. The second time, a couple of guys had stuffed him in his locker and were getting ready to lock him in. Warren just naturally invited that kind of attention—at least, he used to until kids at school saw how Dooley was with him. A year or more ago, Dooley would have been one of the guys whose mission was to make the Warrens of the world miserable. Now—well, Warren had forced him to shift the way he looked at things.

"Then what?" Dooley said. "Once you pay for that, you going to take the summer off?"

"Hell, no. *Then* I start saving up for a car." Warren grinned despite his obvious fatigue. "Well, maybe not a car. There's a computer I have my eye on ..." And off he went, getting all technical about something Dooley didn't care about, until finally Alicia was back with two DVDs, one the new penguin movie Dooley had mentioned, the other a movie about a bunch of wild parrots that she had seen at least a dozen times already. Alicia always went for the animal stuff. She held them out to Dooley.

"Come on up front," he said.

Kevin was behind the counter but not at a register. He was over to one side, his back to Dooley, hunched over his stupid schedule.

Dooley wanded the two DVDs, slipped them into a bag, and handed them to Alicia, who dug in her pocket for the money to pay for them. She always had exact change.

Dooley waved the money aside.

"These are on the house," he said. "Because you're our best customer."

She made a gentle whooping noise that told Dooley how thrilled she was. Kevin turned to look, and for a minute there, Dooley was afraid Alicia would tell him why she was so happy. Kevin scowled at her, annoyed at being distracted from his work. The smile vanished from Alicia's face.

"Why don't you go to the store next door and get a Popsicle?" Warren said gently. "I'll be right there, okay?"

"Get a pink one," Dooley said. "Pink is cherry. Cherry's the best."

Alicia grinned at him.

"She really likes you," Warren said as he watched her go. He turned back to Dooley, his wallet out, thumbing some bills.

"Save it, Warren."

"Won't you get in trouble?" Warren said quietly, one eye on Kevin.

"We get ten free rentals a week," Dooley said. "We're supposed to keep current. We're supposed to have watched everything in the store. It's all good."

"You don't have to do this, Dooley. I can pay—"

"I know you can, Warren. I want to do it, okay? So why don't you forget about it? Go home and get some sleep."

Warren had that same pop-eyed look on his face that appeared whenever Dooley did something to surprise him, usually something nice. Dooley didn't know what to make of that look. He couldn't figure out what Warren expected from him—obviously nothing like this, even though what Dooley had done was such a small thing.

"See you, huh?" Warren said.

"Not if I see you first," Dooley said.

Every chance Dooley got—every time Kevin went into the back room or when he took his break—Dooley tried Beth again. Her cell rang through to voicemail every time. He didn't bother leaving a message. He'd left a couple the night before. She'd never got back to him.

Tuesday afternoon, Dooley was at work again, after calling Beth's cell first thing in the morning, all through lunch, and about a million times between the time he left school and the time he stepped out of the staff room, name tag pinned to his chest, and slipped behind the counter to take over the cash from Rashid, who had a master's degree in chemical engineering and was earning the same lousy wage as Dooley. He called a couple more times when Kevin wasn't looking. In fact, he had just slammed down the phone—still no answer—when a customer about his own age stepped up to the cash. The guy had straight white teeth, hair that fell just so, and was wearing immaculate jeans and a pair of sharp-looking sunglasses hooked on the neck of his form-fitting т-shirt. Nevin.

Dooley looked down for his selection but, big surprise, Nevin's hands were empty.

"Can I help you with something?" Dooley said. It was what he was supposed to say. With regular customers who were friendly, he put real feeling into it. With jerks that treated him and every other video store clerk as if they'd been lobotomized, he didn't even try to hide his boredom. With guys like Nevin, guys who had too much money and the ego to go along with it, he kept it monotone, the message: Whatever.

"Hey, Dooley," Nevin said, nice and perky. He and Dooley each knew who the other was, but they had never spoken. Dooley preferred it that way.

Dooley stared at him.

"How's Beth?" Nevin said, a real needle to his tone, so that Dooley had to fight the urge to grab him by the throat and throttle him. "You talked to her lately? Or maybe she isn't answering her phone." His eyes were sharp on Dooley, and he smiled. "If I were her, I wouldn't, not after what happened."

Dooley couldn't help it—interest flickered in his eyes.

Nevin looked across the counter, waiting for Dooley to ask him what he meant. Dooley felt like kicking the perfect teeth right out of his head.

"What are you talking about, Nevin?"

Nevin shook his head, as if he felt sorry for Dooley.

"She didn't tell you, huh?"

"Told me what?"

"About Parker."

Parker, whose daddy made a killing during the dot-com craze.

"What about him?"

"He was on the trip with us. We stayed over an extra day at his place. He threw one hell of a party."

"Yeah. So?"

"She tell you what happened at the party?"

Dooley stared at him, conveying the message: You're wasting my time.

Nevin sighed. "She didn't, did she?" Dooley didn't answer. "I have to say, I'm disappointed in Beth," Nevin said. "She's always going on about integrity and telling the truth, am I right? And there she is, crying over Parker, and she hasn't even had the decency to tell you."

Beth had been crying over this Parker guy?

"A girl I know saw them go upstairs together," Nevin continued, shaking his head like a disapproving father. "I'm sorry to be the one to tell you this—"-Dooley doubted that—"but they were holding hands."

Beth had been holding hands with a guy, and the worst possible kind of guy at that—a dot-fucking-com heir.

"Parker's one of those guys, he's got girls dropping to their knees in front of him all the time, you know what I mean?" Nevin said.

Dooley was trying to slow down his breathing, one of the so-called coping techniques they'd taught in group.

"She's not the first one he's left crying," Nevin said. "He screws some girl, she thinks she's got it made, and the next thing you know, she's invisible to him. But does that stop the next one from thinking *she's* going to be the one?" He shook his head again. "I never thought Beth would be one of those girls, but I guess you never know."

What the hell was going on? What was Nevin telling him?

"Parker's no gentleman, either," Nevin continued. He was enjoying himself. "He's one of those guys who puts out the details. Everyone at school knows everything there is to know about Beth, if you get my drift."

That pretty much sealed it. Dooley's hands flew out. He caught a handful of Nevin's T-shirt up near the collar and started to drag him across the counter. Nevin let out a yell. His sunglasses clattered to the floor.

The electronic bell above the door bonged. Out of the corner of his eye, Dooley saw a customer, a woman, swing into the store and grind to a halt, staring at him.

"Hey, Jesus, Dooley, what are you doing?" Kevin said, running up the Action / Adventure aisle to the counter. "You want the cops in here?"

Dooley had pulled his arm back and was getting ready to hit Nevin, who was struggling to break free. He was strong, too. It took everything Dooley had to maintain his grip.

"Dooley, let him go or, swear to God, I'll call the cops." Kevin's voice was shaking, like he was terrified what that might lead to. But Dooley had to give him credit. He didn't back down. He reached for the phone on the counter.

Dooley, still holding the front of Nevin's T-shirt with both hands, pulled him in close so that he could smell the fear on him. Then he flung him backward as hard as he could. Nevin fell on his ass with a splat, taking a bin of previously-viewed with him.

Kevin scowled at Dooley, before spinning around, grabbing Nevin by one arm, and helping him to his feet.

Nevin brushed himself off. His face was white.

"You think you're something special," he said. "But I guess

Beth doesn't think so, huh?" He looked down at his shirtfront. "My sunglasses."

They were on the floor beside Dooley. Nevin started for them. Dooley brought one foot down and ground them into pieces.

"It looks like they got broken," he said.

"Fucking animal." Nevin strode out of the store. Dooley watched him climb into his midnight-blue Jag and roar away.

The woman, who had been staring at Dooley, was still rooted to the spot where she had stopped. She seemed uncertain about what to do. Kevin smiled at her.

"Just a misunderstanding," he said. "I'm sorry for any inconvenience. Your rental is on the house today."

The woman looked at him. "I was going to do the three-pack."

"On the house," Kevin assured her.

The woman headed for the new-release display that ringed the inside of the store.

Kevin turned to Dooley.

"What the hell do you think you were doing? What if that guy calls the cops on you?"

"He won't." Dooley was willing to put a week's wages on it. Hell, a month's wages. Nevin had come in with the sole purpose of sticking it to Dooley. The fact that Dooley reacted the way he had was proof positive that he'd succeeded.

"You better pray he doesn't, because assault is a criminal charge, and you get a criminal charge while you're *on shift* and right in front of another customer, for God's sake, and you're out of here just like that, no ifs, ands, or buts." Dooley just stared at him. He was going to have a much bigger problem than being unemployed if Nevin went to the cops. They could lock him up again for that—if there was anything left of him after his uncle got through with him. "Goddammit, Dooley, what is that lady going to think? That we hire thugs here? I mean, for all she knows, the guy was a customer."

"I gotta go," Dooley said. He lifted up the trap to come out from behind the counter.

"Go? Go where? You have four more hours on your shift."

"I have a personal emergency."

"Rashid isn't back from his meal break. I'm alone in the store, Dooley."

Dooley was still breathing hard, still high on the adrenalin rush he'd got from the look of panic in Nevin's eyes. He didn't give a fuck about his job. He didn't—

Jesus.

Act in haste, repent in leisure. How often had he heard that from his uncle? Actions have consequences—that one had been repeated over and over in group. Take a deep breath and think it through—this one from Dr. Calvin, who had a soft voice and a slow, relaxed way of talking. When your eyes are blinded by a red rage, you may think you don't care what happens next. But you'll think differently when you're seeing straight again and you find you're boxed into a corner by your own rashness. You can cut down on a lot of regret by taking a few seconds to think things through ahead of time.

He drew in a deep breath.

"It's Beth," he said. Kevin knew Beth. She came into the store often enough. Even better, she said hi to Kevin whenever he was around, and she did it with a straight face. She even carried on conversations with him from time to time, which seemed to leave Kevin dazed.

"What about her?" Kevin said.

"That's the thing. I don't know." And it was eating him up.

"I'm sorry about that guy. But he's not going to press charges, and it won't happen again."

"It better not." Stern but a little more subdued.

"I have to go, Kevin."

Kevin had no trouble thinking things through. He had no trouble considering consequences.

"Just this one time," he said.

Dooley threw him a curve. He said, "Thanks."

It took Dooley half an hour to get to the building where Beth and her mother lived. He stood in front of the board outside the security door. She hadn't returned a single one of his dozens of phone calls. What were the chances that she'd buzz him up if he rang her apartment? He waited for a few moments, making like he was studying the names on the board. No one appeared either in the lobby or in the foyer where he was. No one opened the door either way, giving him the chance to slip through.

He started pressing top-floor buzzers first.

"Yes?" crackled a voice.

"Pizza," he said into the intercom.

"I didn't order pizza." Brusque, angry.

"Sorry. Wrong apartment." By then he was talking to dead air.

He pressed the next button, then the next, and the next. He was down three floors before someone said, "Well, it's about time," and buzzed him through.

He rode the elevator up to seven where Beth lived, stood to one side of the door, out of sight, he hoped, of the peephole, knocked lightly, and prayed that her mother wasn't home.

Beth's mother answered the door. Thanks a lot, Big Guy.

She looked tired, and for once she didn't regard him with undisguised disapproval.

"Sorry to disturb you," Dooley said. "But is Beth here?"

Beth's mother looked him over, as if she would never understand what her daughter saw in him.

"She doesn't want to talk to you." Her voice was as weary as her face. She started to swing the door shut.

Dooley blocked it with his hand.

Beth's mother met his eyes, but she didn't show the fury that Dooley expected.

"She isn't seeing anyone," she said. "She isn't talking to anyone. I'm sorry."

Sorry? Beth's mother was sorry? What did that mean? Panic rose to choke him.

"Beth!" he shouted. "Beth, it's me!"

Beth's mother stood in the doorway, blocking his way. But she made no attempt to silence him, and that rattled Dooley. What was going on? Why wasn't Beth answering? Why wasn't her mother threatening to call the cops on him?

"Beth!"

A door opened down the hall, and a woman peeked out. Still Beth's mother did nothing to quiet him. Dooley looked at her.

"Nevin came by the store," he said. "He said—" He stopped. He just couldn't make himself say it.

"She doesn't want to see anyone or talk to anyone," Beth's mother said. "But I'll tell her you were here."

Beth's mother, who always acted like she wished she could make him vanish with a snap of her fingers, was going to tell

Beth that he had dropped by? That shook Dooley even more. It was as if he'd stepped into a parallel universe where everything was the opposite of what he was used to: his girlfriend wouldn't talk to him and his girlfriend's mother was actually being nice—well, civil—to him. She swung the door shut and Dooley heard two separate locks click into place.

TWO

Sitting in class the next day was like being staked out naked while fire ants overran his body. Every nerve ending screamed, but there was nothing he could do except sit there and take it. Copy down the bullshit on the blackboard. Listen to the crap that was coming out of his teachers' mouths. Make a note of his homework assignments. Take it and take it and take it until, mother of mercy, the final bell rang. He sprinted down the school steps and made it to the bus just as it was pulling away. He hammered on the door. For once the driver didn't ignore him. He stepped on the brake and let Dooley in. Dooley thanked him as he flashed his transit pass and his student card.

Beth's school had let out before he got there, still breathless from his dash to the bus stop and then from jogging up the tree-lined street to the sprawling building where Beth spent her weekdays. It was a warm afternoon and there were girls everywhere—on the steps and the front walk of the school in knots and bunches, talking about whatever it was girls found to talk about; out on the sidewalk, smoking; farther away, in the parking lot or headed that way, the younger ones climbing into suvs driven by small women who weren't the same color as the girls, the older ones dangling the keys to their own cars. Dooley couldn't believe how many of them were waving lit cigarettes, and these were rich kids in a private school, every one of them university bound; you'd think they'd have enough brains not to smoke.

Dooley scouted them all and then came to a sudden stop.

He didn't know any of these girls. He had no idea which ones were friends of Beth's. He'd never given it any thought. But now that he needed to talk to her best buddies, he realized he had no clue where to start. He'd been going out with Beth for six months. He talked to her practically every day. He saw her at least once a week, sometimes more, depending on his shifts and her home-work load and extra-curriculars. Beth was big on extra-curricu-lars. She was on her school's debating team, yearbook committee, field hockey team, and volleyball team, and she volunteered twice a month at a soup kitchen along with a bunch of other girls from her school. But Dooley had never met any of them. He didn't even know their names. Okay, so she didn't know any of his friends, either, other than Warren, who she'd met a few times. But that was different. Dooley didn't have any friends.

He hesitated, unsure of himself. The girls who were hang-ing out in front of the school were mostly talking among them-selves, but a couple of them had noticed him and were staring at him. He was aware of how different he looked from, say, Nevin. He hadn't arrived by car. His jeans were off-label and worn at the knees. His sneakers were from the mid-price range. His T-shirt was definitely not designer.

But so what? Jesus, he wasn't afraid of what a bunch of girls thought of his wardrobe, was he? What was the worst they could do? Tease him to death? Yeah, well, lock them up in a youth detention facility—as if their daddies would ever let that hap-pen—and see how long they lasted. He pulled himself up straight and marched to the nearest and smallest knot of glossy-haired smokers. A couple of them were already regarding him with curiosity, which made it easier—sort of.

"Hey," he said.

One of them, a blonde with, in his opinion, so much makeup on her eyes that she looked like a starving raccoon, smirked at him.

"Hey," she said, as if she were trying out the word, as if she'd never actually spoken it before.

"I—" Jesus, why was he letting himself get rattled by four girls he didn't even know? "You know Beth—Beth Everley?"

Another blonde, this one more platinum than the first, not even trying to look natural, said, "You're that guy, aren't you?"

That guy?

"You're Dooley," she said.

The other three inspected him closely.

"Are you?" Raccoon Eyes said.

"Yeah."

"I knew it," Platinum said, grinning as she gave him a slow once-over. "No wonder she kept you such a secret."

Kept—past tense. Did that mean anything?

"He's cute," Platinum said to her buddies, "in a kind of classic bad-boy way."

Dooley got annoyed when he realized his cheeks were burning. Jesus. Girls.

"Was Beth at school today?" he said.

All four shook their heads.

"Were the four of you at that Habitat thing with her?"

"That wasn't our home form," Raccoon Eyes said. "But we heard what happened." She smirked at him again. "Guess you're pissed, huh? She was making eyes at Parker all week."

"I thought you said you weren't there," Dooley said, his fists clenching automatically.

"We weren't," said a girl who, so far, hadn't spoken, a scrawny girl with chestnut hair. "But Annicka was."

"Who's Annicka?"

Scrawny pointed at a girl with jet black hair who was leaning on a utility pole across the street, smoking. Annicka glanced at Dooley before crushing her cigarette under the heel of a black boot and heading down the street.

"She was there," Scrawny said. "She saw everything."

Everything? What was everything? What the hell had happened?

"If you want to talk to someone, talk to Annicka," Scrawny said.

Dooley had to run to catch up to her.

"Annicka," he called. "Wait."

He was pretty sure she'd heard him; she didn't have earbuds in, nothing like that. But she had nearly a block's lead on him and the way she was booting it down the street, he was surprised she didn't break into a run. Dooley did and finally grabbed her by the arm. She wheeled around, her expression pure aggression, a cell phone in her hand.

"Let go of me or I'll call the cops."

He jerked his hand away and held them both up in a gesture of surrender.

"I just want to talk to you, that's all."

She had her thumb on the green button on her phone, ready to push. Did she have the cops' number programmed in?

"I know who you are," she said. "I know everything about you."

That stopped him in his tracks. Everything?

"Win is my cousin," she said.

Winston Rhodes. Dooley had heard he wasn't doing too well. He heard that he'd had to relearn how to do things like tie his shoelaces and brush his teeth.

"I'm sorry about what happened to him," Dooley said, even though he wasn't, not one little bit.

"I bet," Annicka said.

"Look, you know Beth Everley, right?"

Annicka's thumb hadn't moved from the green button on her phone.

"You were on that trip with her," Dooley said.

"So? What's it to you?"

She had to be kidding.

"You just said you know who I am. If you do, then you know why I'm asking."

Her thumb stayed on the green button for another few seconds. Then she flipped her phone shut.

"You're checking on Beth, right? You want to know if she spun you one. Right?" She was surly now, snotty. He was starting not to take it personally that Beth hadn't introduced him to any of her friends. What a bunch!

"They said you saw everything. What did they mean?"

"What did they mean? Are you for real?" A grin spread like a stain across her face. "You haven't talked to her, have you? But you heard something. You definitely heard something."

Her obvious enjoyment irritated Dooley.

"Look, I just want to know what happened."

"Okay, sure." She pulled a pack of cigarettes from a tiny purse and lit up. "She was with Parker. That's what happened."

That name again, the same one Nevin had mentioned.

"What do you mean, with him?" he asked.

"They were fooling around all week—you know, flirting with each other. Then, on the last night, he threw this big party at his country place. I saw them go upstairs together. They were holding hands."

Dooley felt sick inside. He wished he'd never asked.

"But you know Parker." Annicka looked at him. "No, I guess you don't." She took a long drag on her cigarette. "Parker's one of those guys who likes to spread it around. And why shouldn't he? He can get any girl he wants. I was sitting across from Beth on the bus on the way home the day after the party. She was staring at Parker the whole time. He was sitting with another girl. Beth looked like she wanted to kill him. I guess she didn't appreciate being dumped so soon."

Dooley felt like he'd been gut-punched by some iron-fisted goon who knew what he was doing.

"This guy Parker, where does he go to school?"

"Why? You want to beat the crap out of him?" She looked and sounded excited by the idea. "You want to do to him what you did to Win?"

Dooley thought, yeah, he'd like to do exactly that. Also, he wanted to see what Parker had that he didn't have, what even Nevin didn't have.

"Where can I find him?"

Annicka glanced at her watch and shook her head.

"He's probably at the tennis club."

The tennis club. Like everyone knew its name—everyone except Dooley.

"What tennis club?"

She told him.

"What does he look like?"

"He's tall. About your height. Maybe a touch shorter." Good. "Blue eyes, blond hair; he's got bangs that keep falling into his eyes, makes him look all sweet and innocent, you know? And dimples. When he smiles, he's got killer dimples. You really would think he was an angel." But the way she said it, Dooley got the impression you'd be a fool to believe it.

He turned to go.

"Hey," Annicka said. "I heard about you, but I *know* Parker. He's in good shape. He's into martial arts—and he's good. I'm not kidding."

◆ ◆ ◆

Dooley followed Annicka's directions to another tree-lined street he had never heard of, the trees all in bud, the houses on the street all made out of stone, all enormous, all surrounded by high fences or hedges, all immaculately landscaped. At the end of the street, right where it made a right-angled turn, was a trim, low-slung building. Beyond that, barely visible from the street, fenced in, were tennis courts.

Dooley walked up to the building and pulled open the door. A man in a blazer and gray slacks looked up at him from behind a counter. Right away his eyes narrowed. He came out from behind the counter.

"How can I help you?" he said, his tone mellow but his eyes sharp. He glanced to his right. A security guard was standing at the only door that led from the lobby into the depths of the club.

"I'm looking for someone," Dooley said. "He's a member here. Parker Albright."

The man clearly recognized the name, but something wasn't computing in his head. He gave Dooley a once-over.

"Mr. Albright didn't mention that he was expecting a guest," the man said.

Mr. Albright. What a world.

"I just want to talk to him for a minute," Dooley said. "Maybe you could—"

"This is a private club. I'm going to have to ask you to leave."

Out of the corner of his eye, Dooley saw the security guard coming toward him.

"Okay." He threw up his hands for the second time in less than an hour. "Okay, I get it."

He was conscious of two sets of eyes on him as he left the building and strode off the property to the sidewalk. He turned and kept going, rounding the nearest corner to inspect the grounds. The whole place was fenced in, not just the courts. But the fence around the property wasn't as high as the ones around the courts. They probably thought it didn't need to be, tucked away like it was in a posh neighborhood. Dooley kept going until he judged he was out of sight of the club house. He hopped the fence and cut across the lawn to the courts.

There were a dozen of them, half of them occupied. Dooley scanned the players and zeroed in on Parker right away. He was exactly as Annicka had advertised—tall, blond, athletic-looking. Dooley studied the chain-link fences around the courts. They were too high to climb, and the only entrance into them was through the club house. That meant he would have to talk through the fence.

Parker was about to serve, but the guy on the other side of the net must have said something to him, because he lowered his hands, turned, and looked across the lawn at Dooley.

"Hey," Parker called. "Hey, you!"

Dooley glanced around, just to make sure. There was no one else on the lawn. He started toward the fence. As he got closer, he thought he recognized Parker's playing partner. He was pretty sure he'd seen him at a party, one of the few he'd been to since he started living with his uncle.

Parker had moved to the fence and was grinning through the chain-link.

"You're that guy Beth was seeing, right?" he said, pushing his bangs out of his eyes.

Was seeing. Past tense again. What had Beth been telling her friends? What had she said to this guy? Dooley looked him over carefully. He supposed he could understand what girls saw in the guy. He was good-looking in a GQ way—well-groomed, obviously loaded, with killer dimples. A real angel, Annicka had said. But there was nothing angelic in his ice-blue eyes.

"I don't know what she told you," Parker said, still smiling, as if he and Dooley were pals, as if they were talking about a ball game they had taken in together, "but it wasn't like I had to twist her arm. She wanted it. She wanted it so bad she practically begged me." Saying it like he was proud of himself. "And that was after I made it clear that I wasn't looking for anything long-term."

Dooley was breathing hard. His heart was pounding. He had to focus to keep the red from blinding him. Those girls at Beth's school had said Beth was making eyes at the guy all week. Annicka had seen her going upstairs with Parker, holding his hand. And now this prick was acting like she was just one more conquest, one more notch on the old headboard.

"I feel for your pain, brother," Parker said, Mr. Sympathetic.

"I can imagine how you must feel. If I *were* into something more long-term, Beth would definitely make the list. She's quite a girl. Tasty, you know what I mean?" He ran his tongue over his lips, and that was it. Dooley lunged forward and managed to catch hold of the collar of Parker's tennis shirt through the fence. He pulled hard on it, yanking Parker so far forward that he had to turn his face to stop his nose from getting mashed against the chain-link.

"Hey!" the guy on the other side of the net shouted.

"You're only going to make trouble for yourself," Parker said, calm, sounding amused.

Dooley pulled harder until the chain-link dug into Parker's cheek. If only he were on the same side as Parker. If only he could—

Someone grabbed him from behind and ripped him away from the fence. The security guard. Correction, two security guards, one of them towering over Dooley, a big block of a man with a grip that bit deep into Dooley's arms and held him while the other one, the one Dooley recognized from the clubhouse, said, "You were warned. Now you're looking at trespass and assault." He pulled out a cell phone.

"It's okay, Tom," Parker said, smooth, unruffled. "We're just having a difference of opinion. I don't think there's any need to press charges."

"Mr. Wiarton already told him he had to leave," Tom the security guard said. "He—"

"I'm *not* pressing charges, Tom," Parker said, the tone of his voice making it clear who was top dog.

"Yes, sir, Mr. Albright," Tom said.

Sir. Mister.

Tom turned to Dooley. "I'm making a security report," he

said. He nodded at the guard who was holding Dooley. The guy started to haul him across the lawn to the clubhouse.

"Hey, Parker," someone called, one of a couple of new guys coming out of the club house, tennis rackets in hand. "We still on for Saturday?"

"You bet," Parker said. He grinned at Dooley. "Come over any time after nine."

"Looking forward to it," the second guy said. "If there's anyone who knows how to throw a party, it's you, Park."

Dooley just bet.

The guard jerked him forward. That's when Dooley spotted her—she was at the edge of the outer fence, half hidden by a trees. Beth. She was standing there so still she was like part of the landscape, and she was looking directly at Parker, who saw her, and nodded, grinning at her. Dooley tried to shake free. He wanted to walk to her. He needed to talk to her.

"Give us any trouble, and I will call the cops," Tom hissed in his ear, "I don't care what that rich-kid son of a bitch says. You hear me?"

Dooley squirmed. He wanted to wave to her, send her some kind of signal to wait for him.

"I'm warning you, kid," Tom said.

The other guard dragged him in through the back door of the club house, into a cramped room labeled Security, where they sat him down, demanded his ID, and wrote up a report on him before escorting him out through the front door and telling him, "If you come back, you'll be arrested."

Whatever.

Dooley ran along the perimeter of the fence to where he had seen Beth.

She was gone.

He checked the nearby streets and the bus stop. There was no sign of her.

THREE

Dooley tried Beth's cell and got voicemail. He tried the landline at her apartment. Voicemail again. He wondered if she had seen him at the tennis club. She must have, unless she'd been unable to tear her eyes away from Parker. He ached to slam his fist into something—a tree, a utility post, a brick wall, *anything*. What the hell was going on? When she'd left, she'd promised to call him every day. But she hadn't done that. No, she'd called him exactly twice. Why was that? Was it true what those girls had said? Had she gone after Parker? Had she come onto him like Parker had said? Had she really slept with the guy? Everyone was saying it, so it had to be true, didn't it? Why else would she have taken off like that at the tennis club instead of waiting to speak to him? Why hadn't she returned any of his calls? Why hadn't she called him as often as she had promised?

Forget it, he told himself. Forget the bitch. What had he expected, after all? That someone like her, someone that smart, that beautiful, that connected—all those private school girls and boys she hung out with, *Nevin*, whom she'd lied about more than once—had he really thought she'd settle for someone like him? What did it even matter? They were both seventeen. It wasn't like she'd been planning to stay with him for the rest of her life. It was just a matter of time. So, okay, she'd made her move. She'd gone after a guy—*the* guy, from the way everyone was talking about him. And she'd fallen flat on her face. It probably served her right. He should be glad.

But he wasn't.

Jesus. Girls! They could really fuck you up. She'd slept with some gonna-be-a-zillionaire. She was refusing to talk to Dooley or even, it seemed, to acknowledge his existence. And what was he doing, pathetic mope? He was aching for her. He was ready to sell his life, his soul, *anything* he could lay hands on, for a chance to talk to her, to see her, to touch her.

Then it hit him like a kick in the balls—he was just like Lorraine. Every time some loser asshole in Lorraine's life ripped her off or cheated on her or just plain dumped her, what did she do? She cried and begged and pleaded, her face all sloppy with makeup and mucus—please, baby, I can't live without you. And when that didn't work, she numbed herself with drugs or booze or both, just like he was wishing he could do now. Well, no fucking way. He wasn't like Lorraine, not at all. He wasn't a pathetic loser. He was smarter than that. But that didn't mean the tug wasn't there. It didn't mean he wouldn't weaken.

Fuck.

He started to jog, his feet pounding the pavement. He cranked up the speed, ran until he was winded, and then ran through that, going and going until he thought he would drop. Until he prayed he would drop. Until the sweat poured off him and his feet hurt. Until he swung into view of his uncle's house.

No one was home.

He let himself in, stripped off, and took a shower. It was easier that way. The water streaming down his face let him pretend that the tears weren't there.

◆ ◆ ◆

He woke to his uncle's voice saying, "Ryan, Jesus, I've been phoning you. How long have you been up here?"

He squinted at his uncle's worried face and then at his clock-radio. He'd been asleep for nearly two hours.

"Sorry." He sat up and swung his legs over the side of the bed. He felt groggy, as if he'd been drugged.

"You hungry?" his uncle said, gruff but clearly relieved to have found him. "It's dried out, but it's probably still edible."

It was chicken baked in peanut sauce, with a side of rice and another of steamed broccoli. He ate it because his uncle had gone to the trouble of making it and keeping it warm for him, not because he was hungry. His uncle studied him from across the table.

"What's going on, Ryan?"

"Nothing." Dooley stood up. "I'll handle the dishes."

His uncle kept his eyes on Dooley for a few moments longer. Finally he sighed and got up, leaving Dooley to it.

Dooley rinsed the plates and glasses and stacked them in the dishwasher. Then he went into the dining room and settled down to his homework, or tried to. The causes of World War II didn't exactly grab him, but he waded through the assigned chapter. Math was even less compelling. If he'd been on his own, he would have abandoned it after a couple of questions, but he was conscious of his uncle behind him in the living room, buried in the newspaper. He was conscious, too, of Lorraine. Maybe too conscious after all those therapy sessions he'd been put through. You can't blame your mother for the rest of your life, Dooley. At a certain point, it's all up to you—they're your decisions, your choices, and you have to live with the consequences. That plus the *big* lesson, the one he should have learned through experience alone but instead had had to have hammered into his head over and over and over: you can drink, smoke, or ingest as many brain-numbing, mood-altering substances as you want and, yeah, all your troubles will go away—for a little while. But they'll come back. They always come back. You can drink, smoke, and ingest some more, keep those ghosts at bay, but sooner or later something always goes wrong. Always. And when it does and when they get you for it, they take all that shit away from you and then you have no choice. You have to live through it again, and worse, and there's nothing you can do about it until they turn you loose again. So, really, what's the smarter choice: learn to deal with it straight up, play the hand you've been dealt, or act exactly like the person you've been blaming for everything all your life, act like Lorraine, which is to say, hide like a coward by drinking, smoking, ingesting, and, in the process, turning yourself into an all-round pitiable, miserable, and completely useless human being?

He closed his eyes and tried to ignore the pressure that was building inside his skull. The thing was, he hadn't seen it coming. He'd thought everything was okay between him and Beth. He'd thought they were good together. He'd thought she was as happy with him as he was with her. Now, in retrospect, he felt like a complete idiot. She hadn't told him there were going to be boys on the trip until he'd said he would see her off at the bus. She hadn't called like she said she would. She'd actively pursued that guy Parker. She'd lied about Nevin. And—he was changing his view on the subject again—she had never introduced him to any of her friends. How many other clues had he missed? It was as clear as gin, as transparent as vodka. She had moved on.

She was through with him.

She wanted something better.

Breathe. Slow it down. Concentrate.

He stared at his math homework for another twenty minutes and then gathered his books.

"I'm going to bed," he said.

◆ ◆ ◆

Dooley's cell phone rang at seven in the morning.

"It's me," the voice on the other end said. He almost dropped his phone. "Meet me in half an hour. At the coffee place across from your school."

"Beth—"

But she was gone.

He dressed, grabbed his backpack, left a note, and hurried out the door.

He was five minutes early, but she was already there, sitting in the back, her eyes on the door. As Dooley approached her, he was shocked by how haggard she looked. Her usually glossy hair was limp and dull. There were dark circles under her eyes. Her skin was pale. She usually looked sharp in clean, smart, fashionable clothes, but today she was wearing sweatpants and a sweatshirt that hid the natural curves of her body. Jesus, all that misery for a guy who didn't give a crap about her?

He pulled out a chair and sat down, but he didn't say anything. She'd gone after another guy. She'd slept with him. She'd been ducking him for days. She had some explaining to do.

She had watched him as he approached, but she stared down at the table top now. His stomach churned. It was worse than he'd thought. She couldn't even look him in the eye.

"Dooley." Her voice was so soft that he had to lean forward

to catch what she was saying. "I have to tell you something." She raised her eyes, and he saw that she was afraid. Of what? Of what she had to tell him? Of how he would react?

He waited. How was she going to play it? Was she going to confess? Was she going to lay the blame on Parker? Was she going to dump him? Or was she going to settle for second-best now that Parker had made his intentions clear?

She hesitated. Her hands were wrapped around a coffee cup. "Nevin was on the trip," she said.

Dooley knew that already. But this wasn't about Nevin. This was about Parker.

"We were assigned to the same work team. He kept coming on to me. It was driving me crazy. I mean, I told him I wasn't interested, but you know Nevin."

Sure. He also knew that Beth's mother liked Nevin. He knew that Beth and Nevin were on the debating teams of their respective schools and that they liked to practice debating together. He knew that the two of them used to hang out sometimes last fall. And he knew that Beth had lied a couple of times about seeing him, which had almost torpedoed their relationship. But then Beth had apologized. She'd told him, "It's not what you think." She'd promised him: no more Nevin. And then she hadn't told him until the last minute that the trip she was going on included Nevin's home form.

Her eyes were anxious on him.

"As soon as I saw it was going to be a problem, I did something about it." He could see she wanted him to believe her, so he nodded. She seemed relieved. Then her eyes clouded again. "You remember I told you about a guy named Parker?"

"The one with the dot-com daddy," he said, and, yeah, he'd

put a spin on it, letting her know exactly what he thought about guys like that.

"Well—" She bit her lip. "What I did is, I asked Parker if I could switch to his team."

Right. And that was supposed to make him feel better?

"He saw what was happening. He asked another girl if she would move to Nevin's team in my place. He took care of it for me."

Uh-huh.

"I did it so Nevin wouldn't drive me crazy. And it worked. Whenever Nevin came around, Parker dealt with it. He found something for me to do away from where Nevin was working. Or he worked with me, you know, so Nevin couldn't do anything."

Good old Parker. If Dooley hadn't already met the guy, if he hadn't already sized him up, he might have been grateful.

"He seemed like a good guy," she said. "He worked hard right from the start, not like some of the guys who had to be told to quit clowning around, that this was someone's actual house we were building and it had to be done right." Dooley could see how Beth would respect that. She took everything so seriously. "He was always the first to volunteer to help clean up after we ate. No one ever had to ask him."

Dooley couldn't even begin to reconcile the Parker Beth was describing with the one he had met at the tennis club.

"I told him all about you," she said. "I told him we were going out."

He stared stone-faced at her.

"He had a party at his country place on Friday night after we finished up for the week." She drew in a deep, shuddery breath. "The party was mostly down on the patio in front of the guest houses. That's where we were going to be sleeping that night. Girls in one of the guesthouses, boys in another. Parker's mother was supposed to be there, but she went out after the party got started."

Uh-huh.

"Everyone was having a good time. Everyone was dancing with everyone else, but mostly it wasn't serious."

Mostly.

"Mostly it was just fun, you know?"

She looked at him as if it really mattered to her what he was thinking. He looked back at her, his face giving nothing away.

"Except for Nevin. He started in again. Only this time he was drinking, so he was really obnoxious."

"And good old Parker bailed you out again, right?" Dooley said.

She looked startled.

"Yes. Because Nevin was—he kept trying to grab me and dance with me, really close." Her cheeks turned pink. Dooley could imagine Nevin, tanked, grabbing her and grinding up against her. "Parker asked me if I wanted to take a walk."

Because, Dooley bet, Parker was a guy who recognized an opportunity when he saw it.

"We just talked. I told him how good I felt about what we had done. He said he did, too. Then he said maybe I should think about volunteering over the summer in a developing country. He told me that he'd done that last summer—he was in Africa for a month, digging wells. He said it was great; he learned so much."

Parker was sounding more and more like that guy in the Batman comics—the one with two faces. There was sweet, considerate Parker, giving the girls what they wanted. Then there was regular, asshole Parker, the one Dooley had met at the tennis club.

"He said he had pictures if I wanted to see them. They were up in his room."

"Jesus, Beth." Talk about the oldest trick in the book.

Her face flushed red. She looked down into her coffee for a moment. When she started to talk again, her voice was shaky.

"So I went into the house with him and we went up to his room and ..." She raised a hand to her face and he saw that she was wiping away a tear. "I told him no, Dooley. I told him over and over. But we were all alone in the house and he was so strong." Tears slipped down her face. "I told him no. I told him to stop. But he wouldn't. He—he—" She pulled a handful of napkins from the dispenser on the table and pressed them to her face. It was a few moments before she could talk again. "I told him I was going to report him, and he said, 'Be my guest.' He said no one would believe me. He'd been a model citizen all week. Everyone saw that we'd been friendly. Everyone saw us talking at the party. Everyone saw us leave the party together. Besides, he said, it wasn't like it was the first time I'd ever done it."

She kept crying and dabbing at her eyes, and Dooley didn't know what to think. She'd said it herself: she'd been with Parker all week. They'd worked together. They'd been together at the party. She'd willingly gone inside with him. Annicka had seen them. They'd been holding hands.

"I've been trying to get hold of you for days," he said.

"I'm sorry."

"You said before you left that you'd call me every day. You didn't."

"It was so hectic. We were so busy."

"But not too busy to make eyes at Parker, huh?" It slipped out without warning, but he wasn't sorry he'd said it.

She looked up at him, stung.

"I wasn't making eyes at him. We were on the same work team, that's all."

"Because you asked to be on his team."

"He was helping me out."

"Sweet guy," Dooley said. "What were you doing at the tennis club yesterday, Beth?"

Her cheeks turned scarlet.

"I didn't mean to go there. I had to think and I just ended up there."

"Think? About what?"

"I had to make up my mind about something."

"About what? What were you going to do? Beg him to take you back?"

Anger flashed in her eyes.

"I told him to stop. I told him no. But he wouldn't listen to me. He forced me, Dooley. He forced me."

"If you didn't want to be with him, why did you go up to his room?"

Her whole body went rigid.

"I told you—"

"Yeah. He invited you upstairs to see some pictures."

"He forced me."

"That's not what I heard."

"You heard? From who?"

"What difference does it make?"

"He *forced* me."

"Yeah? Then why isn't he locked up?"

"I told my mom what happened," she said. He could see she was struggling to get a grip. "She didn't know what to do, so she called Nevin's dad."

Nevin again.

"Nevin's dad was a good friend of my dad's. My mom trusts him. Whenever she has a problem, she goes to him. He's a lawyer. Not criminal. Corporate. But he knows about these things."

Of course.

"She told him what happened." Her voice was shaky again. "He said if I went to the police, I'd have to tell them everything. He asked me a lot of questions. Then he said since I wasn't hurt, maybe I should just let it go."

Well, that explained a lot about Nevin.

"He said unless there were marks on me—"

"Weren't there?"

She refused to look at him when she shook her head.

"There were red marks in a couple of places right after," she said. He wondered what places. "But there were no bruises or anything like that."

"What about on him?"

"I don't know." Her voice was a whisper now. A tear splashed onto the table.

"If you told him no, you must have tried to fight him off, right, Beth?"

"*If* I told him no?"

"Did you scratch him, bite him, anything like that?"

No answer.

Then: "He—Parker—" Her whole body was shaking now. "I heard him tell a couple of guys that he'd nailed me. He told them I got all pissy—that's what he said, all pissy—when he told me it was just fun. He said he'd told me that right from the start. He made it sound like I was the one who was after him. Then Nevin's dad said that unless I could prove what happened, there was a really good chance that the police wouldn't believe me. He said that even if they charged Parker, he would probably have no trouble getting off. He said, because of the circumstances ..." She stared at her coffee for a few moments. "He said I'd have to go into detail in front of a judge, a jury, a whole courtroom about what had happened. He said Parker's lawyer would go into detail, too."

Dooley closed his eyes. He didn't want to think about what kind of detail or what she would say.

"I didn't tell you about it because I didn't want you to know," she said. "Because of what you would think." She looked at him, studied his face. "Because of what you *do* think. Nevin's dad is right. So is Parker. Everyone saw us together. Everyone saw me go into the house with him. No one would ever believe me. I was afraid *you* wouldn't believe me. Then I saw you at the tennis club—I don't know how you found out, Dooley, but when I saw you there and saw how angry you were, I knew I had to do something. So I did it anyway. I went to the police."

Right.

"This happened on Friday night and you waited until yesterday afternoon to go to the police—*after* you found out I knew?" Did she think he was an idiot? "If he scared you so bad, Beth, why didn't you call the police right after it happened? Why did you wait to talk to anyone about it?"

She stared at him, her face white now. She stumbled to her feet.

"You don't believe me."

"You should have called me like you said you were going to.

Like you promised. You shouldn't have gone up to his room with him. Jesus, you were holding his hand on the way up."

She shook her head. She turned and ran from the coffee shop. Shit.

◆ ◆ ◆

Dooley's uncle was at the counter of his original dry-cleaning store when Dooley walked in at lunchtime. He glanced at Dooley and then turned back to the woman who was pointing to a skirt she was holding.

"We'll take care of it," Dooley's uncle said in a soothing voice that Dooley rarely heard around the house.

But the woman wasn't satisfied.

"I paid for good service." Her voice more whiny than sharp. "And I didn't get it."

"We'll take care of that, too," Dooley's uncle said. He waved to Irene, the woman at the cash. "Mrs. Loewen needs a refund." He handed her the skirt with its covering plastic, bill attached. He smiled at Mrs. Loewen. "The skirt will be ready by the end of the day. That's a promise."

Mrs. Loewen nodded brusquely and moved to the cash for her refund. Dooley's uncle waved Dooley over.

"School let out early?" he said.

"I'm on lunch."

"And?"

"I wanted to ask you something."

His uncle waited.

Dooley glanced at Mrs. Loewen and Irene. His uncle got the point. He lifted the trap in the counter to let Dooley in and led the way to the back of the store where his office was. There was a coffeemaker on top of the filing cabinet. His uncle poured himself a cup and added a teaspoon of powdered creamer.

"What's up?" he said, stirring the powder into his coffee.

Dooley hesitated.

"Rape cases," he said finally. "They got someone special to handle those or is it just regular cops?"

His uncle had been lifting the coffee mug to his lips, but stopped and lowered it again.

"Do I even want to know why you're asking?" he said. "And, FYI, it's called sexual assault, not rape."

"Whatever. And it's not about me. I didn't do anything."

His uncle nodded, but Dooley could see he was still chewing on why Dooley would ask such a question. He lowered himself into the chair behind his desk.

"They have detectives who are trained for that."

"You know any of them?"

"I don't know. Maybe. If I don't, I probably know somebody who knows somebody. Why? What's going on?"

Dooley had spent the whole morning chewing over what Beth had told him. She said she'd called the cops. He wanted to know if that was true. He needed to know.

"Ryan? You can't ask me something like that and then clam up."

Dooley looked at his uncle—his uncle who wasn't really his uncle. He was still trying to wrap his mind around that. Why would a straight-up ex-cop like Gary McCormack take on a fucked-up case like Ryan Dooley when he wasn't even related to him? Jesus, he hadn't even wanted to know him for the first fifteen years of his life. What the hell was *that* about? And while he was on the topic, why did life have to be so goddamned complicated? Why was he always having to figure shit out? Deep shit. Why couldn't things run smoothly for a while?

"Ryan, for God's sake—"

"Can you find out if a guy named Parker Albright was charged with rape yesterday afternoon or last night?"

"Who the hell is Parker Albright? Please don't tell me he's some guy you used to know."

"I didn't even know he existed until recently," Dooley said. "Can you find out or not?"

His uncle studied him for a few moments.

"I suppose."

"Will you?"

Another few moments passed before his uncle nodded.

"I'll explain later," Dooley said. "I promise."

◆ ◆ ◆

Dooley was sure his uncle would quiz him over supper. He didn't. He didn't raise the subject at all except to say, "I put a few calls in, but I haven't heard anything back yet."

◆ ◆ ◆

"I was just trying to steer clear of Nevin."

"She was making eyes at him all week."

"He forced me."

"I saw them go upstairs together."

"He scared me."

"They were holding hands."

Don't think about it, he told himself the next morning. She cheated on you, for God's sake, and it wasn't even the first time. She never introduced you to any of her friends. It was easy to see why not. How could he even begin to measure up to the private school kids she spent her days with? Well, fine. Whatever. Pretend she doesn't exist. Pretend she *never* existed. Except, Jesus, how do you pretend a girl like Beth never existed? How do you pretend she never pressed her sweet soft lips against yours? How do you pretend you never ran your hand down the full length of her naked body? How do you remove the memory of her from your head?

Why had she gone up to Parker's room with him? Was she really so naïve? What had she been doing at the tennis club? Was it like Nevin had said—she'd been dumped but wasn't ready to let go? Why had she waited so long to talk to the cops, if she really had? Why had she waited until after she'd seen him at the tennis club to tell him her side of the story?

He kept his head down at school. He didn't look at anyone, didn't talk to anyone, didn't bother to turn on his cell phone—what was the point? He focused every minute on just that minute, nothing more. Concentrated on getting through the next sixty seconds and the next sixty seconds after that. His gut was rock-hard from the tension. His hands kept curling into fists. He wanted to smash something. Someone. Parker Albright. He wanted to hit him so hard in the face that he drew blood. Wanted to keep hitting him until he dropped. Wanted to kick him after that. Did other people ever feel that way, or was it just him?

He got through school. He dragged himself home and ate something, even though he wasn't hungry and the sandwich he made himself sat like a lump in his stomach. Then he set off for the video store, where he was scheduled to work until midnight. The store was in sight. He was ready to walk through the door. But he couldn't stand it anymore.

He dipped into his pocket, pulled out his cell phone, and turned it on. I must be out of my mind, he told himself, but he punched in Beth's number anyway. Voicemail. Again. He left a message: "It's me. Call me." Then he pressed END—and almost dropped the phone when he happened, just happened, to glance across the street. He stepped back automatically, wanting to avoid notice. But the guy on the other side of the street didn't turn his head even once. No, he swung along, an enormous duffle bag over his shoulder. Dooley watched him—front view, side view, back view, the guy getting smaller and smaller until he finally turned a corner and disappeared. It wasn't until Kevin came out of the store, looked around, located him, and said, "I thought I saw you out here. Your shift started five minutes ago," that Dooley realized he was trembling all over. Kevin noticed, too. He said, "You're not going to tell me that you're sick, are you? Because Brendan already called in. It's Friday, Dooley. I don't have to tell you what that means, do I?"

Dooley supposed he must have followed Kevin into the store. He supposed he must have gone into the back room and opened his locker and pulled on his red golf shirt and pinned on his name tag. He supposed he must have taken a shot at doing his job. But it must not have been a good shot because eventually Linelle said, "Who exactly are you expecting to see out there? Dr. Death?"

Dooley looked blankly at her.

"You've spent more time staring out that window than Drea Chappelle spends staring in the mirror," Linelle said.

"Who's Drea Chappelle?"

"She's this princess I used to go to school with."

The words weren't gelling for Dooley. Linelle at school with a princess?

Linelle shook her head. "What's up with you, Dooley? You look like you've seen a ghost—literally."

"I'm fine."

But he couldn't shake what he had seen. Couldn't shake the feeling that had come over him.

◆ ◆ ◆

Dooley heard Linelle say, "Tall. And ripped. Definitely ripped. I want a guy who puts as much work into his body as guys expect girls to put into theirs. And any shade of brown, light or dark, doesn't matter."

He became aware of Linelle staring at him.

"You listening to me, Dooley?" she said. It was slow in the store for a Friday night, and Kevin was on his meal break. Linelle had been talking pretty much non-stop, filling the time, since all they were allowed to play on the monitors was the latest Disney release, and they had both seen it a zillion times already.

"You ripped something," Dooley said.

Linelle gave him the evil eye.

"I was talking about guys. About my type."

"You've got a type?"

"Everyone's got a type," Linelle said. "You obviously like them dark-haired, willowy, with nice perky boobs."

"That's not a type," Dooley said. "That's Beth."

"You're telling me she's not your type."

"She's the only girl you've ever seen me with."

"Well, you're definitely her type. Every time I've seen her, she's with some tall, built dude."

"Yeah," Dooley said. "Me."

"She's a type, despite what you think, Dooley," Linelle said.

"She's every guy's wet dream. They dog her. Like Rhodes. And that dork in the Jag."

"So she's their type. But that doesn't necessarily mean they're her type," Dooley said.

"Right. It's just a coincidence that you and Rhodes and dork-boy all look the same."

"You must mean, we're all white," Dooley said. "Because Rhodes had blond hair and wore glasses and dork-boy isn't anything like me."

"Yeah," Linelle said. "That must be it. You tall, built white boys all look alike. Except that some of you dress a whole lot better than others." She ran a sharp eye over Dooley's red golf shirt, black jeans, and battered boots.

"Yeah. And some of us have to work for a living."

Kevin came back to the store and business picked up. It wasn't until Dooley was on his way home at nearly one in the morning that his brain flashed on the duffle bag. It had words stenciled on it. Little League. The guy was involved in Little League.

◆ ◆ ◆

The light was on in the kitchen when Dooley got home. When Dooley had first started living with his uncle maybe ten months ago now, his uncle had waited up for him every night. He'd given that up after a few months when Dooley never showed up late. Well, hardly ever, and never without a solid reason.

But he was waiting up tonight.

Dooley went into the kitchen. His uncle was sitting at the table, nursing a beer. The look on his face scared Dooley.

"Is it Jeannie?" he said. "Did something happen to her."

"Jeannie's fine," his uncle said. "Sit down, Ryan."

Uh-oh. Dooley sat.

"Why didn't you tell me it was about Beth?"

Oh. Dooley stood up again. He wasn't sure that he wanted to know and wished now that he hadn't raised the matter with his uncle.

"What's going on with you, Ryan?"

"Nothing." And that was the truth.

"Did you talk to her?"

"Who?"

"Who? Jesus, Ryan, who are we talking about here? Beth. Did you talk to Beth?"

"I heard her side of it, yeah."

"And?"

"And what? Look, forget about it, okay? It's not important."

"What? Are you dumping her over this? You're one of those guys? She's damaged goods, and now you're not interested?"

Dumping her? His whole body tensed up again, and again he wanted to smash something—anything.

"She was supposed to call me when she was away. She didn't. Turns out she was hanging out with this guy," he said. "She didn't call when she got back, either. She didn't even return my calls."

His uncle was silent for a few moments. Then: "So you want to know what my contact told me or not?" When Dooley didn't answer, he said, "Sit down, Ryan."

"I'm fine."

"Sit."

"I said I'm fine." He shouted the words at his uncle, surprising him, making him jump a little. His uncle waited a few beats.

"*Please* sit down," he said finally.

Dooley stared right back at him. The guy wasn't even his uncle. But he was the person Dooley was supposed to live with for another couple of months. He was the guy who had agreed to be responsible for him. He was the guy who had bailed him out a couple of times already. Dooley yanked out a chair, its legs scraping loudly against the tile floor, dropped down into it, and crossed his arms over his chest. If his uncle had something to say, he could go right ahead and say it. There was no law that could make Dooley listen.

"I talked to a detective in sex crimes."

"I said it's not important."

"It seems Beth and a bunch of the kids she went on that trip with were at a party at this boy Parker Albright's country house. Parker's mother was there, but the party was outside and she was inside. After the first hour or so, Mrs. Albright went to visit friends. There was a housekeeper present. She was supposed to call Mrs. Albright if anything happened. She spent most of her time in the kitchen, preparing snacks."

It must have been some party.

"Altogether, there were about twenty kids at the party, pretty much an even split between boys and girls."

How convenient.

"It seems that Beth and the Albright kid spent a lot of time together that night," his uncle said.

Dooley squirmed in his seat. He didn't want to hear it again. He didn't even want to think about it.

"Apparently, it was a friendly atmosphere—goofing around, dancing, some underage drinking, probably a little dope. The detective I spoke to, she talked to everybody who was there, and that's what they said—except that no one actually admitted to the dope. Then, sometime around midnight, Beth went upstairs with Parker."

Dooley felt his gut tightening.

"There was a witness who saw them go up." Annicka. "According to her, they were holding hands."

"Jesus!" He couldn't stand it anymore. He jumped to his feet, toppling the chair.

His uncle looked calmly up at him. He got up, circled the table, and set the chair upright again.

"Sit down."

Dooley was breathing hard. He didn't want to have to picture it.

"Ryan ..."

He sat, his whole body rigid in the chair.

His uncle sat, too.

"They went upstairs," he said. "Nobody saw either of them again until the next day."

"I don't want to hear it."

His uncle kept talking, in a slow, quiet voice.

"Beth was in the bathroom for a long time the next morning. One of the girls the detective talked to said she was already in there when everyone else got up. She said she heard the shower running. She said she must have waited for at least an hour, maybe longer, for Beth to come out, and that was after she hammered on the door and asked Beth if she was okay."

Dooley wanted to get out of the house. He wanted to run. He wanted ...

"She didn't talk to anyone on the bus on the way back. She just sat by herself. Another girl said she looked out of it. Those were her exact words."

Annicka had told Dooley that she'd looked like she wanted to kill Parker because he was sitting with another girl.

"Her mother met her at the bus. Beth left without talking to anyone. She went straight home and stayed there for the next few days. On Wednesday evening, she went to the police station, alone, and reported that she'd been raped. They did a rape kit, but by then it was far too late. She'd showered dozens of times. There were no marks on her. They asked if she had washed the clothes she'd been wearing, especially the panties—"

Dooley wanted to clap his hands over his ears. He wished his uncle would just shut up about it.

"It's what they ask, Ryan," his uncle said. "She told them she'd tossed everything—couldn't stand having the stuff around. By the time anyone could look, the clothes were down in a land-fill somewhere. She insisted she was raped. They take date-rape seriously, Ryan. They arrested the Albright kid. He admitted having sex with her." Did he have to keep hearing about it? "But he insisted it was consensual."

Beth had been making eyes at Parker all week. She never called Dooley. She never returned a single one of his calls. She went upstairs with him. She held his hand.

"He made bail, no sweat. Apparently the father's connect-ed—not to mention loaded. You'd have to be to have a place with a couple of guesthouses. A kid like that can afford a hell of an attorney."

"You done?" Dooley stood up to signal that he sure as hell was.

"Have you talked to her?"

He stared at his uncle and nodded.

"What did she say?"

"That she went upstairs with the guy."

"That's it?" his uncle said, surprised.

"She said she told him no."

His uncle looked at him, like, now he got it.

"And you're not sure if you believe her? Well, I'll tell you something, Ryan. A girl doesn't lock herself in the shower for hours after she's had consensual sex with a guy, and she sure as hell doesn't take another dozen or so showers over the next couple of days. Showering like that, over and over, that's something a girl does to get herself clean after she's been raped by some guy. It's what she does to get his smell and his touch off her. To make herself feel clean again. You get what I'm saying?"

Dooley couldn't believe what happened next. He smashed his fists down on the table, making his uncle's beer bottle jump. He smashed them down again and again until he felt his uncle's hands on his shoulders and his uncle telling him softly, "It's okay, it's okay," while he, Dooley, did what he'd never once done before in his life—he wept like a baby in front of another person.

FOUR

"You okay?" Dooley's uncle said when he stuck his head into Dooley's room the next morning at eight o'clock. He was showered and dressed and ready for a day at his dry-cleaning stores.

"Yeah," Dooley said.

"I'm out all day," his uncle said.

A typical Saturday.

"Then I promised Jeannie I'd take her to a fundraising dinner. For the museum." Jeannie loved the museum. She gave money to it. She volunteered there, too, taking visitors on tours of special exhibits, spending a lot of her spare time learning all about whatever she was going to be showing people and taking a lot of pride in what she did. "You're working, right?"

He'd switched with Linelle, his original idea being to celebrate his and Beth's six-month anniversary. Kevin was pissed about that, but as far as Dooley knew, Linelle was still covering for him. If he told his uncle that, though, his uncle would worry, especially after last night. Maybe he'd even cancel his plans so that he could keep an eye on Dooley. So Dooley nodded.

"You closing?" his uncle said, trying to get a fix on when Dooley would get home.

Dooley nodded again. It was easier that way.

"Well, we should be back by the time you're home. You need

anything—even if you just want to talk, Ryan—hit me on my cell, okay?"

Like Dooley had ever called his uncle just to talk. Like he would start now.

◆ ◆ ◆

He made himself get up about an hour after his uncle left. He went downstairs to the kitchen, opened cupboards, stared at the boxes of cereal, including the sugary ones he bought for himself because his uncle refused to waste money on "crap like that." But he wasn't hungry. He poured himself a cup of coffee instead and drank it down, sitting at the kitchen table, staring out the window, and wondering what Beth was doing. He tried her on her cell phone. No luck. He tried her landline. Her mother answered.

"I'm sorry," she said, the first time ever she had said those words to Dooley. "She can't come to the phone. She isn't feeling well."

"Can you tell her I called?"

Her mother let out a long sigh. "All right," she said; another first.

He showered and dressed and left the house. He had no idea where he was going and was surprised when he ended up down at the park, staring at the two baseball diamonds, one on either end. A long, steep slope ran from the street down into the park. Dooley descended halfway and sat on the grass, trying not to think but unable to stop the pictures and thoughts from flooding his mind. That asshole had taken Beth by the hand. He'd led her upstairs. How had that happened? What had she been thinking? Annicka had said it didn't look like anyone was forcing

Beth to go up there. Maybe so. But no matter how you looked at it, no matter who you believed, certain facts were irrefutable. No matter how it had happened, that asshole had touched her. He'd been with her. He'd made ... he'd fu ... he'd been with her.

He'd been with her.

Dooley clasped his head in his hands. He didn't want to be looking at what he was looking at, but he couldn't help himself. Beth had been with another guy. He'd ... he'd touched her.

And after that?

He didn't know. His uncle hadn't said what had happened in the next few hours after that. All he had talked about was the shower, like that was supposed to make all the difference. Maybe it did. Okay, probably it meant something. His uncle wouldn't have said what he had about the shower unless he was sure it did. He wasn't that kind of guy. But that didn't explain why Beth was ducking him. It didn't explain why she hadn't returned his calls. It didn't explain why she had made eyes at the guy all week. It didn't explain why she had gone up those stairs with him or why she'd been holding his hand. It didn't explain what Annicka had said— it didn't explain why she'd done what she'd done—why she had gone up to his bedroom with him when no one had forced her to.

He had no clear idea how long he sat there, head in hands. He didn't care what he must have looked like to the people passing by. Then, somewhere below, he heard excited shouts and roars of approval. He raised his head and saw a baseball game in full swing, little kids in uniforms playing the field and running the bases.

Pacing in front of one of the player benches was the same guy he'd seen on the street the other day, the guy with the duffle bag.

Ralston.

Dooley stared at him. He watched him touch the shoulder of a little kid who had just struck out. Watched him speak a few words of encouragement—at least, that's what Dooley assumed he was doing—to another little kid who was headed for the plate. Watched and watched, until Ralston's team brought it home and parents flooded onto the field, beaming with pride and congratulating Ralston, shaking the guy's hand, for Christ's sake. He watched the kids high-five each other, big grins on their faces. Watched them finally leave, one by one, two by two, with their parents. Little kids, maybe ten or eleven years old. He watched Ralston pack up the bats and the balls. Watched him zip up the big gray duffle bag and hoist it over one shoulder like the weight was nothing. Watched him stroll out of the park, each step he took tugging at Dooley until he got to his feet and made his way down the slope and across the park, moving quickly at first until he was ten or so meters behind Ralston, and then matching his stride to Ralston's so that the distance behind them remained constant. He couldn't believe he was seeing him after all these years. Couldn't believe that he'd showed up right here in Dooley's neighborhood. Was that a coincidence, or was he here for a reason? Dooley shook just thinking about it. Had Ralston come here looking for him? Was that possible?

He followed Ralston away from the park and down a sidestreet, until Ralston stopped and turned, pulling something from his pocket. Dooley ducked behind a massive tree, acting, he knew, like a criminal. He peeked out and saw Ralston unlock the trunk of a beat-up station wagon. Who drove those anymore? Nobody, that's who. Ralston must have fallen on tough times. Either that or ...

Ralston hoisted the duffle bag and threw it into the trunk.

He slammed the trunk shut, or tried to. It didn't take. He had to slam it again, harder this time. Then he circled around to the driver's side and used his key to unlock the door. He climbed in behind the wheel, started the engine, and drove away, right past Dooley, but his eyes straight ahead, like he hadn't seen Dooley or hadn't recognized him. Dooley watched the car until it turned a corner. It took a moment for his body to unfreeze. When it did, he saw a woman standing up on the porch of the yard where the tree stood. She was staring at him, a sour look on her face, like she wanted to yell at him to get off her property. But she didn't. Maybe she lived alone. Maybe she was afraid if she yelled at him, he'd run up her front walk and hit her or drive a knife through her heart, something like that. People didn't trust people anymore. People like the woman who was watching him didn't trust people like Dooley. You heard stories—some guy in one car flips a finger at some other guy in another car who cuts him off on the way to a stop sign, and the next thing you know, the second guy hauls the first guy out of his car and beats the crap out of him. Or pulls out a gun and shoots the guy. He bet that's what the woman was thinking about, that you never know, so it's never smart to yell at strangers. He nodded at her as he stepped off her property. She didn't acknowledge the gesture, but, boy, her eyes were on him like a dog's, territorial instincts on full alert, until he was a couple of doors down the street.

He couldn't say for sure how the rest of the day passed, nor could he say when or how he decided to do what he did. He walked around for a while—it turned out he was on the move for hours—and then, driven by his stomach, ended up at the

Greek place near work where he ordered a chicken souvlaki and a salad heavy with cucumber slices and feta. As he chewed his way mechanically through the meal, he tried without success to think about something other than what had happened.

The idea popped into his head like a spider dropping down from a basement ceiling. He watched the web of possibilities it was spinning. Thought about himself as the fly, helpless, caught up in something he'd had no part in making, then switched it up and thought about himself as the spider, weaving, trapping, ready to pounce. Then, because he was sitting right across from it—had he planned that or had it just happened?—and because that much time had passed without him even thinking about it, he crossed the street and peered in through the store window. Linelle was coming up the aisle from the back room, pinning her name tag to the front of her golf shirt. Kevin was nowhere in sight. Dooley ducked into the store.

"I almost had to call you," Linelle said, slipping behind the counter to take over the cash from Rashid. "I got here and Kevin had a meltdown. He's the most rigid person I know, and I don't mean that in the good way."

Dooley glanced around. "Is he here?"

"Relax. He's in the back, cross-checking the new inventory. You know how that goes."

Dooley nodded. Kevin wasn't just a cross-checking guy. He was a double-checking, cross-checking guy. He'd be back there for an hour, minimum.

"It makes him feel like he has some kind of control," Linelle said. "Jesus, you should have seen him. He went on and on about how I shouldn't even be here; it was your shift and you didn't get it cleared by him. The guy's one hundred percent AR, Dooley"—

her code for anal retentive—"which is why you have to play it his way from time to time. Anyway, he was about to send me home when I reminded him it's the first day of the *Aladdin* promotion."

Every seven years or so, the Disney execs cracked open their vault and re-released some old Disney movie at an inflated price *for a limited time only*, and moms and dads and grannies, especially grannies, rushed in and snapped them up. Normally it was no problem because normally Dooley didn't give a crap. But *Aladdin* was a Robin Williams movie, and you didn't want to get Dooley started on old Robin. The guy was one of those used-to-be-out-there-and-edgy comics who'd gone all smarmy and saccharine. Dooley couldn't shut up about what a sellout Robin was. He was proud of the number of people he'd steered away from *Mrs. Doubtfire* and any number of other lousy Robin Williams movies. Kevin had talked to him about it a few times—"It's your job to give the customers what they want, not talk them out of renting," he said, to which Dooley had replied, "What they want is a good time, not a load of crap." When it was rentals, Kevin let it go. When it was sales, that was another matter. Dooley out of the store on day one of this particular Disney release was a good thing, even if it broke a few rules in the employee manual.

"I need a favor," Dooley said.

"I'm already doing you a favor," Linelle pointed out. "It's Saturday night, remember? You think I couldn't come up with something better to do than help make a shitload more money for those fat-ass Disney execs?"

"My uncle might call."

"So what? You have a cell."

"You know how Kevin is about that. When my uncle wants to get me at work, he calls the store."

"I thought he quit doing that."

His uncle used to call regularly to check that Dooley was where he was supposed to be. But he'd given that up over the past few months, just like he'd abandoned waiting up for Dooley.

"He did, mostly," Dooley said. "But he might call tonight."

Linelle arched an eyebrow.

"Any special reason he thinks you're working when you're not?"

"I'm just saying," Dooley said. "Come on. Please?"

"If he calls, you want me to tell him you're in the can and then hit your cell?"

Good old Linelle.

"What if Kevin gets to the phone first? Or Sonja?"

Sonja, the new girl, was on shift with Linelle.

"Just try to pick up first if the phone rings."

"Right. To make my night complete."

"If Kevin gets it, he gets it. But if you can get to it first—"

"Uncomplicate your life by complicating mine, right?"

"I'll owe you. Anything you say, whenever you say."

"So I keep hearing." She made a sour face. "Okay, whatever." She glanced at the back of the store. "You better get out of here before Kevin decides to stick his head out and check on the troops."

◆ ◆ ◆

He went home, pulled the phone book from the cupboard under the phone in the kitchen and a map book from his uncle's office and looked up Albright. There were a bunch of them, which he cross-checked against the map book until he found the only one who lived in the neighborhood he bet Parker lived in. He considered changing his clothes and then thought, why the hell should he? He switched on the TV—he had at least two hours to kill—but switched it off again almost immediately. He couldn't sit still. He left the house and started to walk up to where Parker lived.

It was early when he got there—too early—and it wasn't the kind of neighborhood where he could park himself against a tree or a utility pole and just wait. Someone would notice him. Someone would see right away that he didn't belong. Someone would call the police.

He walked past the house, trying to tell for sure if it was where Parker lived. The place was big enough—it fit what he'd been told about Parker's father. It was the biggest house on the street and looked a lot newer than the others. But nothing was happening. The place was silent. He kept walking, past other massive houses, until finally he hit a cross street on the bus route. He found one of those five-bucks-a-cup coffee places, went in, and passed the next thirty minutes perched on a stool in the window, watching people while he sipped a cup of fair trade coffee from a country he doubted he could find on a map. Then he headed back down the way he had come.

The place looked more like party central now. There were strings of lights marking either side of the walkway that led up to the front steps and, from there, alongside the house. He heard party sounds coming from around back—music and talking and laughing. He strolled up to the gate in the high wrought iron fence that ran around the whole front of the property. Then he hesitated. What if the gate was locked? What if he couldn't get in?

The gate wasn't locked.

He pushed it open and went up the walk, where he hesitated again. Should he knock or ring or whatever at the front door, or keep it simple and circle around to the back where the party obviously was?

He circled the house.

Jesus, the place was something else. The entire back of the house was glassed in—you could see inside to the tables of food, a bar, clusters of little chairs and tables that spilled out through where the sliding doors had been pushed open onto a patio where music was booming. There was a pool, also under glass— he bet it was heated—with some kids fooling around in it and a few girls in bikinis sitting on the edge. There were more kids on the patio, and more strings of lights that ran on from there to what Dooley assumed was the back of the property. Different lights glinted way back there in the darkness—more houses, Dooley realized, but much farther off. The property must be huge if the nearest houses were that far away.

A girl who'd been standing with some other girls on the patio glanced at him. She detached herself from the group and walked over to him. She was slim and tanned—either she'd browned herself in one of those tanning beds or she'd had herself spray-painted, which he knew about because Linelle had told him, one hundred percent amused by the way white people paid all kinds of money to make themselves look chocolate. She was pretty, too, in that well-kept rich-girl way, Linelle (again) saying that that she could look like that, too, if she had money to throw away on getting her hair and nails and skin done and the time to work out at the gym seven days a week and, oh yeah, Daddy's credit card so she could make sure to keep her wardrobe up to date—this was the same Linelle who was in beauty school and wanted to have her own salon one day so she could cash in on the same rich girls she was always making fun of.

"You a friend of Parker's?" the girl said. The tilt of her head reminded him of Parker. He guessed she was his sister.

Dooley nodded.

She appraised him but didn't say anything and didn't let her face give anything away. Maybe Parker had friends who dressed like Dooley, in jeans and sweatshirts that didn't come decked in someone else's name. Or maybe she was just polite.

"Is Parker here?" Dooley said.

The girl nodded and pointed across the patio and down the lawn to a group of kids, boys and girls with—Dooley squinted—Parker in the middle. Dooley thanked her and headed toward them. He glanced around to see if there was anyone there he recognized. Three of the girls he'd talked to at Beth's school were clustered on one corner of the patio—Scrawny and Raccoon Eyes and Platinum. But they didn't seem to take any notice of him. The girl he thought was Parker's sister, who, Dooley realized, had neither asked for his name nor volunteered her own, started back to the group she'd been talking to. She was intercepted by someone else Dooley knew—Annicka, the witness. Parker's sister broke into a delighted smile. She kissed Annicka lightly on both cheeks, one of those stupid girly pretensions that Dooley hated.

He walked down the lawn toward Parker. Everyone in the enormous yard seemed to be in full party mode. Well, almost everyone. He noticed a girl standing by herself, as motionless as an oversized lawn ornament. She was pretty enough but painfully thin, and she was staring sullenly at Parker. He wondered what her story was. She paid Dooley no notice.

A few of the guests he passed glanced at him, but not many. Most of them were wrapped up in whatever they were doing.

Even Parker didn't pay him any attention at first. He had a tight group of friends around him, and was telling what sounded like a ghost story—"And so then the ghost shows up ..."—but in a strange way for a ghost story, not even trying to be scary, acting more like it was one sorry son-of-a-bitch ghost he was talking about. And instead of being all big-eyed and quiet, wondering what was going to happen next, people started to chuckle, like they already knew where the story was going. Most of them were laughing when Nevin showed up on the fringes, struggling to carry four different drinks without a tray. He was doing a poor job of it. Most, if not all, of the drinks had slopped over the rims of the glasses. No wonder Nevin was holding them so far away from himself. One of the girls near Parker reached out and took two of the drinks from Nevin. She passed them to a couple of guys in Parker's entourage. Nevin gave one of the remaining drinks to Parker and the other to a girl on the other side of Parker. None of them was for himself. The girl who had helped Nevin made her way through the tight little group. She said something to Nevin, but by then Nevin had spotted Dooley up on the lawn.

Dooley had been watching Parker, a real little king there in the midst of his loyal subjects. He had a nice little kingdom, too—both sides of the backyard were surrounded by a high stone wall, discreetly dotted with security warnings—and the lawn seemed to stretch forever. Dooley peered into the darkness, trying to locate its furthest reaches. There was no fence or wall across the rear of the property. It backed onto the ravine.

He glanced at Parker and saw that Nevin was nudging him. Parker raised his glass.

"Well," he said, "if it isn't the notorious Ryan Dooley." He took a long swallow of whatever he was drinking. Everyone around him turned to look. Everyone wanted to check Dooley out.

Dooley approached the group, but kept his eyes on Parker. "I know what you did," he said.

Dooley had to hand it to Parker; he didn't miss a beat. He kept right on smiling, but with a quizzical look on his face, like, shucks, pardner, I don't believe I know what you're talking about. Nevin leaned into him and whispered something. Parker didn't seem to be listening. His eyes were locked on Dooley.

"I don't know what you said to her," Dooley said. "I don't know if you slipped her something, maybe a roofie, but I know you did it, and if you don't fall for it, I'm going to make you wish you had."

Parker looked amused. He laughed and turned to his friends. "This guy is right out of a Tarantino movie. Where did Beth find him?" He swung back to Dooley. "Where *did* Beth find you?" he said, his tone suggesting that he guessed it must have been under a rock.

Jesus, and this was the piece of slime who had touched her. It didn't matter what the details were or who was lying or who was telling the truth. The one thing that had absolutely happened was that this creep had had sex with Beth and then had told his buddies all about it.

Dooley stepped up close to Parker. Annicka was right. He was tall, but not quite as tall as Dooley.

"You standing behind a fence now, smart guy?" he said. "Because if you are, I don't see it."

Dooley took that half step closer, right into Parker territory, and looked deep into Parker's baby-blue eyes. Again he had to hand it to the guy. He didn't intimidate easily. He stared back at Dooley for a good fifteen or twenty seconds. Then he looked sideways, trying to locate his friends, who—this time it was Dooley's turn to be amused—hadn't moved at all, not even the guys.

Dooley wished Parker would do something—throw a punch, bitch-slap him, he didn't care what, just something so that he could slam him back and everyone would see it was self-defense.

"Casper told me all about you," Parker said. Casper? Who the hell was Casper? "He seems to think you're dangerous, but you don't look dangerous to me." He ran his eyes over Dooley. "You look like a loser."

Dooley had known plenty of guys like Parker. Okay, so maybe they didn't have even a fraction of the money Parker had, but they were the same in all the ways that counted. They were bullies and they were talkers. Big talkers.

Dooley wasn't a big talker. He didn't waste his breath on bullies. When he spoke to them, it was to let them know exactly what he was going to do, and that was it. He stared at Parker, letting his eyes carry everything that was in his head and his heart.

Parker stared right back at him. Then, the trace of a smile playing across his lips, he leaned into Dooley, so close that Dooley felt his breath on his ear.

"She wanted it," he said in a voice so quiet that only Dooley could hear it. "And I don't hold it against her, going to the cops the way she did. You want to know the truth? I feel sorry for her. If she doesn't come to her senses and drop the charge, it's going to go hard on her. You know what's going to happen? I'm going to have to get into the witness box and tell them how it went down, what she said, what she told me she wanted me to do, what she did. Because, believe me, brother, she *did* want it. She started the whole thing. *She* came onto *me*, and she did it in front of witnesses."

Blood-red washed across Dooley's field of vision. The prick was goading him. Damned if Parker didn't want the same thing that Dooley did.

"I know where you live," he said to Parker. "I know where you go to school. I know where you play tennis. And I know what you are. I hope you have better friends than the ones standing over there because you need someone to watch your back." He glanced at the kids behind Parker, at Nevin in particular. Then he turned and started back the way he had come, nodding at Parker's sister as he went by. It didn't make him feel any better. None of it did. Hitting the guy, now maybe that would have been something. But it also would have jammed him up, canceled out the whole last year and all the work he had done. But, boy, if he was going to throw it all away, Parker Albright would be the one who would at least make it worthwhile.

A guy shouldered past Dooley at the side of the house. Dooley turned to look at him. His clothes set him apart. His jeans were frayed at the bottoms and his white T-shirt, taut across his chest, had seen better days. He wasn't tall, but he was broad in the shoulders and chest and had sturdy thighs. He looked like a wrestler, Dooley decided, one of those small-ish squat guys who were easily dismissed but who knew how to do real damage. Dooley was about to move on when he heard a husky voice—the wrestler's?—say, "Where is he?" Then a girl: "Get out of here, Brad. Get out or I'll call the cops."

Dooley strolled back to the yard to get a look. Five girls, two of them Annicka and Parker's sister, were standing in front of the wrestler, all of them with their arms out in front of them, trying to push the him back.

"Parker!" the wrestler shouted. "Parker, you asshole! You

fucking asshole! You think you're something? Why don't you come over here and prove it?"

Way down the lawn, Parker turned to look at them. Hey, and what do you know, Dooley saw apprehension on his face. He glanced at his entourage and laughed. But Dooley noticed that he didn't take so much as a step in the wrestler's direction. No, he left that to his sister, who had a cell phone in her hand now and was shouting, "I'm doing it. I'm calling 911. If you don't leave, Brad, you'll be sorry."

A couple of girls Dooley didn't know took the wrestler by the hand. One of them said something into his ear. The wrestler glowered at Parker, looking like he'd give both nuts to get just a piece of him. The girl tugged on his arm again, and the guy backed down. Dooley watched him turn and start back the way he had come. Too bad, he thought. It would have been pleasant to watch Parker get mashed—and to not have to worry about taking any blame for it. It would have been very pleasant.

He probably should have headed home, but he was too stoked for that, too full of what he could have done, what Parker had done, who he had done it to, and how it had all happened in the first place. He had to burn it off somehow, and walking was the safest way. He marched through Parker's front gate, ignoring the dog that lunged at him, the woman who glowered at him, ignoring the young guy with black hair and brown skin who tried to catch his attention, looking like he wanted to ask him something, maybe how to navigate his way out of this neighborhood with its twisting streets and dead ends, which were all advertised on yellow and black signs as *cul de sacs*, ignoring the half-dozen other young guys across the street, also with black hair and brown skin, who were watching the first guy; Dooley figured them for friends, people he had no time for, no interest in. He swerved around the guy, strode down the street, cut through an off-leash park, and followed a set of log and gravel steps down into a ravine. He knew it well—it cut deep into the land between two rows of big houses, snaked down through a couple of parks in one direction, up into an enormous cemetery in another, and, further east, alongside but out of sight of a highway, until it arrived in a sprawling public garden where, if you went at the right time of year, you tripped over bridal parties posing for photographers.

This time of night it was quiet in the ravine. It was dark, too. Not the place you'd want to be if you were a girl alone, but not so bad if you were a guy who knew how to handle himself. You just had to look like you could carry it off so that whoever you might run into would think twice about the risk and would pass until someone else came along who didn't carry himself with the same confidence.

He looked up at all the monster houses as he walked—a lot of them with gazebos overlooking the lip of the ravine, a lot of them not bothering with fences back there because the ravine was steep and the drop into it deep. He moved along quietly between the patches of light that made it down from up above. He rounded a corner in the well-worn ravine path and stopped short. No way. He peered through the gloom. Yeah, it was him all right. What was he doing down here?

Oh.

He wasn't alone.

Dooley hung back for a minute, then started to follow, careful to keep his footsteps light and silent. He saw a piece of tree branch lying on the side of the path—it had probably come down in one of the wind storms that had battered the city over the winter. Dooley bent and picked it up. It was thick and heavy. He carried it with him, swinging it, creeping closer and closer, until the guy turned suddenly, as if he'd felt Dooley back there. He grinned at Dooley and shooed his companion off ahead. Dooley hefted the tree branch. He imagined what he could do with it.

✦ FIVE ✦

Dooley got up early the next morning. His uncle's bedroom door was still closed, and there was a purse on the table in the front hall. Jeannie was still there. Good. His uncle always slept a little later when Jeannie was around.

Dooley snuck down to the basement. The clothes he had put into the washing machine the night before were still in there, damp but clean. He left them where they were, added more soap and bleach, and started the washing machine again. Then he crept upstairs to get dressed. He put on some coffee and ate breakfast while he waited for the wash cycle to end. When it did, he popped everything into the dryer. He was sitting in the kitchen again when his uncle showed up, sniffing the air and looking in surprise at the pot of coffee on the warmer plate.

"I saw Jeannie's purse," Dooley said. Whenever Jeannie was over, his uncle always came down and got coffee for her. Jeannie needed at least one cup, sometimes two, to get her cylinders firing. Only then did she get out of bed. If it was the weekend, she'd come down to the kitchen, usually in a silky robe and a pair of slippers that looked like sandals, and she'd make a big breakfast for Dooley and his uncle.

Dooley's uncle hooked a couple of mugs from the cupboard, filled them, added cream and sugar to one of them, and disappeared back upstairs.

Dooley's cell phone rang.

"It's me," a voice said. "Warren. Did I wake you?"

"No. What's up?"

"I'm at work. They've got me working Emerg. I didn't know if anyone would have called you or what, so I figured I should check and see."

"Call me? What about?"

"Beth."

Everything faded—the cup he was holding, the table, the whole kitchen.

"What about her?"

"They brought her in about an hour ago. I would have called sooner, but it's crazy in here. If they don't have me running the floor-washing machine, they have me sweeping. If I'm not doing that—"

"Beth's in Emergency?" Dooley said. "Is she okay? What happened?"

"I don't know. The paramedics brought her in. I saw them wheel her by."

Paramedics? That didn't sound good.

"Was she bleeding or banged up or anything?" Dooley said.

"I don't think so. I'm not sure. She went by pretty fast, and they had a blanket over her. All I know is, they brought her in and she's still here."

"I'll be there as soon as I can." Dooley flipped his phone shut and ran upstairs to get his wallet.

"Hey!" his uncle thundered through his closed bedroom door. "Keep it down out there, will you?"

Dooley shouted, "Sorry," on his way back down the stairs. He raced to the closest bus stop. No bus in sight. He checked the schedule inside the bus shelter and glanced at his watch. He'd just missed one bus. The next one wasn't due for thirty minutes. He half-ran and half-walked the kilometer and a half to the hospital.

A security guard posted at the entrance to the Emergency department stopped him as he went through the sliding doors.

"What's your business here?" he wanted to know.

"They brought my girlfriend in an hour and a half ago." He was telling the guard Beth's name when Warren appeared, pushing a wide, flat broom. The guard nodded and let Dooley pass.

"She's down that hall," Warren said. "First door on the right, last bed to the left."

"Is she okay?"

"I don't know. I saw them take her in. I haven't seen her since."

Dooley's instinct was to sprint down the hall to her but he forced himself to slow it down. Hospitals don't like civilians racing all over the place, not even when it's a matter of life and death. Two nurses turned and looked sternly at him as he entered the large room. There were five beds in it, each separated by curtains from the ones next to it.

"My girlfriend—" he began, and stopped abruptly when he spotted Beth. She was sitting up in the bed on the far left, just like Warren had said. Her face was pale, but that wasn't what made Dooley's heart slam to a halt in his chest. No, what made that happen were her lips. They were black like coal. Like night. Like death. They were as black as if someone had painted them that color, and when she opened her mouth to say something to her mother, who was sitting on a chair beside the bed, Dooley saw that her tongue was just as black.

Jesus. What had she done? And why? Was it because of him? He should have been nicer to her when he'd seen her in that coffee shop. He shouldn't have asked her those questions the way he did.

Or maybe it was because of Parker.

Either way, he started toward her.

One of the nurses came toward him.

"You can't come in here," she said, her voice brusque, no-nonsense. Beth turned toward the door, saw Dooley, and said something to her mother that he couldn't hear.

Beth's mother stood up. For a moment, Dooley was hopeful. Her mother had been nicer to him than normal when he'd gone to the apartment. Maybe she would intercede on his behalf now.

But no.

She flew at him, scowling, her hands thrust out to push him away. She yelled at the nurse, "Get him out of here. I don't want him near my daughter. Do you understand? I don't want him near her." What was going on? She'd been nice to him the last time he'd seen her. Well, maybe nice was overstating it. But she'd been civil.

Dooley stared at Beth's black lips and white face. She was crying. To his left, he saw the second nurse pick up a telephone handset and speak into it. Her eyes never left Dooley. The first nurse outflanked him and joined forces with Beth's mother to block his way.

"You can't come in here," she said again.

Beth's head was in her hands. Her shoulders were shaking. She was sobbing. How could he not go to her? He tried to push past the two women, but Beth's mother grabbed his arm. She was a small woman, short and slight. Her head barely reached Dooley's shoulder. But, boy, it turned out that she was strong.

She dragged on him like an anchor. The nurse stayed in front of him, moving backwards with his progress and warning him that if he didn't leave, security would put him out. Then Dooley saw relief in her eyes. Two burly security guards appeared, the younger of them looking pumped and ready for action.

"I don't want him here," Beth's mother said. "I don't want him near my daughter."

Dooley looked at Beth over the top of her mother's head. She was hunched over. Her hands covered her face.

"Come on, pal," the older of the security guards said, firm but reasonable. He reminded Dooley of his uncle. "If we have to, we'll call the police."

He couldn't win. No matter what he did, it always came to threats of trouble. Of cops. That was the last thing he needed. He relented and let the security guards steer him out of the room and down the hall to the Emergency entrance, passing Warren on the way. They walked him through the door and stood there, arms crossed over their chests, making sure he left hospital property. Dooley stood out on the sidewalk. He didn't care that the two security guards were watching him. He waited until he saw Warren come through the doors, then he turned and walked down to the stop sign on the corner, out of sight of the Emergency entrance.

Warren joined him a few moments later.

"What happened?" he asked.

"Her mom wouldn't let me talk to her." In fact, she had acted like the whole thing was Dooley's fault. Did that mean it was? Did that mean that Dooley was the reason Beth had done it—Dooley, not Parker? Jesus, as if that even mattered after what she'd done.

"Is she okay?"

Her lips were black. Her tongue was black. Not positive signs.

"Do you clean the rooms, Warren, or just the halls?"

"I clean everything—rooms, halls, shit, piss, vomit."

"What about the room she's in now?"

"I run a mop through there every hour and empty all the trash cans."

"If you find out anything, call me, okay?"

"No problem."

"Any time, Warren. I mean it."

◆ ◆ ◆

Dooley had seen lips like Beth's before. Tyler Brock's lips had been black. His tongue, too, and his gums, all that black making his teeth look whiter than they really were.

Dooley was surprised that they'd let him visit Tyler. They even arranged for someone to run him over to the hospital. True, part of that person's job was to stick close to Dooley to make sure he didn't use the opportunity to slip away. He found out later that no one else had even asked how Tyler was, forget about asking if they could see him. He doubted that he would have asked, either, except for the timing. It had been maybe an hour after Dooley had made his position clear that he'd seen Ralston downstairs, harassing Tyler about laundry detail.

"I did it just the way you told me," Tyler was saying. "Folded everything, too, just like you said."

"Show me," Ralston had said. He'd unlocked the door to the basement and held it to let Tyler go first. Dooley had heard the door click shut behind them. He wasn't positive, but he bet it was locked.

Tyler wouldn't look at Dooley when Dooley was shown into the ward's dayroom. There were other people in the room. A few had visitors, but most were sitting alone in chairs, staring blankly out at the world, like they couldn't believe they were still in it. The youth worker who had accompanied Dooley took a seat by the door, out of the way, and picked up an ancient copy of *Time* magazine. Dooley slipped into a chair opposite Tyler.

"Hey," he said, forcing a cheeriness into his voice that he didn't feel and that he believed Tyler didn't want to hear. "You okay?" Stupid question. Tyler had been Form One'd—they could hold him up to seventy-two hours for a psych assessment. The floor he was on was locked, so he couldn't leave. If he was stupid enough to try anyway, they could forcibly restrain him.

Tyler stared down at the floor. There was a black streak on the front of his hospital smock.

"They made me drink charcoal," he said in a whispery voice. Dooley wasn't sure that he had heard right.

"What?"

"It tasted like shit. They made me drink two bottles."

"Of charcoal?" Dooley was trying to picture it. He found out later that it was powdered charcoal suspended in some kind of liquid.

"Next time," Tyler said, "I'm gonna do it differently. Maybe I'll jump. Or maybe a knife."

Next time?

"Jeez, Tyler—" But Dooley didn't know what to say after that. "Did you tell them what happened?"

"I told them I broke into the infirmary."

Actually, he'd walked into the infirmary, complaining of a sore throat. Dooley knew because Devon Deacon had told him.

Devon was in the infirmary at least once a week. He had stomach problems and kept getting sent for ulcer tests. Once in, Tyler had somehow managed to swipe a bottle of aspirin. Whoever had been on duty would be in shit for that because what if it hadn't been aspirin? What if it had been something that could be used to get a high on? What then?

Tyler had swallowed the whole bottle all at once, with a glassful of water. Dooley had seen him do it. Or, rather, Dooley had seen him swallow *something*, one handful after another, and then lie down on his bed in the room across the hall from Dooley's. Dooley had seen it but had put it out of his mind—what did he care what Tyler did? He hadn't given Tyler another thought until he had to go to the can. He passed by Tyler's room. The kid was sprawled on his bed, his eyes closed. He hadn't moved when Dooley passed by a few minutes later on his way back to his room. So what? Which, of course, is when he spotted the empty aspirin bottle on the floor. Dooley stood there for a moment before going into the room and pressing two fingers to the side of Tyler's neck. He was still breathing. Dooley hesitated. The thought in his mind: it was none of his business. But a whole bottle of aspirin? Dooley wasn't positive how much was needed to kill a person, but he'd heard of people getting themselves into serious trouble with aspirin. He found out later that as few as (or as many as—it all depended on your point of view) twenty tablets was serious enough to cause seizures, comas, and, yup, the one Tyler had been going for, death. He looked for and found a counselor playing two-on-two ping-pong in the rec room and told him what he'd seen. The counselor dropped his paddle and hurried out of the room. The paramedics showed up five minutes later to take Tyler to the hospital. Two days later, Dooley was in the psych ward dayroom, pulling a chair up so he could sit opposite Tyler.

"I mean," he said, "did you tell them what happened before you ... did what you did?"

Tyler refused to look at him.

"I don't know what you're talking about."

Right. Okay. He was probably embarrassed. Who wouldn't be?

"If you want, I could say something," Dooley said, even though he didn't want to. Thing number one: What if no one believed him? Thing number two: Why did he even have to? Why didn't Tyler just stand up to the guy? That's what Dooley had done, and if he could do it, so could Tyler. He looked at Tyler's pale face and enormous eyes, black and glazed like a doll's, all big-eyed innocence, until you studied them and realized there was nothing behind them. You'd never guess that he'd been locked up for violent assault. What Dooley had heard: Tyler had grabbed a kitchen knife and stabbed his foster mother with it. A guy who could do that should be able to tell another guy to fuck off, shouldn't he? "You want me to talk to my uncle?" Dooley said. He barely knew his uncle then—Gary McCormack was just some hard-nosed ex-cop who had showed up one day and was on Dooley's case, once a week when he visited, to shape up, for Christ's sake, think about his future and what he was going to do when they released him into the community, where did he see himself living, what did he see himself doing? Always pushing Dooley for answers when, mostly, Dooley was thinking that the very first thing he wanted to do was celebrate—by which, of course, he meant get high. Still, his uncle used to be a cop, which meant he would probably know how to handle Tyler's situation.

Tyler shook his head. "I'm okay."

What did that mean? Dooley had seen him go into the basement with Ralston. He knew, because he knew Ralston, what that was all about.

"You should say something to someone."

Tyler stared at him. He didn't say a word. Dooley didn't get it. Maybe Tyler was afraid to go up against Ralston on his own. That was understandable. But to turn down help when it was offered? If you did that, you had no one to blame but yourself.

Dooley reached into his pocket, pulled out the couple of candy bars he had picked up in the gift shop, and set them on the table in front of Tyler. Tyler didn't so much as glance at them. Dooley asked him how long he would be in the hospital. Tyler didn't answer. Dooley said if they kept him any longer than seventy-two hours, he would see what he could do about visiting him again. Tyler was silent. When Dooley stood up to leave, Tyler didn't seem to notice.

Two days later, Tyler came back from the hospital. He had to report to the infirmary every morning for some pills. Dooley wasn't clear what they were for. Tyler hardly ever spoke. Ralston stopped by his room regularly and stood in the doorway, talking softly to him. Dooley never heard Tyler answer.

◆ ◆ ◆

Dooley climbed his uncle's porch steps and sank down onto one of the Muskoka chairs his uncle had out there. He still couldn't believe it: Beth was in the hospital, and it looked like she had done more or less what Tyler had done. He thought back over everything he knew about her. She was bright and driven to succeed. She took school seriously. She'd been traumatized as a kid—her father had been murdered and she'd been right there.

The wounds had been deep. She hadn't been able to shake the memories. But when her brother had died, she'd shown herself to be a tiger. She'd pushed hard to get to the bottom of what had happened to him. Nothing had stood in her way. So, suicide? It didn't make sense. Beth was a fighter, not a quitter. Suicide was the ultimate surrender. No, it didn't add up. What had led her down that path?

The front door opened, startling him. It wasn't his uncle. It was Jeannie. As usual, she was well put together, hair neatly styled, just enough makeup to look fresh and elegant, never too much that she seemed desperate to recapture her youth. She was wearing black slacks, a form-fitting blouse, and black loafers. She looked terrific for a woman her age.

"Oh," she said, surprised to see him sitting there. "I thought I heard someone come up the steps. I thought it was Gary. He went out to run some errands." She looked him over. "Is everything okay?"

"Yeah."

Maybe it was the fact that she didn't take his response at face value but stood in the door, looking at him. Maybe it was the concern in her eyes. Or maybe it was that she was a woman, an okay one at that, and he trusted her.

"You remember Beth?" he said.

Jeannie's smile was swift and soft.

"Of course."

"She's in the hospital."

"Oh?" Jeanie let the screen door shut behind her. She perched on the edge of the Muskoka chair beside his as if to reassure him that she wouldn't stay if he didn't want her to. "Is she okay?"

Dooley struggled with how to answer the question. He had no idea what, if anything, Beth would want him to say. He was hoping she hadn't done it because Parker had dumped her like Annicka said. But would it make things any better if she had done it because of Dooley instead, because of the way he had reacted, what he had said?

Jeannie placed a hand over his and let it lie there for a moment.

"I won't pry, Dooley. That's not my style. But if you want to talk, I'll be inside. And Gary should be back soon." She got up and moved toward the door.

"She tried to kill herself," Dooley said.

Jeannie turned and stood motionless.

"But she's okay?"

"I don't know. I guess so. I saw her, but I didn't get a chance to talk to her. They wouldn't let me. They called security."

Jeannie sat down again and squeezed his arm.

"I don't know why she did it," Dooley said. He glanced into Jeannie's quick, compassionate eyes. She was a good person. She'd taken his side before. So why was he lying to her now? "She went away for a week. To work on a community project. Her school is very big on community projects. Stuff like building houses for underprivileged families."

"Probably to teach them how over-privileged they are," Jeannie said quietly. Yeah, Jeannie was a good person. She always got it.

"There was this guy on the trip with her," Dooley continued. And before he knew it, he was spilling out the whole story—not the part about going to the tennis club or to Parker's party, but the rest of it, about Nevin and Parker and what the girls at Beth's school had said, about what Beth had said. About what he had said to Beth.

"I should have told her straightaway that I believed her," he said. But the thought was still there, burning in his brain like an ember: what if she'd swallowed all those pills because of Parker, because he'd fucked her and then dumped her? What if she'd heard about the trash Parker was talking about her? What if what she'd done had nothing to do with Dooley at all? He didn't tell Jeannie that part, either.

"But she's going to be okay?" Jeannie said when he had finished.

"I sure hope so," Dooley said. Tyler hadn't been okay. They'd kept him under lock and key for a while. They'd put him on medication. They'd made him see a shrink regularly. But, in the end, Tyler had gone ahead and finished the job, differently, just like he'd said he would, not with pills but with a twisted up bed sheet and a plastic milk crate pilfered from the kitchen.

"I don't know Beth as well as you do, but what I've seen, I like," Jeannie said. "Maybe she's not perfect. Who is? But she seems to have a good heart."

Jeannie was right about that, Dooley thought. Look at the effort she'd put into her brother. Or how she'd listened to the worst about Dooley and had still stayed with him because, she said, she believed she saw what other people didn't, maybe she saw the other side of him. Maybe that was the problem. Maybe, after all this time of looking at him the way no one else did, she'd come to a decision. She'd kept quiet about who was going on the trip with her and, once she was gone, she'd made a play for someone different, someone more like what she was used to, someone with promise.

Maybe.

"Her mother won't let me near her. She's the one who got them to call security on me and throw me out of the hospital."

"I remember her mother," Jeannie said. The two women had met under less than optimal circumstances. "If I were you, I'd talk to her, Dooley. I wouldn't give up." She squeezed his arm again and then got up and went inside.

◆ ◆ ◆

Dooley's uncle came into Dooley's room later that night, after Jeannie had gone home.

"Jeannie told me about Beth," he said. He didn't ask why Dooley hadn't told him himself, but Dooley could see the question in his eyes. "You want me to talk to her mother, see if she'll cut you some slack?"

"No, it's okay," Dooley said. "I'll do it myself. It's probably better that way."

"You sure? Because I don't mind."

"I'm sure. But thanks."

His uncle nodded and closed the door quietly behind him.

SIX

"A couple of years ago, it was guns," Dooley's uncle said from behind the newspaper the next morning. "Kids were running around shooting each other and the papers were all over it, calling it the summer of the gun. Remember?" Dooley didn't, and, in any case, his uncle didn't stop to wait for an answer. "Now it's knives," his uncle said.

Dooley poured himself a bowl of cereal and a cup of coffee.

"Every Tom, Dick, and Harry has a knife, and they all seem to be using them to carve each other up. Kids especially."

Dooley glanced at the page his uncle was reading. "Teen stabbed to death in front of local mall." There was a picture of the kid, but that wasn't what caught Dooley's attention.

"Can I see that?" he said.

"When I'm finished. And since when did you start reading the paper at breakfast?"

"Whatever," Dooley muttered. He added milk to his bowl and sat down to eat.

His uncle moved through the pages slowly, as if he were committing each one to memory. Dooley drank a cup of coffee while he waited. Finally his uncle put the paper down. Dooley grabbed it. He read the news brief next to the picture of the fatally stabbed teen: *Body found in ravine.* The story was exactly one paragraph long. It said an off-duty cop had found a body while he was out jogging on Sunday morning. It referred to the deceased as a white male whose name the police had not yet released, "pending further investigation."

He realized his uncle had said something.

"Sorry, what?"

"I said, you're going to be late for school."

Dooley put the paper down.

"You're sure you're okay?" his uncle said.

"Yeah." He was as sure as anyone could be after a week from hell.

"The offer still stands. If you want me to call Beth's mother—"

"It's okay." If Beth had wanted to see him, nothing, not even her mother, could have stopped her. But she hadn't even looked at him when he was at the hospital. She'd just sat there in bed, her head buried in her hands. "I gotta go."

◆ ◆ ◆

He found Warren at his locker, but Warren didn't have any news.

"All I know is they put her up on seven," he said. When he saw that Dooley didn't get it, he added, "The pysch ward is on seven. I'll see if I can get up there, but I can't promise anything."

"If you find out anything or see her—"

"I know," Warren said. "I'll do my best."

Dooley spent the afternoon wondering where Beth's mother would be. He knew she worked, but Beth was in the hospital and the way Dooley saw it, attempted suicide was as bad as it could get, short of having some terminal disease. Beth's mother seemed to him like the kind of person who would stick pretty close. After all, Beth was her only child now, all she had left. She would probably take time off work. Minimally, she would be at the hospital every chance she got, so he went directly there after school and was startled to see Beth's mother in the lobby, queued up at the Tim Horton's kiosk, which was doing brisk business.

"Mrs. Manson?"

She turned, startled to see him.

"How's Beth?"

"Next!" the counterperson said.

"Coffee, black," Beth's mother said.

"Medium? Large?"

"Medium."

Dooley waited while she got her coffee and paid for it. She didn't look at him but instead searched the lobby for a place to sit. There were a couple of uncomfortable plastic chairs against one wall. She headed for them and sank down. Dooley hesitated before claiming the one next to her.

"Is she okay? Do they have any idea how long they're going to keep her in here?" he said, keeping his voice quiet, doing his best to convince her of his concern, conveying, he hoped, I'm a nice guy and I care, I really care.

She looked him over as if he were a total stranger. He supposed, in a way, he was. She had barely ever spoken to him, and had judged him purely on circumstances (catching him in bed with Beth hadn't helped, nor had all those times he'd been questioned by the police) and on his past (he couldn't blame her for that; he supposed he would do the same if he had a daughter who was seeing a guy with his history). Still, Beth must have told her a few good things. She and her mother had locked horns over him more than once, which meant that Beth had to have said *something* in his defense.

"She thinks it's her fault," Beth's mother said finally. "And she thinks, for some reason I don't even pretend to understand, that she let you down in some way." Her voice got louder. "That's why she did it." She was angry—at him. She blamed him. "The irony is, Parker Albright is much more her type, and if it wasn't for you—" She broke off. Maybe she didn't want to finish her sentence. Maybe she didn't think she had to.

Dooley focused on his breathing, filling his lungs slowly and emptying them again, another coping technique. It slowed him down, pushed his anger back into its black hole.

"I'd really like to see her, Mrs. Manson."

"No." No hesitation there. The old Dooley would have strangled her. The new Dooley merely wished he could.

"Could you at least ask her if she wants to see me?" he said, working even harder now to keep his anger in the black place where it belonged.

She shook her head. The worry, the fear, the shadow of a prayer he had originally seen on her face were gone now, replaced by the ferocious protectiveness of a mother.

"Getting involved with you was the worst thing that ever happened to Beth," she said. Dooley knew for a fact that it wasn't. "Look where it's led."

Terrific. Beth blamed herself, her mother blamed Dooley, and old Parker was walking around without a care in the world.

Dooley stood up. His heart beat like a battle drum in his chest. He told himself over and over: breathe. Breathe. With a curt nod, he left Beth's mother alone with her coffee.

◆ ◆ ◆

His uncle was watching the news when Dooley got home. He muted the sound.

"So?" he said.

"I talked to her mother."

"And?"

"She turned me down."

"Now what?" His uncle was clearly apprehensive, worried, probably, that Dooley would do something stupid.

"I don't know. I guess I wait and see if she calls me." Or, he thought, I could try to get a message to her through Warren. He sat down in an armchair and glanced at the TV. "So, what's new?"

"Some politician spouting more BS," his uncle said. "Although that's not really news. Price of gas is up again for no damned reason that I can see, other than pure greed on the part of the oil companies. And another kid bites the dust—doesn't look like it's gang-related, though. No knives or guns."

Dooley stared at the TV screen, even though he didn't care about the news. All he cared about was Beth.

"The kid must have pissed off someone really good," Dooley's uncle said. "His head was stove in by a rock. Someone pounded him and didn't stop until he was good and dead. Are you even listening to me, Ryan?"

"Yeah," Dooley said.

He'd been thinking about Beth all day. More than that, he'd been thinking about something that Dr. Calvin had told him more than once. Life was all about control, about understanding what was in your control and what wasn't. Basically, what it boiled down to was that shit happens. It happens all the time. Sometimes you can see it coming and sometimes it rains down on you with no warning. And pretty much the only thing you can do once you're neck-deep in it is make a decision: wallow in it or grab a shovel and dig yourself out. The shit-happens principle applied to other people, too. Other people think what they think. They do what they do. Sure, you can argue with them, you can fight them, but, fundamentally, you have no control over their thoughts and actions. The only thing you can control, the only power you have, is how you react to them: again, you can wallow in whatever bullshit they put on you or you can suck it up and move on. "The way I look at it," Dr. Calvin had said once, "there are more than enough assholes in the world. You can join that crowd or you can be a good guy, Dooley. You can decide to do the right thing just because it's the right thing to do, no matter what anyone else thinks—no matter what that little voice in your head is telling you about revenge, or payback, or just desserts." He'd had that on his mind all day and had decided that the right thing to do if he loved Beth was to take her at her word, to do anything it took to back her up, and to make sure Parker Albright got exactly what was coming to him.

"So?" his uncle said, irritated now. "What did I just say?"

"Some kid got his head bashed in." His uncle harrumphed, disappointed, Dooley thought, that Dooley actually had been listening. "You know him or something?"

"They haven't released his name," his uncle said.

So what's the big deal, Dooley wanted to ask.

His uncle clicked off the TV. "You hungry or did you already fill up on junk food?"

Dooley hadn't thought about food since he'd had lunch at the Chinese restaurant he liked because the only other diners were old Chinese men. No one from school ever ventured into the place.

"I could eat," he said.

"Good." His uncle heaved himself up off the couch. "I made a barley casserole."

"Barley?"

"Jeannie's interested in eating more vegetarian. I thought I'd try out a few things." The look on his face dared Dooley to make something of it. Dooley knew better.

Dooley trudged across the flagstone to the main entrance of school the next morning. There were kids milling around outside, smoking, flirting, giggling, gossiping, texting—all the stuff they were going to have to stop doing when the bell rang. Warren was up near one of the doors. He perked up when he saw Dooley and started down the steps toward him. His eyes flicked to someplace behind Dooley, and Dooley saw a puzzled look on his face, which quickly turned to concern when he shifted his gaze back to Dooley and gestured with a tip of his head, wanting Dooley to look. But before he could, a hand fell on Dooley's shoulder and a voice said, "Ryan Dooley?"

Dooley turned to face two uniformed cops.

"Yeah, I'm Dooley."

"You're wanted for questioning."

Well, he couldn't say that he hadn't been expecting them.

"Questioning about what?"

"Do you know Parker Albright?" said the cop who had put his hand on Dooley's shoulder. He was the older one of the two, nearly as old as Dooley's uncle, which meant he was either a total fuck-up or one hell of a dedicated cop if he was still on patrol at his age.

"I know of him," Dooley said cautiously. Jesus, now what?

"Well, a couple of detectives want to talk to you about him."

Detectives?

"Is this about Beth?" he said. "Is she okay?"

"All I know is, we were told to bring you in for questioning."

Dooley glanced at Warren, who wore a worried-mother expression. Most of the kids milling around outside school were staring at Dooley. Dooley bet there wasn't a single one of them who was surprised to see the cops on him again.

Dooley nodded and walked with them back to the police car at the curb, where the older cop recited his rights to him, covering his ass. Whatever.

They stuck him in an interview room and let him sit there for a while. He wondered if Beth was okay. He pulled out his cell phone and was about to call directory assistance to get the hospital's phone number when the door to the interview room opened and a detective walked in. Detective Randall, the same cop who had investigated Lorraine's death. But he was Homicide, not sex crimes. No way, Dooley thought. He must have heard that Dooley had been picked up and had dropped by to see what was going on. That had to be it.

Randall pulled out a chair and sat down.

"Hello, Ryan," he said.

Dooley nodded.

Randall ran through Dooley's rights. Dooley's fingers tingled. Then his arms. His chest tightened. What was going on? Why was a Homicide cop reading him his rights?

"What's this about?" he said.

"Are you sure?" Randall said, meaning, was Dooley sure he didn't want his uncle there and didn't want to call a lawyer?

"I'm sure. I'm also sure I'm going to get up and walk out of here unless you tell me what's going on."

"First things first," Randall said. He made Dooley sign the paper before he leaned back in his chair and said, "Do you know Parker Albright?"

"Yeah. Sort of." Had Parker laid a complaint? No, that couldn't be it, unless Randall had transferred to another unit.

"Sort of?" Randall raised an eyebrow. "You want to elaborate?"

"I know who he is. I met him a couple of times. Why?"

"Did you kill him?"

"What?" Jesus, Parker was dead?

Randall stared at him. He let the silence between them grow, hoping, Dooley knew, to make him so uncomfortable that he would feel compelled to go on, maybe hang himself.

"Where were you Saturday night, Ryan?" Randall said at last.

"I didn't kill him."

"I talked to your manager at the video store. He said you were supposed to work on Saturday night, but that you didn't turn up. He said you switched your shift with one of your co-workers, even though he told you that you couldn't." That was Kevin, all right, complaining about Dooley to the cops. "You know what that makes it, right, Ryan? It makes it premeditated. First degree murder."

"I didn't do it."

"Where were you Saturday night?"

"Out. I was out."

Randall shook his head as if he were disappointed. He seemed even more disappointed when Dooley let the silence stretch, forcing Randall to say in a weary voice, "Let me be a little more specific, Ryan. What did you do Saturday night *after* you left Parker Albright's back yard?"

"I went home."

"What time did you get there?"

If Randall knew Dooley had been at the party, then he probably had some kind of timeframe. Someone—he wouldn't be surprised if it was Parker's sister—would have had an idea when he'd showed up at the party and someone else—again, it wouldn't surprise him if it was Parker's sister—had probably noticed when he'd left. For sure, his uncle would remember when he got home—his uncle, to whom Dooley had spun a lie, telling him a panhandler had puked on him on the way home from work.

"It was late," he said. "I don't know. After midnight. Probably closer to one."

"Can anyone verify when you got home?"

"My uncle." But, boy, Dooley wasn't looking forward to Randall having that conversation. Nor was he looking forward to what would follow that little chat.

Randall digested this piece of information.

"Where were you between the time you left Parker's house and when you got home?"

"Walking around. I was just walking around."

Randall sighed. "Walking around *where*, Ryan?"

"Just around."

"Just around. Your favorite place, as I recall. What were you doing at Parker's party in the first place? Did he invite you?"

"No." But Randall already knew that.

"So why were you there?"

"I wanted to talk to him."

"Talk to him? You mean, threaten him?"

"Threaten him?" There was no way anyone had heard what he'd said to Parker. That meant that Parker must have told someone. He might even have told everyone at the party.

"Come on, Ryan. I know you did."

"I wouldn't exactly call it a threat."

"Not exactly?" Randall sat motionless, his hands clasped together on the table. When Dooley didn't elaborate, he said, "Did you go to the Millbrook Tennis Club on Friday afternoon and assault Parker Albright?"

"I didn't assault him," Dooley said. How can you assault a guy through a chain-link fence? "I just talked to him, that's all."

"By slamming his face into a fence? Sounds like it was a nice, friendly conversation."

Dooley said nothing.

"Four witnesses, including two security guards, saw you, Ryan. That wasn't a conversation. That was an assault, attempted, at least."

Dooley kept quiet. Randall stared at him for a moment.

"How's Beth?" he said finally. "You still seeing her?"

Dooley had no intention of discussing Beth with a cop.

"You know she pressed charges against Parker, don't you, Ryan? You know she's saying it was date-rape?"

Blood was pulsing through Dooley. He had to work hard to sit still, to show nothing.

"Where were you between nine-thirty and the time you say you got home on Saturday night, Ryan?"

"I told you. I took a walk."

"Where, exactly, did you take this walk?"

Dooley looked into the detective's eyes. They didn't give away a thing, but Dooley had this idea that Randall knew. He was that kind of cop. He didn't ask questions that he didn't have the answer to.

"Come on, Ryan. You expect me to believe a smart guy like you can't remember where he was a few days ago?"

Silence.

Randall leaned across the table, his eyes harder than Dooley had ever seen them before. "If you want to see outside again, Ryan, tell me where you were and make me believe it."

"In the ravine. I took a walk in the ravine."

"The ravine that runs behind Parker's house?"

Fuck.

"It's the same ravine," Dooley said. "But I wasn't in that part of it." He knew Randall wasn't kidding. If Dooley didn't make him believe it, he wasn't going to walk. No way.

Randall eyed him again.

"I paid a visit to Parker's house," Randall said. "It's quite a place. His dad's one of those dot-com millionaires. Did you know that?"

Everyone was so impressed with Parker's dad's money, Dooley thought. They all mentioned it.

"Beth goes to a private school, right?"

Dooley just stared at him.

"I bet she meets a lot of rich boys," Randall said. "Boys like Parker. Did you see that pool while you were up there at that party? It's one of those indoor / outdoor deals. They use it all year round. There's a hot tub, too. I bet Parker knows how to put that to use, what do you think?"

What Dooley thought was that Randall was trying to get a rise out of him. Well, nice try.

"I've met a fair number of kids like Parker over the years," Randall said. "A lot of people think that because they live in the best neighborhoods and go to the best schools, they're good boys. Real little angels. But you and I both know that's not true, don't we, Ryan? Parker and a lot of guys just like him are spoiled rotten. They don't appreciate what they have. You think Parker got up every morning and thanked his lucky stars that he lived in a house like that? You think he realized how lucky he was? No. In my experience, guys like that know nothing about gratitude. They're all about entitlement. A guy like Parker thinks he deserves all the good things in life. And you know what? There's not much in his life that tells him otherwise. His parents give him everything his heart desires. His teachers aren't hard on him—they wouldn't dare, not with all that tuition money his parents pay to that fancy school. And girls? Well, come on, what kind of girl wouldn't want to land a guy like Parker? She'd have it made. She wouldn't have to work. She wouldn't have—"

"I didn't kill him," Dooley said.

"She says he raped her, Ryan. You know what that means, right?"

Yeah, he knew. Did Randall think he was stupid?

"I read the complaint," Randall said. "I read Parker's statement, too. One thing no one's denying is that he had sex with her. How did you feel when you found out, Ryan? That's why you went to the tennis club, isn't it? And to the party? Because you knew that Parker'd had sex with Beth."

Dooley felt a swirl of cold blackness begin to rise in him. He wished Randall would shut up.

"Beth told you he raped her. So you went looking for Parker to punish him, didn't you? You went there to make that rich son of a bitch pay for laying his hands on your girl. Isn't that right, Ryan? I bet it drives you crazy, picturing him with her, doesn't it? Something like that could drive a guy crazy enough to want to beat someone's head in. Is that what happened? You pictured him with Beth. You pictured what he did with her and grabbed the nearest thing you could lay hands on and you—"

Dooley stood up. He wanted to punch something.

"Sit down," Randall said.

Someone knocked on the door to the interview room. Randall grimaced in annoyance and went to open it.

"The kid's lawyer is here," said the cop at the door.

"He didn't ask for a lawyer," Randall said.

"I want a lawyer," Dooley said.

"I heard that," a voice said. Annette Girondin stepped into the room. She gave Dooley a concerned once-over before turning to Randall. "Is he under arrest?"

Randall glowered at her. "No," he said finally.

"Right," Annette said. "Come on, Ryan."

Her high heels clickety-clicked to the elevator. She didn't say a word until they were out of the building and in her car.

"What did you say to them?" she asked.

"Nothing."

"Why didn't you call me? You forget my number?"

"No. I just thought—"

"You thought you could handle it on your own? For God's sake, Ryan. You think you know the law better than they do?"

"No, but—"

"Next time, call me."

Which gave Dooley an opening to ask, "How did you know I was there, anyway?"

"Your uncle," she said. "He has more sense than you do. He called me."

His uncle? How did he know?

Dooley got a bad feeling.

SEVEN

Annette pulled up in front of Dooley's uncle's house. She reached into her purse, pulled out a small silver case, opened it, and handed him a business card.

"Put that in your wallet," she said. "It has my cell number on it. You can get me 24/7."

He nodded.

As he got out of the car, he saw his uncle come out the front door and stand on the porch. Alarms went off in Dooley's head. His uncle should have been at work, but there he was, looking down at Annette's car, his fist to one side of his head, index finger and pinkie finger extended, gesturing to Annette that he would call her later. He stood aside to let Dooley into the house, closed the door after him, and followed him into the kitchen, where Dooley busied himself looking in the fridge, mainly so he wouldn't have to look at his uncle. He felt his uncle's eyes on him. Sure enough, when Dooley backed out of the fridge with a container of orange juice, his uncle was standing with his hands on his hips. Dooley edged by him to the cupboard to get a glass. He poured himself some juice and drank half of it. His uncle was still staring at him.

"How did you know?" Dooley said finally.

"That vice principal at your school called." He must have meant Mr. Rektor, who held Dooley in about as much esteem as Dooley's uncle held Rektor. "Said he didn't know whether I knew it or not, but a couple of police officers from the local division had picked you up outside the school. You want to tell me why I had to hear it from him? You forget what I told you to do if the cops started hassling you again?"

Dooley didn't answer. He knew his uncle well enough to know the question was rhetorical.

"I got in touch with Annette," his uncle said. "But she hadn't heard from you, either. So she said she'd go down there and check it out. What did they want?"

"They wanted to ask me some questions."

"About what?" his uncle said, his tone making it clear that he was in no mood to coax the information out of Dooley one piece at a time.

"About some guy."

"Jesus Christ, Ryan. Either you spit the whole thing out right now or I'll get someone on the phone who will."

"It's none of your business."

"I'm responsible for you. You're under a supervision order. It damn well is my business."

You're not even really my uncle, Dooley wanted to say. I didn't ask to be here, so get off my case. He caught a picture of himself in his head, looking and sounding like some pissed-off little kid: I didn't ask to be born. Except that he'd accepted his uncle's offer. He'd lived in his uncle's house; he'd eaten his uncle's food; he'd let his uncle go to bat for him more than once; and, in exchange, he had agreed to play by his uncle's rules.

"They wanted to talk to me about some guy who was killed."

"Killed?" It took his uncle a moment to digest what Dooley had said. Clearly, it was the last thing he had expected. "What guy? What is it with you, Ryan? Someone gets killed and the next thing you know, the cops are looking at you."

"Parker Albright," Dooley said.

His uncle was as still as stone. Dooley wondered if he was having a stroke or something.

"Parker Albright, who supposedly sexually assaulted Beth?"

"*Supposedly?*"

"Allegedly," his uncle amended. "You telling me he's dead?"

"That's what Randall said."

"Randall?" Dooley's uncle knew him well.

Dooley nodded. He wished he was anyplace else but in his uncle's kitchen—well, or that interview room.

"What, exactly, did Randall say to you?"

"He asked me if I killed Parker."

"You told me you didn't even know the Albright kid existed until you found out what happened to Beth. I took that to mean you'd never met him. Was I wrong?"

"I met him," Dooley said. "I talked to him." Then, since his toe was in the water, he plunged deeper. "A couple of times."

His uncle's face was rigid. It was not the answer he had been hoping for, but it seemed to be the one he'd been fearing.

"Circumstances?"

Dooley shifted in his chair. He was living in his uncle's house. He would be there for another six months, until his supervision period was over, assuming he hadn't screwed that up already. His uncle—he still hadn't come to grips with his uncle not really being his uncle. He didn't want to be like Lorraine. She had been messed up ever since she found out she was adopted—well, *and* since she'd learned the circumstances of her adoption. She'd never got over it. Dooley had known plenty of guys who were adopted and who were uneasy in their skin because of it. He'd figured they were lucky. He'd figured, hey, they're not your real parents, so you don't have to listen to them; they've got nothing on you, so what's your problem? How many times when he was little had he wished that he was adopted, that Lorraine wasn't his real mother, that there was someone out there who wasn't Lorraine, and who maybe regretted that they'd given him up, and who maybe was even looking for him? And now here he was, living in the house of his uncle who wasn't really his uncle, who had despised his adopted sister and all her bellyaching. His uncle, who had taken him in despite all that, who had taken responsibility for him. Who was taking responsibility for him now, when, really, when you came right down to it, Dooley didn't think it was his uncle's business, not now, not when they weren't even related.

But there he was, looking at him and waiting for an answer. And, for some reason, Dooley felt he owed him one.

"I wanted to see what he looked like," Dooley said.

"That's it?"

Lorraine would have accepted what he said and let it go, assuming she'd asked in the first place, assuming it had even occurred to her to ask. But Dooley's uncle? He'd been a cop. He pressed and pressed until he had a picture in his head that satisfied him.

Dooley met his eyes.

"I wanted to see what he had. You know?"

He was skating around the edges of the truth—he knew it and, judging from the set of his uncle's jaw, his uncle knew it, too. Christ, why was he sitting here and subjecting himself to this? Why did he care what some old ex-cop thought? He drew in a deep breath.

"I wanted to see ... you said it yourself. That girl"—Annicka—"saw them holding hands. I just wanted to see him, that's all."

His uncle nodded grimly. "Anything else you want to tell me?"

Dooley shook his head. But it didn't stick. The next thing he knew, he was telling his uncle what had happened between him and Parker at the tennis club. He told him he'd stopped by Parker's house, too, although he didn't go into all of the details. It would just complicate things. He told himself that he was spilling the story because people had seen him—a lot of people—and that his uncle would find out anyway. But he wasn't sure that was the whole reason.

"How did this kid die, anyway?" his uncle said.

"Randall didn't say." But no, that wasn't quite right. "He said something about beating his head in."

His uncle frowned. "This Albright kid—where did he live?"

Dooley told him.

"Like that kid they found in the ravine," his uncle said.

"What?"

"The kid I was telling you about last night. The one they found in the ravine with his head stove in. It'd be quite a coincidence if there were two kids who died like that."

His uncle stared at him. He was doing his cop scan, reading Dooley's expression, what he was doing with his eyes, what he was doing with his hands, the way he was sitting, every detail of his bearing, and was comparing it to every thief, robber, assailant, and murderer—liars, the whole lot of them—that he had ever met and wrung a confession from.

"According to what I heard on the news, which wasn't much—and what little there was in the paper—he was killed

Saturday night." Dooley could see him remembering and doing some mental calculations. "You were working Saturday night. You closed. You telling me a smart guy like Randall didn't bother to check that out?"

"About that—"

"Jesus!" his uncle said. "Don't tell me you *weren't* working."

"I kind of switched with Linelle."

"Kind of?"

"I switched with her, okay?" Christ, his uncle could be such a pain.

His uncle glowered at him.

"Look, I'm sorry I wasn't upfront with you," Dooley said. "But I didn't kill that guy."

His uncle studied him, his lips pressed together.

"I've been straight with you about Parker. I told you I went to his tennis club."

"To pick a fight with him."

"I went to his house, too."

"To pick another fight with him."

"You don't get it," Dooley said. "You should have seen Beth. She—she was all messed up. And the way that jerk-off talked about her—" Rage pulsed through Dooley, even now.

"You let him get under your skin, didn't you?"

"Wouldn't you, if it was Jeannie?" He knew his uncle would. He pictured some slick guy, starting in talking to his uncle about Jeannie the way Parker had talked to Dooley about Beth. Slick would be talking through a mouth full of broken teeth before he finished his first sentence. There was no doubt in Dooley's mind about that.

"Yeah," his uncle said after a moment. "Okay, so I can see

how that could happen. But that doesn't make it right." Dooley could see that he had to say that. He'd been a cop for most of his life. If it hadn't been hard-wired into him from the start, it had been pounded into him over thirty on-the-street years. "I can see you needed to see the guy. I understand what you were looking for. But, for the love of God, why did you go back a second time? And to a party, no less, where, I assume, there were plenty of witnesses."

Dooley didn't have an answer to that, at least, not one that made sense.

His uncle studied him for a few moments, his mouth working like it was about to spit out something unpleasant.

"I'm assuming that if you weren't at work, then that story about the guy who threw up on you was just some more bullshit that you decided to throw my way. Am I right?"

Dooley had been hoping that wouldn't come up. But here it was, another stupid move come back to bite him in the ass.

"That part's true," Dooley said. He looked his uncle in the eyes. It scared him how good he was getting at that, giving cops and ex-cops that sincere, I-got-nothing-to-hide gaze, steady, unwavering. "Only it was on the way home from Parker's, not on the way home from work."

His uncle stared at him. He didn't say a word—another cop trick. The same damn trick Randall had used—let the silence hang between them for longer than was comfortable. Nine times out of ten, it ate at a guilty mind and made the perp talk, trying to solidify his story. Dooley waited him out.

"So," his uncle said finally, "if it comes down to the cops asking me if I noticed anything unusual that night, that's what you expect me to tell them—that some panhandler barfed on you."

"Tell them what you want," Dooley said. "I had nothing to do with what happened to Parker."

His uncle kept up his cop stare.

"I know you're hiding something from me, Ryan. And I know that if you try that with the cops, you're going to be in big trouble."

Dooley peered evenly into his uncle's steely gray eyes.

"You think because they let you walk out of there with Annette that they're done with you? How do you know they're not messing with you? How do you know they didn't let you walk because they just got a lead on an eyewitness who can put you at the scene at or near the time of death? How do you know they're not going to come back at you tonight or tomorrow or the day after that with an airtight case that's going to see you go away for murder?"

"I didn't do it," Dooley said. Jesus, wasn't he listening?

"I sincerely hope that's true."

Right. Dooley calmly walked up to his room, quietly closed the door, and beat the crap out of his pillow. His uncle let him be.

◆ EIGHT ◆

Warren, bleary-eyed and clutching a travel mug that Dooley assumed was filled with coffee, was standing in front of school the next morning. As soon as he spotted Dooley, he waved to him.

"I tried to call you yesterday, but I couldn't get through."

He must have called while Dooley was with the cops, and then, after Dooley got home, he hadn't checked his voicemail.

"What's up?"

"I got called into work early yesterday. I did a double shift." Warren lifted his mug, tilted it back, and took a good, long swallow. Dooley waited patiently. Warren never wasted his time. There was a point to everything he said. "A guy up on seven called in sick. They asked me to cover for him."

Dooley perked up. Beth was on seven.

"Did you talk to her?"

"For a couple of minutes, yeah," Warren said.

"And? How is she? Did you ask her to call me?"

Warren blinked at him from behind his glasses.

"She didn't smile at me the way she usually does." That seemed to bother him. "She looked sad. But she asked about you."

"She did?"

"Yeah. She asked how you were."

"Did you tell her to call me?"

Warren nodded.

"And? Did she say she would?"

"She didn't say anything. Then I got called away. Some guy down the hall had an accident, and I had to go clean it up."

"Accident?"

"Mostly the job's okay. But sometimes the patients have accidents, then they call for a cleaner. It was all over the floor. I thought I was going to puke."

"Did you see her again?"

"I tried to. But she had a visitor."

"Her mother?"

Warren shook his head. "Some guy."

"What guy?"

"She was crying and the guy was trying to calm her down."

"What guy, Warren?"

"A tall guy—your height. Your build, too, kind of. Toothy guy. I think she called him Kevin."

"Nevin?"

"Yeah," Warren said, surprised but nodding. "That's what it sounded like, but I thought I must have heard wrong. I never heard of anyone called Nevin."

Dooley wished he hadn't either.

"What was she crying about?"

"I wasn't eavesdropping, Dooley. I was mopping the floor out in the hall."

"You didn't hear anything?"

"I don't know why she was crying. But I heard her mention the cops. She wanted to call them, and that guy—Nevin—he kept asking her what she meant."

"What *did* she mean?"

"I don't know. I heard her say he deserved it."

"He? Who?"

"I didn't hear a name. She said he deserved it and that she was going to call the cops and was going to tell them. Then one of the nurses called me. They needed me downstairs. They're so short-staffed there, you can't believe it. Anyway, by the time I was finished down there, it was time to go on my regular shift down on two. I never got back up to where she was. Dooley, I think maybe I—"

The bell rang.

"Thanks for trying, Warren," Dooley said.

◆ ◆ ◆

Dooley dragged through math, which he was turning out to be reasonably good at, even though he didn't see what good it was, and English, which he liked for some of the stuff they had to read but didn't like because his teacher, a maternity-leave replacement who, Dooley had observed, was tight with Rektor, made a point of not looking at him. After English, Dooley was heading to his regular lunch place when his cell phone trilled in his pocket. He pulled it out and looked at the display. Private number. He was about to stuff the cell back into his pocket when he thought, what the hell. He flipped it open.

"Yeah?"

"Dooley?"

His knees buckled. His stomach clenched.

"Beth." Thank God. "Beth, I'm sorry. What I said—it was stupid. I wasn't thinking. I didn't mean it. You know that, don't you?"

"I know," she said, her voice so soft that he had to stick a finger in his other ear to drown out the buzz of tires on pavement, the rumble of the streetcars, the buzz of conversation as people breezed by him in both directions. Even then, he couldn't hear her. Had she hung up? Had they been disconnected?

"Beth?"

Still nothing.

Then: "I saw you, Dooley."

What? What was she talking about?

"That night," she said. "I saw you."

That night? *What* night?

"I was there," she said. "I was in the ravine."

Sweet Jesus.

"I saw what you did."

He felt like a comic book superhero whose Achilles heel had just been discovered. He's battling the villain when, all of a sudden, he starts to turn to stone or ash or ice, it doesn't matter which, they all turn to something, and it always starts with the feet. His feet don't move, and the superhero looks down and realizes why: they're petrified or burned to the bone or frozen solid. And as he watches, the immobilization creeps up his ankles, his calves, to his knees, his thighs, his hips, and there's nothing he can do about it except dread the moment when it reaches his heart.

"Beth—"

"Dooley, I—" She broke off. For a few seconds Dooley heard nothing. Then a noise—male, muffled, vaguely familiar. "They're here," she said. "I have to go. I love you."

Then nothing again. Dooley punched in her cell number—and couldn't get through. She must have been calling from a hospital phone, but what the hell was the number? He spun around, sweeping the street for a pay phone. There weren't any. He thought of the restaurant. There was a pay phone in the back, between the men's room and the ladies' room. He loped down the street, pushed open the door, and nodded at the woman who was there every day at lunch to take orders. He thought maybe she owned the place or was married to the owner. He'd been coming so regularly that she smiled at him now, although he hadn't broken through her limited English to make real conversation. He kept going, to the back, to the phone. A thick city phonebook, dog-eared and ragged, nestled in a nook under it. He pulled it out, looked up the hospital phone number, and fed a couple of quarters into the slot. He had to listen to a long message before the option presented itself—press zero for the operator.

"I'd like to speak to a patient," he said. "Beth Everley"

"Everley," a brisk female voice said. There was a pause. "I'm sorry, I can't put you through."

"Why not?"

"I can't put you through."

"I just—"

But by then the phone was dead.

He bet Beth's mother had something to do with it. He could see her issuing the order: nobody gets through to Beth. Nobody. He could go down there, but he wouldn't be allowed to see her, either. Her mother had that nailed down, too.

He dropped the phone back into its cradle and stood there a moment, his forehead against the cool, hard pay-phone box. When he finally straightened up, he saw the woman looking at him, her forehead furrowed. He went back to the main room and slumped into his regular booth. The woman was at his side almost immediately.

"Same?" she said, her black eyes peering at him, a tiny but motherly smile on her face. "All same?"

He wasn't hungry any more. But she was smiling and nodding at him. Maybe all she wanted was to sell a lunch. But maybe—Dooley had the feeling this was so—she was like one of those TV moms. Maybe she thought a good meal would make him feel better.

He nodded at her. "Same as always," he said. "Thank you."

She was back faster than usual with a bowl of soup that he hadn't ordered.

"Special," she said. "All good for you."

He accepted it and thanked her again. The soup was thick and hot and spicy and—he never would have believed it if he hadn't tried it—it spread a warmth through every part of him that let him move again, let him think. And when he started to think, his heart began to race. Easy, he told himself. Easy. Think it through.

But, Jesus, all the thinking in the world brought it back to the same place every time.

Warren had heard her tell Nevin that she wanted to call the cops.

Beth had been in the ravine that night.

She had seen him.

She had seen what he did.

And the kicker—even after that, she had said, "I love you."

Warren had also heard her say that she wanted to tell the cops that he deserved it. Who deserved it? Dooley? But if he deserved to have her call the cops on him, why had she said she loved him? She'd meant it, too, as far as he could tell. He'd heard it in her voice. She'd said it in that quiet way she always did, only with real hurt this time. Because she was separated from him? Or because she wanted to call the cops? Or—he remembered the muffled male voice—because she had already called them? He thought hard about the voice. It had sounded familiar.

Randall.

He was sure of it. Beth had been down in the ravine. She had seen him. She loved him. But she had done what she felt she had to do. She had called the cops.

The woman was back with his meal. She beamed when she saw the empty soup bowl.

"All good," she said. "All good."

♦ ♦ ♦

He sat in history class, his ears tuning out the drone of his history teacher's voice and, instead, hyper-attuned to every footstep that passed in the hall. If he was right, if it really was Randall's voice that he'd heard, something would happen soon.

The bell rang.

He made his way to his next class through the din of the crowded corridor, and sat waiting again, his eyes darting to the glass in the classroom door every time he thought he heard something out in the hall.

They still didn't come.

He went to his locker to ditch his textbooks and binders and to round up his homework. He walked down to the main floor slowly, thinking that as much as he hated this school, at least it was a real school, not just a rundown classroom in a juvenile detention facility.

There was no patrol car outside. No unmarked police car, either.

No Randall.

Maybe he was waiting for him at his uncle's house. Maybe Dooley would round the corner onto his uncle's street and see the dark-colored sedan that screamed, "Cop on Board."

Randall wasn't waiting for him on his uncle's street, either. What was taking him so long?

He sat at the dining room table, where he could hear what was going on outside and could look through to the living room and out the picture window onto the sidewalk beyond. Even so, he was caught off guard when he heard a car door slam. He sprang to his feet, but before he even got to the living room, he heard footsteps on the porch. Here we go, he thought. Then a key turned in the lock.

It was his uncle, home from work, half a dozen bags of groceries hanging from his hands.

"You gonna stand there gawking at me or are you going to give me a hand?" he said, kicking the door shut behind him.

Dooley took half of the bags and carried them through to the kitchen. His uncle followed with the rest of them. He didn't say a word as he moved around the room, putting some things away, leaving others out.

"You want some help with supper?" Dooley said when all the groceries were stowed.

"I'm good," his uncle said, without looking at him. Was he still pissed off from last night? Jesus, when it rained, it definitely poured. "Go do your homework."

After Dooley got through his math homework, his uncle called him to eat. He cleaned up the kitchen, just like always, and went back to tackle his history assignment.

His uncle sat on the couch with the newspaper.

"You can take that upstairs if you want," he said.

"I'm good here," Dooley said.

His uncle shrugged and disappeared behind the pages of the business section.

The doorbell rang at nine o'clock, jolting Dooley like an electric current.

His uncle started to lower his paper.

"It's okay," Dooley said, jumping to his feet. "I'll get it." He was out of the room before his uncle could speak, a vain attempt, he knew, to stave off the moment he had been dreading all day.

He swung the front door open. It wasn't who he had expected.

◆ NINE ◆

Her hand landed on his cheek before he even registered what she was doing.

Smack!

The blow resounded in his ear and, Jesus, it smarted. He stared at Beth's mother in disbelief. She had thrown her whole body into the slap and was unsteady on her feet, but her eyes were focused and were blazing into him. She hurled herself at him, raining slaps and punches on him. Dooley had never been hit by a woman before. He couldn't believe how strong she was.

"Hey!" he said. He caught one of her wrists, then the other. He was taller than her, with more muscle. But she had rage on her side. She wouldn't quit. She wrenched and struggled to break free. Then she spat at him, landing an enormous gob of saliva on his face.

"What the hell?" his uncle's voice rumbled. He moved in between the two of them, thrusting Dooley back out of the way.

Beth's mother lunged at him again, but this time was intercepted by Dooley's uncle.

"What the hell is going on here?" he demanded. "Lady, you want me to call the cops?"

"She's Beth's mom," Dooley said. Jeannie had met Mrs. Manson, but Dooley's uncle never had.

"It's all your fault," she screamed at Dooley, craning to look around his uncle at him. "It's because of you. I told her over and over, I told her, he's a criminal, he's no good."

"Why don't we all calm down here," Dooley's uncle said.

"Is Beth okay?" Dooley said. Something must have happened. Something he hadn't expected. If Beth had called the cops on him, Beth's mother would have been dancing in the street. Dooley would be put away. It would be her dream come true.

"She says it wasn't because of you, but I know better. This whole thing is about you. Everything is about you. You've ruined her. You've ruined her life. I wish she'd never met you. I wish you'd never been born."

"Look, lady," his uncle began. He glanced at Dooley, searching for a better way to address her.

"Mrs. Manson," Dooley said.

"Look, Mrs. Manson, I don't know what's happened, but—"

Beth's mother zeroed in on Dooley's uncle for the first time. Her eyes, her mouth, the set of her of her jaw, they all painted one cohesive picture of hatred.

"You're as bad as he is," she said. "You brought him here."

She turned, crossed back over the porch, and marched down the walk. Dooley saw her get into a waiting cab. He watched it drive away.

"What the hell was that all about?" his uncle said.

All Dooley could do was shake his head. Maybe Beth had told her mother what she had told Dooley on the phone. But if she had, why was her mother so angry with him? Why had she come all the way over here to slap him? Why hadn't she gone out to celebrate instead?

"Well, something flew up her nose," his uncle muttered.

"I'm going to bed," Dooley said.

He went upstairs but didn't get undressed. Instead, he lay on his bed fully clothed, waiting for the police to show up.

◆ ◆ ◆

Dooley's uncle was on the phone when Dooley went down to the kitchen the next morning. He turned and looked at Dooley, his face somber. Dooley's ankles felt icy. The cold radiated upwards to his calves, his knees.

"You're saying it all fit?" Dooley's uncle said into the receiver. He turned away from Dooley to scrawl something down on a pad of paper on the kitchen counter. "Yeah. Yeah, okay."

It was quiet as Dooley's uncle continued to listen and to scribble on the pad of paper. Dooley poured himself a cup of coffee and sat down at the table. His stomach was queasy. He'd barely slept. He kept thinking about Beth. He was sorry he'd said what he had in the coffee shop. He wished he could be with Beth. He wished he could hold her and make her feel better—except that probably the last thing in the world she wanted right now was some guy holding her. He wished she'd never gone on that stupid trip. He wished she hadn't been down there in that ravine. He wished she hadn't seen him. She had accepted a lot of things about him, but this? There was no way. He wished he could talk to her. He wished he could see her face so that at least he'd have a shot at figuring out what she was thinking.

And he wondered what exactly she had told the cops.

"Yeah, thanks," Dooley's uncle said. "I owe you one." He dropped the receiver into its cradle and turned to look at Dooley.

"That was Joe DeLucci," he said.

Joe DeLucci was a cop friend of his uncle's.

"What did he want?"

"He didn't call me. I called him." His uncle freshened his coffee and dropped down in the chair across from Dooley. "They made an arrest in the Albright murder."

Dooley knew he should have been relieved, but the tautness in his uncle's eyes and profound regret in his voice put Dooley on full alert.

"It's Beth."

Sometimes, back when Dooley used to get wasted, he'd get on the bus and head for a friend's house or wherever he happened to be sleeping. Sometimes there was no place else to go, so he aimed for home. And, if he was wasted enough, he'd fall asleep and not wake up again until he was so far past his stop that he had no idea where he was. It always jolted him. He'd look out the window at scenery he didn't recognize, and he would panic. He felt like that now, like he'd nodded off for a moment and had missed something important. One minute his uncle had been talking about Parker Albright and the next minute he was saying it was Beth. What was Beth? What had Dooley missed?

"What do you mean?"

"Beth is the person they arrested. It's in the paper, but they don't refer to her by name." Well, they wouldn't. She was seventeen. She'd be covered under YCJA, assuming—and Dooley didn't want to believe it, couldn't bring himself to even contemplate it—his uncle had just said what Dooley thought he had heard.

No, it couldn't be right. There was something going on here, something that was messing with his brain.

"She called the police herself," his uncle said, shaking his head slightly, as if he were also having trouble believing what he was saying. "She confessed. She told them everything."

"What do you mean? Are you telling me Beth killed Parker?"

"I'm telling you what Joe DeLucci told me." DeLucci and Dooley's uncle were tighter than brothers.

"It has to be a mistake," Dooley said.

"She called the police. She told them she did it. She gave them the when, why, and how. And apparently they have a guy who saw someone matching Beth's description running out of the ravine the night it happened. They've arrested her, Ryan."

"Where is she? Did they—"

"She's still in the hospital, but she's being arraigned this morning. I don't know where she'll end up. It's murder, and they don't usually grant bail for murder. But considering what's happened and the fact that she was still in the hospital when she called them ... I'm sorry, Ryan. I don't know what else to say."

His uncle asked him if he wanted to talk about it, but he didn't. What was there to say? Beth had called the police. She had confessed.

"I'm at the new store all day today, in case you need me," his uncle said. He looked at Dooley as if considering how he would hold up—*if* he would hold up—before getting up and setting his coffee mug in the sink.

Dooley went to school and looked at the faces in the hallways— familiar faces now, even though he couldn't say he was friends with anyone there except Warren—and wondered what kind of day was unfolding for some of them. Maybe a fair number of them sucked, just like his day. But he seriously doubted that anyone else was dragging through math and history and French while contemplating the fact that a loved one had just been arrested for murder.

He couldn't wait for the day to be over, but, in his experience, the worst days never seemed to end.

After school, he reported for work and went through the motions, scanning returns, shelving them, processing customer purchases, all of it without putting anything of himself into it. He kept thinking about Beth. She had confessed. She had told the police that she'd killed Parker. He could imagine how Randall was looking at it. Girl is sexually assaulted (at least, that's what she claims). The guy who allegedly assaulted her has a different story (like any guy ever says, yeah, that's right, I raped her). The girl has no bruises, no scratches, no physical evidence to show that she was assaulted. She didn't report the assault until a couple of days after it happened. Witnesses say the alleged assault victim was flirting with her alleged assailant all week. A witness says the alleged victim went willingly up to the alleged assailant's room and that the two of them were holding hands. So already there's serious doubt: was she assaulted or not?

The guy involved has high-powered parents, which means he can afford a high-powered lawyer. The girl can probably imagine what she's in for if the case goes to court. Already it's a he-said, she-said setup. The guy's lawyer is going to present the guy as a good student, an upstanding citizen, etcetera ad pukedom. Maybe a few of the guy's teachers will be paraded in front of the court. Maybe the guy volunteers somewhere—for sure, he's dug wells in Africa and has helped to build houses for the needy. That's how the whole thing got started. The girl herself will tearfully tell her side of the story. Then she'll be cross-examined. Isn't it true that you flirted with the defendant all week?

Isn't it true that you asked to switch to his work team? Isn't it true that you went up to his bedroom willingly? Isn't it true that you were holding his hand? What did you think was going to happen up there? And isn't it true that you became upset when the defendant indicated that he wasn't interested in a long-term relationship? Isn't that why you were sullen and withdrawn on the bus all the way home and why you were staring at the defendant? Isn't it true that you were planning how to get back at the defendant? And did you finally come up with a plan—you were going to accuse him of sexual assault? Isn't that why you didn't mention anything about sexual assault to anyone until after you were home from your trip? And what about your boyfriend (assuming that was how she'd presented Dooley)? Isn't it true that you didn't tell him what happened until after someone else told him what you'd done, that you'd gone up to the defendant's room willingly? Isn't it true that you told him about this alleged sexual assault only when it was obvious he knew something had happened? Isn't it true that you were afraid of what he might do to you if he found out you'd had sex with another boy? Isn't it true that he has a history of violence? Isn't it true that you rolled the dice and lost with the defendant and that you were afraid that if the truth came out, you'd lose your boyfriend, too?

What girl would want to go through that? What girl would seriously think that she had a chance of being believed, that she would come out of it with her dignity and her reputation in tact? How would she feel when the guy was acquitted, which, of course, he would be, and walked out of court with his head held high while she would be viewed as a pathetic case of a young woman spurned—or worse, a young woman who had been spurned and refused to accept that fact? Because there was also the incident at the tennis club. What had she been doing there? Why had she been lurking around?

And then, of course, there was the bottle of aspirin.

Dooley could see Randall leaning across the table, a look of sympathy on his face. You took an overdose of aspirin, Beth. You did it the same night that Parker was killed. Maybe he assaulted you and maybe he didn't. Maybe you were afraid he was going to get away with it, or maybe you were afraid that he was just going to get away from you. Either way, it must have eaten at you, a guy like that, rich, good-looking, girls lining up to throw themselves at him, and he treated you like that. That's why you went to the tennis club, isn't it, to let him know that he couldn't get away with it. You went to his house that night, too, didn't you? Did you sneak into the yard from the ravine, Beth? Did you get him to agree to talk to you in private? Did you tell him how you felt? And then what happened, Beth? Did he laugh at you? Did he tell you that girls like you are a dime a dozen? He did, didn't he? He made you feel as bad as you'd felt after you slept with him, didn't he? Then what? Did you get angry? Did you decide you were going to make sure he didn't get away with it? Did you kill him, Beth? Did you smash his head in? You did, didn't you, Beth? Someone saw you in the ravine that night.

Randall would look her straight in the eye, telling her he understood. You're not a bad person, Beth. That's why you swallowed that bottle of aspirin, isn't it? Because you killed Parker and then you couldn't live with what you had done, because you're a good person. I talked to some of your teachers and to the principal at your school. They all said the same thing—she's a good student and a fine human being. But Parker got under your skin, didn't he? He hurt you, and you wanted him to feel as bad as you felt. You didn't mean to kill him, did you, Beth? You just wanted to talk to him. But he laughed at you, didn't he, and things got out of control? You're not a bad person, Beth. You proved that when you called us and said you wanted to talk with us. Tell me exactly what happened. You'll feel better if you get this off your chest. I know you're the kind of person who takes responsibility for what she's done. That's why you called us in the first place, isn't it?

And Beth had spilled the whole story—assuming that she'd needed any encouragement in the first place. She'd told him the when, the where, the why, and the how.

Jesus, was he responsible for what she'd done? She'd called him and said she'd seen him. Did she get the idea from seeing him in action? She'd also said she loved him. What had he done lately to show his love except make her cry by saying absolutely the wrong thing when she'd finally told him what had happened? No wonder her mother was so furious with him. No wonder she'd slapped him. To her, he was nothing but a criminal with whom her daughter insisted on associating. And look where it had landed her.

He could see how Randall would be certain that Beth was the one. All the pieces fit together. She had the motive. She admitted she'd been there. She'd admitted she did it. She'd told him how it had happened. It all hung together, a pretty and deadly package wrapped up in a big red bow. Jesus, even he could see it.

Except for one thing.

Dooley found it impossible to picture Beth as a killer.

◆ TEN ◆

Dooley thought he was going to go crazy. He'd thrashed around in bed all night, unable to get comfortable, unable to sleep, antsy to do something, anything, to help Beth, and jittery because he couldn't figure out what that something was. Up until he hadn't heard from Beth while she was away and then just after she came back, it had been a while since he'd yearned for a drink or a hit. He'd been too wrapped up in Beth. Sure, things were a little rocky back before Christmas. But they'd smoothed that out. They got together whenever Dooley wasn't working. If Beth's mother was out for the night, Dooley went over. He was always afraid that her mother would walk in on them again, but she never did. And he always—always—made sure that he was out of the apartment a good fifteen minutes before she was due home. When Beth's mother was home, Beth came over to Dooley's uncle's place. His uncle wouldn't let them hang out up in his room, which kind of surprised Dooley. After all, his uncle knew they fooled around. More than a couple of times he had asked Dooley if he knew about safe sex. But, whatever. He wasn't with Beth just for the sex. Not even close. He was with her because ... well, because he couldn't stand not to be with her. Because he always felt better when he was with her. Or when he knew that he was going to see her. And, to be honest, because she always seemed so happy to be with him.

He loved the way she smiled when she saw him. He loved the way she nuzzled up against him when they were watching a movie on TV. And the way she called him up even when she didn't have anything special or important to say. Or when she sent him text messages asking him how his English test had gone or if he'd finished the history essay he was working on. She remembered what he was doing. She cared enough to ask. The only other person who did that was his uncle, and his uncle did it as a homework cop, not out of pure interest. He loved her because she loved him—or said she did. And looked like she did. And acted like she did. Whoever would have thought?

And then she'd got fucked over—literally—by some asshole, and how had he reacted? He hated himself for that. He hated what he'd said the very last time he'd seen her. She'd gone out and swallowed a bottle of aspirin. And now here she was under arrest for murder.

He gave up any idea of sleep and sat upright on the edge of his bed at a quarter to five in the morning, staring into the gloom. It wasn't right. It couldn't be right. Killing herself, or trying to, that was one thing. But caving in some guy's head—even if it was Parker Albright's—no way. So why had she confessed? Why had she called up the cops and told them she'd done it?

He dressed and slipped out of the house. The sun peeked over the horizon as he started down the path into the ravine and headed north up to where it ran behind Parker's house. He passed a couple of people out walking their dogs and nodded at the ones who nodded at him. He walked quickly, burning off some of the nervous energy that had been building up ever since his uncle had given him the news. By the time he looked up at the big houses and picked out Parker's, his jitters had subsided a little.

Down in the ravine behind Parker's house, ribbons of yellow-and-black crime-scene tape hung from shrubbery and trailed, broken, on the ground. Okay, so that was where they'd found the body—in the shrubs and scrub that ran along the edges of the ravine floor, directly to one side of the promontory that jutted out from the back of the Albright property. What had Parker been doing down in the shrubbery? Likely answer: he'd been dead by the time he got there.

Dooley looked upward. There was no crime-scene tape up top, but that didn't mean there hadn't been any. Parker had been found down in the shrubbery, but Dooley bet he'd started out up top. The Albrights had probably removed the tape as soon as it was no longer needed. He imagined they didn't want to look out their windows and see it fluttering there to remind them that someone had done something so heinous to their son. But he bet it had been there.

It had to be thirty-five or forty feet from the floor of the ravine to the promontory. Thirty-five or forty feet of reinforced concrete slabs at a more or less ninety-degree angle that gave little or no purchase for climbing. Dooley waded through the brush to the base of the concrete and reached up, feeling for a handhold. He managed to dig a couple of fingers into the narrow, shallow indent between one slab and the next one above it, but it took all his strength to chin himself up because there was no place to dig his feet in. The best he could do was press the toes of his sneakers as hard as he could against the concrete, while he reached up one hand to feel for another handhold. He held himself there, fingers sweeping the concrete above him, for about ten seconds before his muscles gave out. He landed on his feet and looked up again, frowning.

His uncle had said that the cops had a witness who had seen a girl matching Beth's description down in the ravine. Beth had told Dooley she'd been in the ravine that night.

In the ravine.

His uncle hadn't said anything about her being at the party. If she had been there, wouldn't someone have said something to the cops? But his uncle hadn't mentioned that. No, he said she'd been seen down here.

Dooley had been up there. He had seen the wall around the Albrights' backyard—and all the security stickers. No, there were only two ways for Beth to have gotten up there—either she'd joined the party the same way Dooley had, by walking past Parker's sister and all the other guests who were there, or she had climbed up, unseen, from down in the ravine. He looked around again. Beth was in good shape, but she wasn't as strong as he was. If he couldn't climb up the sheer wall, he didn't see how she could. He wondered what she had said to Randall about that. Randall was smart. He wouldn't believe just any story about what had happened. She must have been pretty convincing. And what had his uncle said—she had given the cops the when, the why, and the how. What she'd said must have fit with whatever the cops had found—how Parker had died, where he'd been found, where he'd been originally, what and where the murder weapon was. Randall would have asked about all of that, and Beth must have given answers that made sense. How could she have done that unless she'd been involved in some way?

Dooley didn't like it. He didn't like it one bit.

He stood in the shrubbery for another few minutes, thinking it over, and then headed home again. He was climbing out of the ravine when he thought about her phone call to him. I was in the ravine that night, she'd said. I saw what you did.

He stopped and thought it through. Where exactly had she been? What exactly had she seen?

What the hell was going on?

He ditched his last class of the day so that he could get to Beth's school before it let out for the weekend. This time he was bolder. He was waiting at the bottom of the main steps when the big oak doors opened and girls began to stream out of the building. He stepped in front of the closest one, forcing her to a halt, and said, "I'm looking for friends of Beth Everley."

The girl stared at him in silence for so long that Dooley thought she must be deaf. Then her eyes scanned the growing crowd of girls and she pointed to a willowy blonde.

"Ask Kate," the girl said. "Maybe she can help you."

At the sound of her name, the blonde glanced in Dooley's direction. He hurried over to her before she could make a get-away.

"Are you Kate?" he said.

She nodded. Just then he saw a familiar face. Annicka, still looking nothing like the rest of these girls. But he'd already spoken to her and hadn't liked what she'd said. If Parker was still alive and if Beth ever got him in court, Annicka would be up there, a witness for the defense. He turned his attention back to Kate.

"You're a friend of Beth's, right?" he said.

He saw her processing the name behind impossibly pale blue eyes.

"Beth Everley," he clarified.

"I know who you mean. I know her, but I wouldn't say we were friends."

Dooley looked around for the girl who had directed him to Kate, but she was long gone.

"You're that guy, aren't you?" Kate said. "The guy she's been seeing."

Jesus, how did they all know about him?

"I'm looking for some of her friends," he said.

Kate arched a perfectly shaped blonde eyebrow. Her face was like cream, with rose-colored lips and mesmerizing eyes. He had never seen such a delicate-looking creature.

"*Friends* of Beth?" she said. She skimmed the crowd. "Cassie," she called, her voice like a small silver bell. "Cassie, over here."

Dooley looked from girl to girl to girl until finally he saw one who had turned questioning eyes on Kate. She said something to the girl she was with, then broke away from her and made her way over to Kate.

"This is Beth's boyfriend," Kate said. "He wants to talk to you."

Dooley caught the blatant superiority in Kate's voice and was surprised. Sturdy Cassie could probably whip fragile Kate's scrawny little ass, but little Kate clearly believed she had something that trumped physique.

"There you go," she said to Dooley before continuing on down the steps. Dooley tracked her to the parking lot with his eyes and wasn't surprised to see her pull out a set of keys to a little cherry-red Lexus. When he turned back to Cassie, he saw the hardness of a slave in her expression.

"You and Kate, you're not—"

"Friends?" Cassie said. "Please! I'm here on a scholarship."

It made sense that it was something like that, a caste thing, a line that marked the division between true elite and pretender elite—like old money versus new money or banking money versus porno money.

"How about you and Beth?"

"Beth pays full tuition, not that that matters to the Kates of the world. Look, I have to train, so ..."

"You heard about Beth?"

"You mean about her being arrested for killing Parker? Yeah, I heard."

"Were you on the trip with her?"

Cassie shook her head.

"Have you talked to her since she got back?"

"Just once. I called her when I heard what happened. Everyone was talking about it. They were all saying that she—" She broke off abruptly. Her cheeks turned apple-pink.

"I know what *people* were saying," Dooley said. "What did *she* say?"

"That Parker raped her. She was really upset. She said he wasn't anything like the way he came across. I don't know what he did or said to her, but it sounded to me like he really scared her." That's what Beth had told Dooley: *He really scared me.* "She said she told the police and that they were nice to her. But all the questions they asked—she was afraid if it went to court, everyone would believe Parker and no one would believe her." She stared him right in the eyes. He wondered what her sport was, whether it was a team sport or something individual. Whichever, he had the idea she was a fierce competitor. "She said you didn't believe her."

Jesus, is that what Beth thought? And even still, the last thing she had said to him was, "I love you."

"I believe her," he said quietly, "even if it didn't come across that way to her. I believe her. That's why I'm here."

"If she was with Parker, it was only as a friend," Cassie said. "She wasn't interested in him."

"How do you know? I mean, I hear the guy was loaded."

She gave him a withering look. "How long have you been going with Beth? Six, seven months? And you think that's what she's interested in? Money?"

It wasn't what he thought. It was what he was afraid of. It was what still mystified him. Beth knew plenty of Parkers—guys who weren't just loaded, but who were good-looking, who had real futures, the sky was the limit, who could give her anything and take her anywhere; guys who hadn't spent time in lockup; guys whose mothers weren't fucked up, at least, not the way Lorraine had been; guys who hadn't beaten a woman so hard with a baseball bat that she ended up in a wheelchair. Why wasn't she with one of those guys? Why was she with him?

"She loves you," Cassie said, her tone straight-ahead, not pulling any punches, like she had believed it when Beth had said it, but now that she was face to face with him, now that he was asking these bone-headed questions, she was beginning to think that Beth had given her heart to altogether the wrong guy.

"I need to talk to some of the girls who were on the trip with her and who knew Parker," Dooley said. "Girls who might have been at that party he had last weekend. But I have no idea who they are."

She studied him for a moment before finally relenting.

"I guess I could ask around. My mom has my class list at home somewhere. Give me your number. I'll call you later tonight."

He would be at work later, and Kevin would have a meltdown if he caught Dooley on his cell. But so what? Let him fire

Dooley. Let him try. He gave Cassie his number and thanked her. He started down the steps. She called him back.

"You don't think she did it, do you?" she said. "You don't think she killed Parker?"

"No." It was the first time he'd said it out loud. He liked the way he felt saying it, confident, sure of himself. "No, I don't." Beth wasn't a killer. And when you came right down to it, Dooley bet there were a lot of people who'd like to see old Parker dead.

◆ ◆ ◆

The store was busier than usual for a Friday night, and Friday nights were second only to Saturday nights. Dooley had no trouble keeping himself occupied, but Cassie was never far from his mind. She'd seemed okay when he'd talked to her. But would she come through? Eight o'clock passed and he hadn't heard from her. Kevin went on his break, and Dooley mouthed a prayer: Now would be a perfect time for her to call.

She didn't.

Kevin came back and slipped behind the counter with Dooley so that Rashid could take his break. Rashid did what he always did: he stepped out onto the sidewalk, stood right on the other side of the store's big front window, wearing his red video-store golf shirt, and lit a cigarette. Kevin rapped on the glass and waved at Rashid, the gesture meant to shoo him away from the store.

"It's a family place," he muttered to Dooley. "Parents don't want their kids to see customer sales associates smoking."

Rashid waved back, a big smile on his face. He took another long drag on his cigarette but didn't move from the spot where he was standing. Dooley couldn't tell if Rashid was being a rebel or if he genuinely didn't understand Kevin's gesture. He didn't know how Rashid had got the job in the first place. If anyone ever asked him about a movie, it was a given that Rashid had never heard of it. He was also useless fielding questions about the latest release featuring whatever actor a customer was interested in. To tell him the plot of a movie you were looking for in the hope that he could supply the title was a sure route to disappointment. But Dooley got a kick out of how he got under Kevin's skin. Kevin kept glancing over his shoulder as he scanned customer picks, took their money, and handed them their receipts. Only when Rashid had finally smoked his cigarette down to the filter did Kevin's shoulders sink below his ears. When Rashid took another cigarette out of his pocket and used the first one to light it, Kevin's whole body clenched again. The woman who stepped up to his cash looked at Rashid, then at Kevin, and said, "You people set a poor example." Dooley chuckled. Kevin scowled at him.

Dooley felt his cell phone vibrate in his pocket. He turned away from Kevin so that he could check the display. Cassavettes, J. He didn't recognize the name, but he had a feeling.

He glanced at Kevin, who had disposed of his last customer and had slipped out from behind the front counter to hurl the door open. He marched over to Rashid. Dooley turned so that his back was to the two of them and answered his phone.

"It's Cassie," the voice on the other end said. "You got a pen?"

Dooley said yes while he scrabbled for one. He grabbed a promotional flyer, flipped it over, and scrawled the names and phone numbers Cassie gave him. He asked for and got addresses, too. There were four altogether.

"I'm not a hundred percent sure if they were all at the party," she said. "But I know they were all on the trip with Beth and I've seen at least three of them with Parker."

"Thanks," Dooley said. "I really appreciate it."

"Yeah, well, good luck."

"Cassie? You still there?"

"Yeah."

"Have you talked to Beth?"

"Not this week," she said. "Sorry."

The electronic bell above the door beeped, and Kevin and Rashid came in. Dooley flipped his phone shut and slipped it back into his pocket.

"But I was on my break," Rashid was saying. "And I wasn't in the store."

"You're wearing a store shirt. People know you work here. It creates a negative impression."

"I read the employee manual Mr. Fielding gave me when he hired me," Rashid said. Dooley was surprised to hear it. "It says the store is smoke-free, but it doesn't saying anything about not smoking on a public sidewalk."

Dooley had read a few pages of the employee manual. Like most people with most manuals, he only opened it when he had a problem, usually with Kevin, and needed ammunition he could shoot back with. He supposed it was possible that Rashid had done the same thing.

By the time Dooley got out of the store, it was too late to start calling girls he didn't know. He would have to wait until the next morning. If there was one thing he hated, it was waiting.

◆ ELEVEN ◆

Dooley got out of bed early for a Saturday morning, not that it did him any good. He figured he should wait until at least ten o'clock before he started calling the girls whose names Cassie had given him. Then he thought, what if they weren't home when he finally called? Cassie had said she was going to look at the class list her mother had at home. That meant she'd given him parents' phone numbers, not girls' cell phone numbers, which made sense when he thought about the way Kate had spoken to Cassie and what Cassie had said to him. She went to the school but she sure wasn't part of the in crowd. She probably didn't have a lot of cell phone numbers.

A woman with an accent—he thought maybe she was Filipino—answered the phone at Monique Norton's house.

"She is not available now," the woman said.

"Do you know when she will be available?"

"Sorry, no. May I take a message?"

Dooley thought it over and decided no. If he managed to get Monique on the phone, she might talk to him. If he left a message, she might not call him back. He thanked the woman and moved on to the next number.

"Yes?" a sleep-hoarse voice said.

"Marie Beddoes?" The first name on the list Cassie had given him."

"Yes?" The voice was slightly more alert. "Who is this?"

He took a deep breath. "My name is Dooley. I'm a friend of Beth Everley's."

He heard a chuckle.

"I heard you were more than a friend."

"And I heard you were on that school trip with her."

"Yeah? So?"

"I was hoping you could tell me what happened, you know, between Beth and Parker."

"They hung together almost the whole week. Then she went up to his room with him."

"Did you see them?"

"Go up to his room? No. But I saw them at the party. And I saw them leave together. And I saw Beth on the bus the next morning. She was sitting by herself. She looked upset. But, really, what did she think?"

"What do you mean?"

"If she wanted to put out for him, that's her business. But thinking she was going to score Parker as a boyfriend? Not a chance."

"Did she say that was what she wanted?"

"It's not what she said. It's how she acted—she stuck pretty close to Parker all week. It was obvious what was on her mind."

Was it?

"Were you at the party at Parker's house the night Parker was killed?" Dooley asked.

"Thanks a lot!" she said, sounding annoyed. What had sparked that? "I saw you there, so, yeah, I was there. Why?"

"Did you see Beth there?"

"No." There was a strong hint of confusion in her voice now.

"What about Parker?"

"What about him?"

"What was he doing?"

"What Parker always does. Having fun. Parker loves to have fun."

"What time did you leave the party?"

"Jesus, what are you, the cops? Who, by the way, I've already talked to."

"You mind telling me what you told them?"

He heard a long, impatient sigh and was afraid she was going to hang up on him.

"I was at Parker's until maybe one in the morning," she said finally. "The party was still going strong when I left, but I had a headache. I said goodbye to Deecee when I left."

"Deecee?"

"Parker's sister," she said, like, what kind of idiot was he that he didn't know that. "I didn't see Parker, though."

"Do you know where he was?"

"Oh, stupid me. If I'd known you were going to ask me that, I would have turned on my x-ray vision."

So that was a no.

"You remember what time it was the last time you saw him?"

"I don't know. Ten, maybe ten-thirty."

"Did you notice who he was with?"

"I don't remember if he was with anyone special. There was a bunch of kids around him, like always. I just saw him, that's all."

"Okay. Thanks," Dooley said.

The line went dead. She didn't even say goodbye.

Rachel Silverman was next on the list.

"She's at her class, dipshit," said the kid who answered the phone at her house. Dooley would have bet anything he was Rachel's kid brother.

"I was hoping to catch her before she left. I'm supposed to pick her up after class, but I lost the address."

"Then your ass is going to be in a sling," the kid said.

"Do me a favor? Help me out. Where's her class?"

"How would I know?" the kid said. "I got better things to do than keep track of stupid ballet classes."

Dooley sensed he was about to hang up.

"Do you at least know the name of the place?" he said.

"Danse Classique Academy," the kid said. "You guys get stupider and stupider. By the way, she's not a natural blonde."

"I know," Dooley said, even though he had never met Rachel.

Danse Classique Academy was in the phone book and was located—big surprise—up near the tennis club that Parker had frequented. Dooley took the bus. When he got there, he tried the front door. It was locked. He walked around the place and heard someone playing a piano inside. It sounded like the kind of music he had heard in a movie that Beth had made him watch about a kid in England, a boy, who wanted to be a ballet dancer. The music he heard through the window stopped every so often and then started again, the player hammering out the same piece of music over and over. Dooley pictured skinny girls in leotards making frou-frou moves. Why did they bother? Who even went to the ballet? He circled back around to the front and waited. The better part of an hour passed before the door opened and girls started coming out. There weren't that many of them—eight or nine at the most. Half of them were blondes, but which one was Rachel? He said her name out loud. Only one head turned. He moved toward her.

"Rachel Silverman?"

She looked him over.

"I've seen you around my school," she said, large hazel eyes looking frankly into his. "You're that guy Beth was seeing, right?"

He nodded and glanced at the girl beside Rachel, who was shorter and who, unlike Rachel, refused to meet his eyes. Dooley didn't know her name, but he recognized her right away. She was the girl who had helped Nevin hand out the drinks that night at Parker's party.

"What are you doing here?" Rachel said. Dooley was amazed at how direct the girls at Beth's school were. He wasn't amazed at the demanding, bitchy quality of their voices. He bet most of them were used to getting what they wanted when they wanted it.

"You were on the trip with Beth," he said.

"We both were." She nodded at the other girl, who peeked up at Dooley for all of a split-second before staring again at the flagstone under her feet.

"I was wondering ..."

"You were wondering how it went down between Beth and Parker, right?" Rachel smiled smugly at him when Dooley nodded. "Well, I'm sorry to tell you, Studly, but she's the one who started it. She's the one who wasn't happy with the team assignments. She's the one who asked to switch to Parker's team. And she's the one who went into the house with him that night. Nobody was twisting her arm."

How many times had Dooley heard that? How many times had he wondered about that whole week—Beth and Parker working together, eating together, talking together? And then that party. If it hadn't been for that party ...

"So she and Parker were pretty friendly, huh?" he said. He hated himself for it, but he asked it anyway, even knowing what all those girls were like, how they loved to talk, how they would be back at it on Monday, if not before, telling each other about him, about Beth's boyfriend Dooley.

"Extremely friendly," Rachel said. "She knew what she was doing—and what Parker was interested in. There's no way she couldn't have known what was going to happen."

"Maybe she thought he was going to show her pictures from when he was in Africa," Dooley said. "That's what he told her."

Rachel laughed. "Get real. She makes happy with him all week, he invites her up to his room to show her pictures, they get it on, and the next thing you know, she's crying rape? Please!"

"So, you don't believe her?"

"She's intense, you know?" She looked him over again. "I hear you're pretty intense, too."

"Beth told you that?" Jesus, what had she said?

"Beth doesn't talk about you. But I heard it around, you know?"

No, he didn't know. But he could imagine. A girl like her, maybe she'd known Winston Rhodes or some of the guys he hung around with.

"Parker likes to fool around," she said. "Beth's not the first girl who slipped between the sheets with him, thinking she'd landed him. But she hadn't. His sister told me that Parker told her he'd made it clear from the start. They were just fooling around, that's all. It wasn't like a lifetime commitment."

"You know she's been arrested?" Dooley said.

"Yeah. And I'm not surprised. My dad's a shrink, you know."

Okay. And what the hell did that have to do with anything?

"He says someone like Beth, with her past, it was just a matter of time. You know about that, don't you? About what happened to Beth's dad and what her brother did? Beth was right there. She saw the whole thing. The way I heard it, it really messed her up. She was just a kid when it happened, and my dad says that when kids experience that kind of trauma, it can come back and bite them in the ass when they're older." Dooley bet her dad had a fancier way of saying it. "He says sometimes people who go through what Beth went through sublimate their feelings. You notice how she's always perfect, right? Always prepared. Always keeps things neat and tidy. Totally anal. She's trying to keep her life under control. Trying to keep it nice and clean and orderly—you know, keep the demons at bay."

Dooley thought about Beth's bedroom. He had been in awe the first time he saw it. It was completely white—the walls, the ceiling, the curtains, the bedding, the floor, all the furniture. It was like being in a house made of snow, except that whenever he was in there, he was hot all over, not cold. Did all that pure white mean something to Beth?

"You can only do that for so long," Rachel said in a know-it-all tone that Dooley bet made for a lot of bitchy behind-her-back sniping among the girls at her school. "Eventually, something's got to give. If you want my opinion"—which Dooley did not, in fact, want—"that's what happened to her. She went in expecting something from Parker, and when she didn't get it, she snapped. She tried to punish him by crying rape. When it became obvious that didn't work, well, like you said, they arrested her for Parker's murder."

She sounded convinced of what she was saying. Dooley wondered how many other people thought the same thing.

"Were you at the party at Parker's house the night he died?" he asked.

"Yeah."

"Did you see Beth there?"

"No. But I didn't see Parker, either, for most of the night. What does that prove?"

Maybe nothing. There was just one more thing he needed to know.

"Have you talked to the cops, Rachel?" He was pretty sure Randall would want to check with all the kids who knew Beth, all the ones who had been on the trip with her, all the ones who had been at Parker's party that night.

"Not yet. But they called me. They asked me to come down so they could ask me some questions. I'm going in on Monday, with my dad's lawyer."

Terrific, Dooley thought. He could just picture what Randall would make of Rachel Silverman's opinion.

After he left Rachel, he tried Ellie Davis. There was no answer at her house, and he didn't leave a message. He tried Monique Norton again, too. She was still unavailable. He could think of only one other person who knew Beth and who had been on the trip and at both parties. But, boy, that was the last person in the world he wanted to talk to.

He went home and stared at his homework assignments for a couple of hours, the whole time thinking about Beth and wishing he could see her. He tried Ellie Davis and Monique Norton a few more times each. He tried Warren, too, and got him right away.

"She's still up on seven," he told Dooley. "I heard one of the aides say she was going to get an assessment on Monday, and if that went okay, they were going to transfer her somewhere else, you know, until she has her court date."

"Any chance you can get to see her?" Dooley asked.

"There's no way to get onto that floor without someone unlocking the door for you, and no one is going to unlock the door unless I'm there on legitimate business."

"You can't switch with someone?"

"I don't know. It's a big hospital. The scheduling is crazy." He fell silent for a moment. Dooley waited. He heard a sigh. "There's a guy who usually works up there—I switched shifts with him one time when he asked me. His brother was having a bachelor party and he told me he was going there specifically to get wasted, so no way did he want to come to work the next day. He said he owed me one."

"Think you can collect?"

"I'll know in an hour. I should see him in the locker room. I'll do my best."

Dooley had no doubt of it. He didn't think Warren was capable of doing less.

Someone knocked on his bedroom door—his uncle, dressed in a suit, his aftershave wafting its way to Dooley's nose.

"I'm going. I have to pick up Jeannie. You're working tonight, aren't you?"

"I gotta be there in an hour."

"Well, just so you know," his uncle said, "I'll be calling the store to check on that. And I won't be talking to that girl, what's her name?"

"Linelle."

His uncle nodded. "Linelle, who for some reason I'll never understand seems to like to lie for you." Linelle had covered for

Dooley a few times, back when his uncle didn't trust Dooley to be where he said he was going to be. "I'll be talking to that manager of yours."

Aw, shit.

"You're going to call *Kevin* and ask if I'm at work?"

"It seems I don't have much of a choice if I want to know where you are."

"Come on! I've been straight with you, just like you wanted."

"Is that right? Does that include the night this Parker kid was beaten to death?"

Okay, so, no, it didn't.

"Except for that," Dooley said. "I've been straight with you except for that."

"Funny thing about trust," his uncle said. "It can take a long time to establish it. A very long time." His eyes drilled into Dooley. "But you can blow it all away in a second."

Which is what Dooley had done.

"I'll also be calling you here after you get off shift," his uncle said. "You screw up, Ryan, and I'm going straight to Al Szabo." Dooley's probation officer. "I'm not putting up with any bullshit. Do I make myself clear?"

"Yeah," Dooley said. "Whatever."

His uncle hung there a moment before turning and shutting the door behind him. Dooley heard his footsteps on the stairs, then across the hall. He heard the front door open and close. The house was silent.

He felt like putting his fist through a wall. After all this time, his uncle was back to doubting him. But so what? Why did he even care? He was almost eighteen. Once his supervision order was up, he could move out. He could do whatever he wanted.

He could call his own shots.

But the thing was, he did care. He didn't know why, but it mattered to him what his uncle thought. The past couple of months, when things had been going smoothly with both Beth and his uncle, had been the best months of Dooley's life. When he was with Beth, it was like being in what he imagined heaven would be like, assuming it really existed. And when he was with his uncle, well, it was like being home. Or what he imagined being home felt like to the rest of the world. He walked into the house after school or after work, and he could count on a greeting instead of a "Get lost." He could count on good food, too, and didn't mind one little bit that it was his job to clean up afterwards. He didn't mind any of the chores he had to do around the house, either. In fact, he was more than glad to do them in exchange for having a clean place to sleep, regular meals, and someone to ask him how his day had been and what he learned. Even better: someone who actually listened when he answered. Someone to care. And Jeannie? He smiled whenever he thought about her. Jeannie was the icing on the cake.

◆ ◆ ◆

Kevin was in Dooley's face the minute he walked into the store, but instead of giving him a hard time about something he wanted him to do, he grinned and said, "Your uncle called me."

Dooley kept walking, headed for the back room to change into his red golf shirt with the name tag attached.

"He said he wanted me to call him when you got here," Kevin said, keeping pace with Dooley. "He also said he wanted me to call him if you didn't show up or if you left early."

Dooley pushed open the door to the back room. Kevin came in behind him.

"You know," Kevin said, "your uncle's a lot nicer than I thought." Kevin used to shake at the thought of Dooley's uncle, ever since the time his uncle had showed up in response to one of Kevin's calls to customers who were overdue in returning items.

Dooley pulled off his T-shirt and pulled on his golf shirt.

"He said I should keep an eye on you until further notice," Kevin said. "Sounds like he doesn't trust you, Dooley."

Dooley went back out into the store and slipped behind the counter to relieve Rashid. Kevin stood and watched him for a while. He seemed disappointed that Dooley didn't react. Well, good.

Kevin watched him all night, which shouldn't have bothered Dooley, but it did. When he told Kevin he was taking his meal break, Kevin said, "I guess I'd better call your uncle and let him know." Dooley wanted to put a fist in Kevin's face, but he held back. One thing he'd learned: sometimes that second or two of pleasure he got from acting on impulse, from doing the things that other people only dreamed of but were too chicken-shit to do, sometimes it just wasn't worth the retribution that, in his case, invariably followed. He went to the Greek restaurant across from the video store and told himself he didn't care what Kevin did.

His phone rang as soon as he sat down. It was probably his uncle, calling to check in and give him a hard time about something else. He checked the display. It wasn't his uncle's number. It was one he didn't recognize.

"Hello?" he said.

"Who is this?" the voice on the other end demanded. A girl's voice.

"You should know," Dooley said. "You called me."

"No, you called me." She sounded pissed off, whoever she was. "Anna said she talked to you, like, three times."

Anna? Who the hell was Anna?

"I got your number off the phone memory," the voice said. "Who are you and what do you want?"

It started to click. She was one of the girls on Cassie's list that he hadn't talked to yet. She had to be Monique because no one had answered at Ellie Davis's house.

"Look, Monique ..."

"Would you mind introducing yourself?" she said, her tone pure acid.

"I'm a friend of Beth's. I wanted to ask you a few questions about what happened."

There was utter silence on the other end.

"Hello? Monique?"

"I'm here." Her voice was even frostier now. "Just so you know, *I'm* a friend of Parker's. At least, I was. I've known him since we were kids. We went to the same kindergarten. We had play dates together."

Which meant she probably wasn't going to be all that helpful. At least, not over the phone. Maybe if he could see her in person, and if she could see him.

"I wanted to talk to you about Beth," he said, choosing his words carefully. "About what happened?"

"You're that boyfriend of hers, aren't you?" Monique said. "The criminal."

"Yes." And no.

"Why should I talk to you?"

Good question.

"Because, like you said, you were friends with Parker. Look, Monique, I know you know what happened on that trip. I just need to talk to someone who was there. Someone who can help me sort this out. Beth and I ..." He let his voice trail off and sighed heavily. "Maybe we could meet tomorrow? Please? I won't take a lot of your time. I just ... I need to talk, that's all."

Silence. Then: "There's a Starbucks on the corner two blocks south of my school. Meet me there tomorrow at noon."

"How will I recognize you?"

"I'll recognize you," she said.

The line went dead.

♦ TWELVE ♦

Dooley felt as unsettled on Sunday morning
as he had the night before. He had talked to a few people and,
so far, all he had gained was greater insight into why Randall
had arrested Beth after listening to her confession. He had lain
awake thinking about everything he knew, which, when you
came right down to it, wasn't much.

He rolled out of bed, pulled on a pair of jeans and a T-shirt,
and headed downstairs to make coffee. Halfway down, the aro-
ma hit him, and he knew he was too late. Sure enough, there was
his uncle in the kitchen, pouring skim milk into a cup, which
was how Dooley knew that Jeannie was in the house.

"You must have been out late," he said to his uncle. "Either
that or you tiptoed up the stairs, because I didn't hear you."

His uncle poured another mug of coffee, this one black, for
himself. "What do you have planned for the day?" he said.

"I have to meet someone at noon. Other than that, not
much. Why?"

"Jeannie's making supper tonight. She's making pie for des-
sert. She was hoping you'd be here."

Dooley smiled. Jeannie made the best pie he had ever tasted.

"You can tell her I wouldn't miss it for anything," he said.
Especially since Jeannie always served her pie warm from the
oven, with a good-sized scoop of expensive ice cream on top.

"All right then." His uncle carried both mugs out of the kitchen. Dooley heard him pad up the stairs.

Dooley got himself some cereal and coffee. It was only eight-thirty by the time he finished both. Now what? He was going to go crazy sitting around with nothing to do. He prowled through the house for a few minutes, then went out the back door to the garage. His uncle was always grousing about what a mess it was. He kept saying that one of these days he was going to drag Dooley out there and the two of them were going to clean the place out. Dooley looked over the interior. No wonder his uncle hardly ever parked in here. There was junk everywhere. Dooley thought for a moment about how to proceed and then waded in.

Three hours later, he dashed into the kitchen to wash his hands.

"I thought you were out," his uncle said.

"I was. In the garage. I gotta go. Tell Jeannie—" But there she was in the door to the kitchen, still in the long silky robe that she kept in his uncle's bedroom. "I'll be back in time for supper, Jeannie," he said. "I'm looking forward to it."

She beamed at him. "Don't fill up on junk food. I'm making a roast. With gravy."

Dooley loved Jeannie's gravy. He would have hugged her, except that he didn't know what kind of reaction that would get.

◆ ◆ ◆

The Starbucks near Beth's school was doing a brisk Sunday afternoon business. Dooley glanced around. There were a couple of small groups of girls around Beth's age. A few of them looked at him, but none of them waved him over. He lined up at the counter to order a coffee. His cell phone rang.

"I'm around the corner."

It was Monique.

"I'm inside," he said.

"I know. I saw you go in. But there are friends of mine in there, and I don't want them to see me talking to you."

Oh.

"I'll be right out."

He scooted out of line just as the barista behind the counter asked him what he wanted. A slim brunette in gigantic sunglasses, tight jeans, and a cropped jacket that showed off her skinny butt was pacing up and down out of sight of Starbucks. When she saw him, she waved him over and then turned and walked briskly up the street, forcing him to jog to catch her. That bugged him, but what choice did he have?

"I don't even know why I agreed to meet you," she said.

They were headed in the direction of her school. She turned and glanced at him, but he couldn't tell what she was thinking, not with her eyes hidden behind those massive dark glasses.

"I was hoping you could tell me what happened on that trip," Dooley said.

They reached the school and Monique turned up the path that ran along one side of the ivy-covered building. There was a playing field in back, with bleachers on one side of it. She led the way. They sat down side by side.

"I know you talked to Rachel," she said. He should have expected that. Girls liked to talk. They liked to fill each other in on all the details of their lives. "I can't tell you anything that she hasn't already told you."

"Are—were you and Beth friends?"

"Not really."

"Were you at the party at Parker's country house?"

"Of course. I told you. I've known Parker all my life."

"Did you see what happened there?"

"I saw Beth dancing with him. If you ask me, she was having a good time." He had the feeling she was peering into his eyes and trying to assess the damage she was doing. But those damn sunglasses ... "And I saw them leave the party together. They were both smiling, you know what I mean? Someone said they were holding hands."

"Someone said? You didn't see that yourself?"

"I didn't see a lot of things, but that doesn't mean they didn't happen." Her tone was snotty, like, who did he think he was, questioning her? "She didn't have to go into the house with him if she didn't want to. It's not like he threw her over his shoulder and carried her in, kicking and screaming. They left the party together, and I didn't see either of them again until the next morning when Parker came down for coffee."

"What about Beth? Was she with him?"

"No. I heard she was hogging one of the bathrooms. I didn't see her until we got on the bus. She was sitting way at the back, pouting and staring at Parker. I remember thinking she was looking at him like she wanted to kill him. But when I thought it, it was just an expression. Who knew she was really going to do it?"

"What about the party at Parker's house the weekend after you all got back? Were you there, too?"

She looked at him for a long time before she said, "You walked right past me on your way to talk to Parker."

Oh. He bet she was one of the kids who had talked to Randall.

"Did you see Beth there?"

"Look, I don't know what you want from me—"

"I'm just trying to figure out what happened. Was she there or wasn't she?"

It rattled him a little when she said, "I told the cops I wasn't sure. I thought it was her—it sure could have been her—but I didn't get a good look. It was dark and they were far away."

"They?"

"She and Parker."

Shit.

"When was that? When did you see them?"

"What am I? A timekeeper?" He'd never met anyone so prickly, and he was afraid she was going to call it quits. "I can only tell you what I told the cops. I went inside a little after ten, you know, to use the facilities. I passed Parker on the way. He was at the food table, grabbing a bottle of champagne and some glasses." Champagne. Of course. "When I came out again, he was way back at the end of the yard, and there was a girl with him. She was shorter than him." So was Beth. "She was slender." So was Beth. "And she had long, dark hair." Just like Beth's. "But that's all I could see for sure. There's some bushes back there, just before where it drops off into the ravine. It's nice and quiet back there. No one can see you. I've heard girls say they went back there with Parker." He could picture it. "I saw them back near those bushes. I didn't see Parker again before I left." Another strike against Beth.

"You told the cops you weren't sure it was Beth," he said slowly. "But if you had to guess, what do you think? You think it was her?"

She looked across the tidy, litter-free playing field and

shrugged.

Dooley got up and stood in front of her. He reached out and removed the enormous sunglasses from her face. She wasn't bad looking, but she was gaunt and the only color on her face was two smudges of unnatural pink on her cheeks and black liner around her eyes.

"Monique, do you think the girl you saw was Beth?"

She met his gaze.

"Like I already said, I told the cops I couldn't swear to it. But it could have been her. It definitely could have been."

"Did you see Beth at the party before then? I mean, really see her, so that you could swear to it?"

She was still staring into his eyes.

"No."

"Did anyone else mention seeing Beth there?"

"Not that I heard of."

"If she had been there, who would have seen her arrive? As far as I could see, there was only one way in."

Monique cocked her head to one side. Her lips curled up into a tight smile.

"I guess Deecee would have seen. She's a year younger than Parker, but she's the responsible one. She was watching everyone who came into the yard. She was afraid word had got out that there was going to be a party, and she didn't want a bunch of troublemakers showing up and trashing the place. Yeah, Deecee probably would have seen. She was keeping an eye on everyone who went in or out."

And, for sure, the cops had talked to her. In fact, they'd probably talked to her first thing. But who had the cops dragged in for questioning? Dooley—not Beth. Deecee must have told them that Dooley was at the party. But she must not have mentioned Beth, which had to mean that she hadn't seen her. Still, it would be good to talk to her.

"Thanks," he said. He held out her sunglasses. She took them and slipped them back on.

"You still love her, don't you?" she said.

He didn't answer. There were some things that were no one's business but his own.

"You seem like an okay guy," she said. "But just so you don't get the wrong idea, I'm glad the cops arrested her. I only wish she was eighteen instead of seventeen. If she was eighteen, she'd be locked up for life. At seventeen, the most she'll get is ten years, and a third of that will be served in the community, on probation. Her name will never get mentioned, her record will stay sealed. No one will ever know. Ten years and then she can get on with her life. But Parker? He's gone and he's staying gone."

Dooley was thankful she had her sunglasses back on. He didn't want to see the eyes that matched the words she had just spoken because, if he did, he might do something that he would regret.

◆ ◆ ◆

He walked back down to the main street. What now?

Against whatever common sense he possessed—he was pretty sure his uncle would have said that it wasn't much—he found himself headed to Parker Albright's house.

A small brown woman answered the door. When Dooley asked if Deecee was in, the woman asked for his name.

"I'm a friend of Parker's," he said.

The woman asked him to wait. She did not invite him to

step inside. She closed the door in his face and left him standing on the wide stone steps for so long that he began to think that the answer was no, Deecee wasn't in, and that he was supposed to figure that out for himself.

Then the door opened again and there stood the girl who had greeted him at the party. The look in her eyes went from friendly to hostile the moment she took in his face.

"You're not a friend of Parker's," she said. She began to swing the door shut.

"Wait! I just want to talk to you for a minute, about what happened."

The door was already half closed.

"I know who you are," Deecee said. "You're *her* boyfriend."

"Yeah, that's right." He wasn't going to deny it, especially not to Parker's sister. "Was she here the night of the party, Deecee? Did you see her?"

"What difference does it make? She confessed. She told the police she did it. She even told them how she did it." Her voice broke when she said the last part, and tears gathered in the corners of her eyes.

"All I want to know is, did you see her that night?" he said, talking low and gentle, as if he were talking to Beth. "That's all."

She wiped a tear from her cheek. "No. No, I didn't. I told the cops that, too. But that doesn't mean she didn't sneak in. I was keeping an eye on who was coming into the yard, but it was a party, you know? I didn't see everything."

"I talked to your friend Monique."

Deecee's expression sharpened. Monique was probably in for an earful.

"She said she saw Parker leave the party with a girl around

ten o'clock. She said the girl had long dark hair. Do you know who that might have been?"

"Beth has long dark hair," Deecee said.

Dooley forced himself to stay calm.

"Was there anyone else there with long dark hair?"

Deecee stared at him.

"There were nearly sixty people at the party. A lot of them had long dark hair."

"Can you tell me who?"

It was as if she hadn't heard the question. Maybe she really hadn't. Or maybe she hadn't wanted to.

"It wouldn't surprise me if it was Beth who Monique saw. She'd been saying all those horrible things about Parker and what he supposedly did at our country place. Because of her, the police arrested him and charged him with sexual assault." Her eyes drilled into him. "Girls line up around the block to get with Parker. He's a good person. He's considerate and sweet and good-looking. He didn't have to force anyone. But he got arrested because of her, and she refused to drop the charges."

"What do you mean, refused?"

"She's crazy," Deecee said. "I've heard people talk about her. I know all about her brother and his friends. I'm not surprised what she did, showing up like that and luring Parker away from the party and killing him. I'm not even remotely surprised."

The look in her eyes was one of pure hatred. Jesus, he wondered what Beth would have done if she'd seen all the looks he had seen in the past couple of days. These people had all judged her. Who she was and who she had been was colored now by the lies they were all convinced she had told and the revenge she had supposedly exacted. Beth had crossed the line, whether she realized it or not. She had a big neon sign flashing above her head that set her apart from civilized society. Beth was just like him now—except that he refused to believe that she had done what they thought she had done. What she herself had confessed to doing.

He met Deecee's eyes. "Thanks for talking to me."

He was turning away from the door when he heard a man's voice.

"Lena said a friend of Parker's was here," the voice said.

"Lena was wrong, Dad. He isn't a friend of Parker's. He's a friend of Beth Everley's."

One part of Dooley's brain told him to get the hell out of there, now. Another part, the part that reminded him of his uncle, told him who this man was and what he had been through, told him to do the decent thing. He turned to see Parker's father, who was tall, like Parker, and looked surprisingly fit for a guy who probably never had to lift a finger if he didn't feel like it.

"I'm sorry for your loss, sir," Dooley said.

Mr. Albright stepped out in front of his daughter. Dooley saw then that he was much taller than Parker had been, taller than Dooley, too, and bulky. Dooley didn't know whether that bulk was muscle or fat. It didn't matter. A man that tall, carrying that many pounds, with that half-crazed, half-grieving look on his face, was a threat. Dooley stepped back a full pace. His heart was pounding in his chest when he finally turned and started down the wide stone steps. Every muscle in his body clenched as he waited for Mr. Albright to make a move. But nothing happened—until he turned the corner onto his uncle's street nearly an hour later.

◆ ◆ ◆

Dooley's antennae started to tingle when a dark-colored sedan slid to the curb beside him—on the wrong side of the street. He made it for a cop car before he saw who was behind the wheel.

Randall.

Dooley glanced up the street. His uncle's house was out of sight. He waited. Randall stepped up onto the sidewalk and moved in close, inside Dooley's comfort zone, trying to make Dooley squirm. Dooley wanted to step back, but he knew it was pointless. Randall would only step in close again.

"What have you been up to, Ryan?" Randall said.

Right. Like Dooley was going to answer any cop questions without having a clear idea of where the questioning was going.

"I got a call from Patrick Albright." Parker's dad. Boy, the guy hadn't wasted any time. "He tells me you were at his house, harassing his daughter."

Oh. So it was that game.

"I wasn't harassing her. I asked her a couple of questions, that's all."

Randall chewed this over silently, or pretended to. Dooley knew that trick, too.

"Why?" he said at last.

"Why?"

Geez, what was it with detectives? You knew they were smart guys because they'd made the grade. They knew they were smart, too. They got off on it. But they never quit playing dumb, like they thought that would trip you up.

"Why do you think?"

"Well now, that's a good question," Randall said, talking slowly, like he was some kind of moron. "Maybe you were talking to her because you're trying to find out what we know—and what we don't know."

Gee, you think?

"We've already got your girlfriend, Ryan. Maybe you're checking around to see what we've got on you."

Randall gave him that look, the one his uncle gave him sometimes, the one that told you that he knew whatever it was you were trying to hide, he had it all figured out and he was just waiting for the right time to spring it on you. The thing was, though: Dooley had dealt with enough cops and had lived with his uncle long enough to know that most of the time that look was bullshit. He figured they'd had to practice it in front of a mirror at the police academy—the fake-out-the-suspect look. Make him think you know everything, make him feel the doom that's waiting for him, fill him with such despair that the only thing he can think of to do is to give it all up and hope he'll be shown some mercy. Dooley would have ignored that look, except that this time he wasn't sure what Randall was up to. He must have turned up something if he was here talking to Dooley. But what?

"I'm going to ask you again, Ryan, and this time I'd like an answer. Why were you asking Deecee Albright about what she saw the night her brother died?"

Part of him wanted to like Randall. After all, he'd ended up being okay when Lorraine had died. But that first time he brought Dooley in to talk to him about Parker, it was like they were back to square one, like everything that Dooley had done that wasn't completely fucked up, all of a sudden didn't matter. Still, giving him attitude wasn't going to help. In fact, giving a cop attitude pretty much guaranteed that he'd go out of his way to mess you up.

"You talked to Beth," Dooley said, talking to Randall the way he would talk to his uncle, trying to make him think—despite everything he had heard from the girls he had talked to. "You think she would actually kill someone?"

Randall's eyes remained guarded, which told Dooley something. Randall wasn't in shoot-the-shit mode. He wasn't going to let it be just two guys having a conversation. He was in full investigative mode. Mr. Detective.

"I've been doing this job a long time, Ryan," he said. "Most people who kill someone, it's not a huge surprise. They're leading the life. Or they're time bombs, you know, like those guys who all of a sudden lose it and do the murder-suicide thing. But every now and then it happens. Every now and then, some ordinary citizen, some seemingly perfectly nice individual, takes a life. Sometimes it comes out of the blue. Sometimes there's a reason that's been festering for a while."

Like being assaulted by a pig like Parker Albright.

"The real question is," Randall continued, "how did a petite girl like Beth bash a big guy like Parker over the head with a rock that must have been a struggle for her to lift once, never mind a couple of times." Randall was having doubts, at least about part of it. "How did she get up and down a sheer drop as high as the one behind the Albright house without any help?" Which meant that no one had been able to say for sure that Beth had gone to the party the regular way—around the side of the house, the way Dooley had got there, or maybe through the house. "You think maybe she might have had an accomplice?"

Now Dooley got it.

"She seems like a nice girl," Randall said. "Pretty, too. And from what I hear, she's been seeing you against her mother's wishes. Her mother says she's obsessed with you."

If Beth so much as waved at Dooley, her mother read it as obsession. What else would explain what a nice girl like her was doing with a criminal like him?

"I bet you didn't meet many girls like her before you moved in with your uncle, huh, Ryan?"

Dooley just looked at him. Anything he said would just give Randall another way to get at him. The smart thing to do, he realized, was to simply walk away. He wasn't obliged to talk to Randall. But he wanted to know exactly what Randall was thinking. Randall knew it, too. He'd probably been counting on it.

"I bet you never met such a sweet girl before. Polite, too, even when she was sitting there in that hospital room giving me chapter and verse on how she killed Parker Albright."

Dooley could picture it—Beth in her soft, husky voice, probably calling Randall sir.

"So it must have ripped your guts out when she told you her story about what Parker did to her," Randall said. "Did you talk about it, Ryan?"

"Yeah, we talked." But the thought of that conversation—of Beth, pale, fidgety, sitting across from him in that coffee shop—made him want to go back in time. He should have listened more carefully. He shouldn't have said what he did. He should have ... Jesus, Dr. Calvin was right. You could drive yourself crazy with should-haves, but they didn't get you anywhere. They didn't erase what had happened. They couldn't make it go away. All you could do was learn from them. Dooley knew how it went. *How did it make you feel, Ryan?* Like shit. *Did you like that feeling?* No. *Do you want to feel that way again?* No. *How are you going to make sure you don't feel that way again?* Next time, I'll do it differently. It was the right answer, but it never seemed like enough when he said it. Next time was next time. How the hell did you make good on *this* time?

"Did you and Beth talk about what should happen to Parker?"

Dooley felt himself go on full alert. He would have to be careful now.

"She said she'd talked to the cops," he said. "I heard Parker was arrested and then made bail. But he was charged and was going to court for it."

"That's not what I mean, and you know it, Ryan. Did you and Beth talk about what would happen if Parker beat the charge? There was a good chance he would. I know about the witnesses. I've read their statements. I also know about how long it took for Beth to report the incident and what the rape kit turned up on account of the time lag. It was going to be hard to get a conviction, Ryan. She told you that, didn't she? She was sure Parker was going to beat it and she hated that. So did you, didn't you?"

If Randall knew what Dooley had really thought, if he knew what Dooley had said to Beth, he'd have an even lower opinion of him than he already did.

"Did you plan it together?" Randall said. "Is that why you showed up at the party? Were you getting a look at the layout? Were you figuring out how to get Beth in there without being seen?"

Dooley bet that Randall wished Monique had been able to positively identify the girl she'd seen with Parker. But she hadn't. And it looked like either no one else had seen the girl, or, like, Monique, that no one was able to identify her.

"Did you help her get up onto the promontory?" Randall

said. "Did you help her kill Parker?"

Jesus.

"I don't have to talk to you."

"No, you don't. Not now, anyway," Randall said. "But how about doing everyone a big favor? How about telling me exactly where you were and what you were doing when Parker Albright was killed?"

Randall's eyes searched his. Well, let them. Dooley met them square on. He didn't have to tell Randall anything. He certainly didn't have to tell him anything that would get him locked up.

"If you were in on it, I'm going to get you," Randall said.

That was it. Randall had nothing but suspicions. Dooley stepped past him and walked as calmly as he could down the street to his uncle's house. His heart was racing when he opened the front door. Jeannie's head popped through from the kitchen.

"Smells good, huh?" she said, beaming at him.

"Yeah," Dooley said, forcing a smile. "Smells great."

♦ THIRTEEN ♦

Jeannie had just called Dooley and his uncle to dinner—she'd set the dining room table with a white lace table cloth and his uncle's mother's silverware—when Dooley's cell phone rang. He dug it out of his pocket.

"Let them leave a message," his uncle said as Jeannie appeared carrying a roast on a platter.

Dooley checked the read-out. It was Warren.

"I'll just see what he wants," he said.

His uncle took the platter from Jeannie and set it on the table. Jeannie dashed back into the kitchen. Dooley stepped out into the front hall.

"Warren, what's up?"

"It's not Warren," a soft, slightly husky voice said.

Dooley felt like he'd been punched in the stomach.

"Beth?"

"They won't let me call anyone except my mother and my lawyer. And they always insist on dialing for me. I think my mother told them to."

"Where's Warren?"

"He's cleaning outside my room. He's going to tell me if anyone comes." There was a long pause. "He said you wanted to talk to me, Dooley."

"I love you, Beth."

"I love you, too. You don't have to worry."

"Ryan," his uncle called. "Time to eat."

"In a minute," Dooley called back.

"It was all my fault. My mom got me a lawyer. He doesn't know any of her friends, so that's good. He listens to me, Dooley. He doesn't try to pressure me."

He didn't understand what she was talking about. Why would a lawyer pressure her? Pressure her to do what?

"He says that under the circumstances—you know, because of what Parker did and then because of what I did—"

An image of her with black lips and a black tongue flashed before his eyes.

"—that he might be able to get me a suspended sentence. Maybe he can even get me off. I told him I don't care. And I don't, Dooley. It never would have happened if it wasn't for me. I know that." There was another pause and then she was speeding along as if she was in a race with time. "I saw you, Dooley. At first I thought—"

"Ryan!" his uncle thundered. "Dinner. *Now.*"

"Saw me?" Dooley said. It wasn't the first time she had said that. "Saw me when?"

"That night. With Parker." Her voice broke. It was a moment before she spoke again. "I wanted to tell you ... I love you, Dooley. And I won't say a word to anyone. I promise."

His uncle appeared in the front hall, hands on hips, fury on his face. Dooley turned away from him.

"Beth—"

His uncle perked up, frowning.

"Dooley? It's me."

"Warren? Put Beth back on."

"No can do," he said. He had dropped his voice so low that Dooley could hardly hear him. "The cops just showed up. I gotta go."

The phone went silent. Dooley stared at it.

"Was that Beth?" his uncle said, no longer angry. "Is everything okay?"

"I don't know."

His uncle laid a hand on his shoulder. "We can talk later, if that's what you want. But right now, Jeannie is sitting in there waiting for us. She knocked herself out making a spectacular meal. You think you could come back in there with me and show her some appreciation?"

He was asking, not telling. This was important to him, Dooley realized.

They went into the dining room and tucked into Jeannie's meal. If it had been any other day, any other day at all, Dooley would have thought he'd gone to heaven. Roast beef, gravy, little roasted potatoes, green beans with almond slivers, a green salad on the side, and, afterwards, homemade apple pie, warm from the oven with a scoop of ice cream on the side. Any other day, any other day at all, he would have eaten until his stomach exploded.

Dooley's uncle said he would take care of the dishes. He asked Dooley on the sly if he wanted to help out, maybe catch up on things. Dooley said no.

◆ ◆ ◆

His uncle told him not to worry about it. Dooley thanked Jeannie for the meal, excused himself, and went upstairs to his room.

Sitting at the table, making small talk with Jeannie, had been torture. But he'd done it, not because his uncle had asked him to—well, maybe that had been part of it—but because he liked Jeannie and he didn't want to hurt her feelings. But even still, he'd had to force himself to pay attention to what she was saying, none of it very important, because all his brain wanted to do was replay what Beth had said: *I saw you. With Parker.* Jesus, did she mean what he thought she meant?

He sat on the edge of his bed, his stomach churning, until he couldn't stand it any longer. He pulled out his cell phone and punched in Warren's number.

"What happened? Why were the cops there again? What did they want?"

"I don't know," Warren said.

"Were they uniforms or plainclothes?"

"Plainclothes. I recognized one of them. He was that guy that was on your mother's case."

"Randall?"

"Yeah."

"Did you hear what he said to her?"

"I couldn't. The door was closed."

"How long was he in there?"

"I don't know. At least twenty minutes. I couldn't hang around and wait, Dooley. I stayed as long as I could, but ... Sorry."

"It's okay. You did good," Dooley said. "Thanks. I mean it, Warren."

◆ ◆ ◆

He heard Jeannie leave and his uncle pad up the stairs to his room. Then nothing for a moment. Then his uncle coming down the hall toward his room and a soft knock on the door.

"Yeah?" Dooley said.

His uncle pushed the door open. "I just wanted to thank you for how you behaved at dinner."

"It's no problem. I was glad to do it. I like Jeannie."

"And she likes you." For a moment, he seemed about to say something else on the topic. He hung in the doorway, studying Dooley. "How's Beth?"

"Okay, considering."

"Nothing new?"

Dooley shook his head. He wondered why Randall had gone back to the hospital to talk to her. Whatever the reason, he was pretty sure Beth hadn't told him anything new. Maybe she'd even been smart enough to insist on the presence of her lawyer. He hoped she'd been even smarter and had kept her mouth shut altogether. Dooley was pretty sure, based on what she had said on the phone, that she wouldn't have told Randall what she'd told Dooley.

He could drive himself crazy, imagining what might have happened, but imagining wasn't the same as knowing. The only way he was going to know for sure what happened was when Randall came looking for him again to ask more questions or maybe to slip the handcuffs on him.

❖ ❖ ❖

When Dooley woke up the next morning, the roof still hadn't caved in. That's good, he told himself. Every day that Randall didn't come after him was one more day he had to figure out what to do. But where to start?

Someone hammered on his door. What the hell? Dooley sat up just as the door burst open.

It wasn't the cops.

It was his uncle, with a pissed-off look on his face, which was just as bad as if it had been the cops.

"For Christ's sake, Ryan, you're going to be late for school."

Dooley glanced at his clock-radio. Whoa! How had that happened? He jumped up and reached for the jeans that lay in a heap by the side of his bed. His uncle stood in the doorway, harrumphing while Dooley zipped up.

"I'm sorry, okay?" Dooley said. "I had trouble getting to sleep." He sniffed his armpits and dug in his dresser for a clean T-shirt. His uncle's shoulders untensed a little.

"I know things haven't been easy lately," he said.

No kidding.

"But school's a non-negotiable."

"I said I was sorry." What more did his uncle want?

"What I meant was—"

"I know what you meant." He shoved his feet into a pair of boots and then did a three-sixty, scanning for his backpack. It was under his desk. He grabbed it and headed for the door.

His uncle was still standing there.

"Why don't you come by the store after work?" he said. "We can talk."

"I got stuff to do."

"Ryan, this thing with Beth—"

"I'm gonna be late." He started to squeeze by his uncle, but his uncle stepped back and let him pass.

Dooley walked as fast as he could, breaking into a run from time to time, but the bell had already rung by the time he got up the school steps and through the door. Worse, Rektor was standing outside the school office. When he saw Dooley, he waved him over.

"Home form is almost over," he said. "That makes you late, Mr. Dooley."

Mr. Dooley. Dooley hated being called that. Rektor called all the other male students by their last names, but as soon as he knew that that was what Dooley preferred, he stuck a Mister in front of it and added a sarcastic little spin when he said it.

Dooley didn't bother to offer an excuse. The one he had was lame, and he knew that Rektor wouldn't believe it anyway. He looked at the vice principal, waiting to see what he was going to do.

The bell rang, signaling the end of home form. The hall flooded with students. If Dooley joined the crowd, he would make it to his first class on schedule, with no need for a late pass. He glanced at Rektor and then thought, Fuck it. If Rektor wanted to bust his balls, he could call him down to the office. Dooley took the stairs two at a time, ignoring Rektor's voice behind him, and was in his seat in math class before the next bell rang.

Math class passed in exquisite suspense. He kept glancing at the door, expecting to see either Rektor or Randall on the other side of the glass.

Neither showed up.

He found Warren at lunch time. The poor guy was nodding off over a pair of peanut butter sandwiches.

"Hey," Dooley said, nudging him gently.

Warren's head shot up. There was a look of panic on his face, as if he'd been caught snoring in class.

"You need to get some sleep," Dooley said.

"Tell me about it." Warren picked up a sandwich. "It's the schedule. It's crazy. I haven't been able to figure out the formula. Sometimes you work three shifts and get three shifts off. Or they give you four shifts and three shifts off. Then all of a sudden they hit you with six shifts straight with only two shifts off to recover. It doesn't make any sense."

"You doing six now?"

Warren nodded. "Five down and one to go. Then I get two glorious nights to catch up on my sleep—after I catch up on my homework." He bit into his sandwich. From the look on his face, it might just as well have been a shitwich.

"How's Beth?"

"If you think I look tired, you should see her."

She'd looked exhausted when Dooley had talked to her in the coffee shop. She'd looked even more drained when he had caught a glimpse of her in Emerg. He ached to hold her.

"Is she still at the hospital?"

"She was when I left at six this morning. But I heard she has to make a court appearance. After that, I don't know." He blinked at Dooley from behind his glasses.

"What?" Dooley said.

"Nothing."

"You were going to say something, Warren. What is it?"

"It's nothing. I'm tired, too. That's all." He started to raise his sandwich to his mouth again. Dooley caught his hand and lowered it to the table.

"What is it, Warren?"

Warren shrank back a little.

"It's that guy.

"What guy?"

"The one I told you about. The guy who comes around all the time."

"Nevin?" Jesus, he hated Nevin. "What about him?"

"He shows up all the time with Beth's mother. She really likes him, doesn't she?"

What? What was Warren telling him?

"Beth's mother, I mean," Warren said quickly. "She's crazy about the guy. He comes to the hospital with her all the time, and he's always rushing around, getting her coffee, taking her down to the food court and making sure she eats something, telling her it's okay, he'll keep Beth company if she has to go to work, all that kind of stuff."

"Yeah, I know."

"You do?"

"Yeah. It's okay." Dooley let go of his hand.

"If it's any consolation," Warren said, "I don't think Beth likes him as much as her mother does. She talks to him like a friend, but it's nothing like the way she talks to you."

For the first time in a long time, Dooley felt a surge of hope in his heart.

"Thanks, Warren."

◆ ◆ ◆

School ended for the day, and the roof still hadn't caved in. He was on his way out when his cell phone rang. He checked the display. It was the store. Boy, it had better not be Kevin.

It was Linelle.

"There's a girl here asking for you," she said.

"What girl?"

Dooley heard Linelle ask the girl for her name.

"Ellie Davis," came the answer.

"She's there now?"

"Yeah."

"And she asked for me?"

"You ever known me to bullshit you, Dooley?"

"No."

"Well then?"

"Tell her I'll be there in ten minutes. Ask her to wait."

There was a pause while Linelle relayed the information.

"She says she'll be in the Greek place across the street."

"How will I recognize her?"

Another pause.

"She says she'll recognize you."

Dooley ran most of the way.

When he pushed open the door to the restaurant, he was thinking, how do all these girls I've never met know what I look like when I couldn't pick a single one of them out of a lineup if my life depended on it?

In Ellie's case, it turned out to be no mystery.

She was the girl who had been with Rachel Silverman at the ballet school.

She was sitting at a table for two near the back. He ordered a Coke on his way to her.

"I've been calling you," he said as he sat down across the table from her.

She looked startled.

"I didn't get any messages."

"I didn't leave a message. I've been calling your home phone. No one ever answers. I was beginning to think you were out of town or something."

"Sula doesn't answer any number that isn't on the list."

"List?" he said. Sula? he thought.

"The housekeeper. My mom doesn't let her answer unless

the person who's calling is someone we know. Anyone who's not on the list has to leave a message and my mother decides whether or not she wants to call back."

In that case, Dooley was doubly glad that he hadn't left a message. He could imagine some uptight mom who, if you asked him, desperately needed a hobby, listening to whatever message he might have left.

"How did you find me?" he said.

"I heard Nevin say one time that you worked at that video store."

Dooley bet that there'd been a sneer in his voice when he said it. He bet old Nevin would rather die than work in a video store. If he ever did a job like Dooley's—fat chance—he'd be fired on his first day for being condescending to the customers.

"What did you want to talk to me about, Ellie?"

A waitress appeared and put a Coke in front of Dooley. She glanced at Ellie's coffee cup to see if she wanted a refill, but it looked to Dooley like she hadn't touched what was already in there. Ellie waited until the waitress had left.

"Beth has always been nice to me," she said. She was looking at Dooley's Coke, not at Dooley. "Rachel doesn't like her. I don't really know why, except that Rachel doesn't like a lot of people."

Dooley bet the feeling was mutual.

"That's just the way she is," Ellie said.

Dooley wondered why Ellie, who seemed nice enough, would hang out with someone like Rachel. Low self-esteem, maybe. She'd been like a shadow the first time he'd seen her, letting Rachel do all the talking. And now she looked flat-out uncomfortable, like she was afraid that if she looked at Dooley, he would bite her.

She drew in a deep breath. Her eyes came up to meet Dooley's.

"It's all my fault," she said. Her focus jumped back to the tabletop.

"What's all your fault?"

"Everything," she said, so quietly that Dooley had to strain to hear her. "I ... I feel terrible. If it hadn't been for me ..."

"What do you mean, *everything*?"

She stared resolutely at the tabletop for long enough to make Dooley lose his patience. But he forced himself to wait.

"I was on Parker's team," she said.

She was talking about the trip.

"Parker wasn't even interested in her."

"In Beth?"

Ellie nodded.

"He was sort of dogging this other girl on our team. He was like that. He'd set his sights on some girl and then go after her, you know, until he got what he wanted. It was like a game to him." Some game. "Anyway, after the first day, Beth came up to Rachel and me at suppertime and asked if she could sit with us. Rachel was going to say no, but I said sure." She glanced up at Dooley. Her cheeks turned pink. What was going on? "Nevin was on her team," she said. Her voice took on an even softer quality when she said his name. "I thought maybe if she sat with us at supper, Nevin might sit with us, too."

Maybe what they said was true. Maybe there really was someone for everyone, even old Nevin.

"He tried to join us," Ellie said. "He came over and asked if he could sit with us. But Beth said no. She said the other chair at our table was already spoken for, even though it wasn't."

Oh?

"Then Rachel said, no, it wasn't. She invited Nevin to sit down. I could see Beth was upset, but she did her best to hide it." She ventured another glance at Dooley. "She's like that. She's nice. She doesn't like to hurt people's feelings." Her eyes shifted away again. "When I got up to leave, she came with me. She told Nevin we had something we had to do. We walked away. Then she told me that she didn't understand why Nevin was acting the way he was."

"What way was that?"

She hesitated.

"He was hitting on her," she said at last. "She said he should have known better. She said he knew she had a boyfriend." Her eyes met Dooley's fleetingly, and her cheeks turned pink again. "She told me a little about you. She said you weren't at all the way most people thought you were. She really loves you." There was a touch of awe in her voice that made Dooley sit a little taller in his chair and made him ache all that much more for Beth. "That's when I made a suggestion."

"Suggestion?"

"I said I would talk to Parker. I said maybe we could arrange to switch teams. That way Nevin wouldn't be able to bother her so much. And, well, I thought ..."

"You like Nevin, huh?" Dooley didn't understand it. He thought Nevin was an over-privileged, overly pampered, conceited little weasel. But what did he know about the kids in Beth's life, other than that they lived in a different world from his? A world where, apparently, shy girls with a shortage of self-esteem developed serious crushes on twits like Nevin.

Ellie confirmed it with a nod.

"I talked to Parker that night."

He tried to imagine it—mousey little Ellie trying to pry a favor out of hotshot Parker.

"He didn't act like he was even remotely interested. I tried to tell him—I said she had this boyfriend back home and that Nevin was bugging her and that she just wanted to be able to get through the week without being harassed. Finally, he said he would think about it. I was sure he was going to say no. But first thing the next morning, he went to talk to Mr. DeLisle—he was in charge of the project—and he arranged for Beth and me to switch teams. I was really surprised. I didn't think he'd been paying attention to what I was saying."

"Why the change?"

Ellie shrugged. "But Beth sure was grateful to him. And he really turned on the charm, you know?"

Dooley didn't, but he sure could picture it.

"I could tell that Beth liked him," she said. "But it wasn't the same way that she likes you." This time when she looked at him, she held her gaze steady. "I was at the party that last night after we finished the project. I didn't see her go into the house with him, but someone who did said they were holding hands."

"Do you remember who that was?"

She thought for a moment.

"Rachel told me that that's what she heard, but I don't know where she heard it. I could ask."

"It's okay," he said. He already knew who it was.

He remembered what his uncle had told him after he'd talked to a cop friend of his. Parker had insisted that Beth had gone willingly up to his room. He'd insisted that he hadn't done anything that she hadn't agreed to. And, his uncle said, it was going to be hard for Beth to prove otherwise because *there was only one witness who saw them go up.* And that witness said they were holding hands.

Annicka.

Annicka had told Dooley that she had seen Beth and Parker together. She was the one who had seen them go up the stairs. She was the one who had seen them holding hands.

"You know a girl named Annicka?" he said.

Ellie nodded.

"You know her last name?"

"Charles."

"You know her phone number or where she lives?"

She shook her head.

He stood up abruptly.

Ellie cringed in her chair, as if she were afraid of what he was going to do.

"How'd it work out for you, anyway?" he said, partly to get that scared look off her face, partly because he was curious. "With Nevin?"

"It didn't," she said. "He wasn't interested in me. I should have known. I should never have suggested that Beth switch teams with me."

"You thought you were helping her out," Dooley said, even though that probably hadn't been even close to the reason she had done it. "How did he take it when he found out about her and Parker?"

"I think he felt bad about that."

Dooley could see that.

"But not the way you think," Ellie said. "See, that's the thing about Nevin. He can be really sweet. He heard about Beth going upstairs with Parker—everybody heard about it. And he saw how upset she was the next morning. But instead of ignoring her, the way I know I would if I found out some guy I had a crush on had gone and slept with another girl, he went and sat with her on the bus. He tried to talk to her, but she wouldn't say a word. She just kept staring at Parker. After a while, Nevin got up and went to sit somewhere else. I switched seats to talk to him. He said she made a mistake, that's all."

"A mistake?"

"By sleeping with Parker. He said a lot of girls made that same mistake. He said they found out the hard way that Parker wasn't the kind of guy you could count on."

"Did he say that or did he say that Beth said that?"

"I don't know. But it's what everyone was saying. Everyone knew about it. And I guess Beth took it hard."

"What do you mean?"

She looked surprised. "Well, she pressed charges. She went up to his room with him, holding his hand, and as soon as it became obvious to her that he'd got everything he wanted and wasn't interested in her anymore, she accused him of rape."

"You think that's what happened?"

"Isn't it?" Her eyes were wide, innocent. "Nevin said maybe she was practicing what to say to you, you know, in case you heard about it."

Dooley's first reaction: How would I hear about it? I don't know any of these people. Then it came to him: Nevin. Nevin hadn't wasted a minute. He'd come straight to the store to tell Dooley.

"Wasn't he mad at Parker?" he said.

"Nevin?" More surprise. "No. Nevin and Parker are friends. Nevin would do anything for Parker. He knows how it is. You think that's the first time Parker has taken some girl up to his room at a party? Nevin even covered for him a couple of times."

"Covered for him?"

"One time, there was this girl who was seeing another friend of Parker's. But you could tell she was also interested in Parker. Rachel says she got close to Parker's friend just so she could have a chance at Parker. We were all at a party together, and this girl was making eyes at Parker. The next thing, I see that the girl has dragged Parker into his father's den and Parker is winking at Nevin. Nevin was on the boyfriend just like that, keeping him occupied until Parker and the girl came back. It was the last time I saw the girl. But Parker's friend? He's still Parker's friend. I don't think he ever knew what happened."

He looked at Ellie again, at the sad little Nevin-struck look on her face. Had she even listened to what she had just told him? Didn't she see what kind of pandering opportunist she was stuck on? Jesus. These guys, Parker and Nevin, they had something that dazzled women. Was it just the money or was it something else? And Parker, well, he seemed to have the same effect on guys as he had on girls. It wasn't every guy who could screw some other guy's girl and get away with it. There had to be some advantage to it, but Dooley couldn't see it. Except for with Nevin. Good old Nevin. He had heard the same thing everyone else had. He'd heard that Beth had gone willingly with Parker. He'd drawn the same conclusions as everyone else: that she'd been upset when she found out that all Parker had been interested in was fucking her. He'd seen his opportunity. He had tried to comfort her on the bus. He'd gone to see her all those times in the hospital—Nevin, in there nice and tight with Beth's mom. The little weasel had even come to the store to tell Dooley. He'd wanted Dooley to know what had happened. He probably loved it that Dooley knew he was right there at Beth's elbow, comforting her, helping her pick up the pieces. And never once had Beth told him to get lost. She probably didn't even know about that visit to the store. Dooley hadn't mentioned it, and he was willing to bet that Nevin hadn't, either.

"Thanks for coming by," he said to Ellie. "Thanks for talking to me."

He put some money on the table to pay for his Coke and her coffee.

On his way to the restaurant door, he pulled out his cell phone. Cassie's mother had a class list. Cassie would be able to tell him how to get in touch with Annicka. He was scrolling through calls, looking for her number, when his uncle called.

"Where are you, Ryan?"

Shit. He had forgotten he was supposed to stop by his uncle's dry cleaning store.

"I'm sorry. I got hung up—"

"I need you at home. Right now."

◆ FOURTEEN ◆

Dooley's uncle didn't go into details. He said he needed Dooley at home. He said, "Right now." And that was that.

Dooley stood outside the restaurant for a moment, staring at his phone. What was his uncle even doing at home? Why wasn't he at the store where he was supposed to be, where Dooley was supposed to have met him? Something must have happened.

Dooley hurried home.

His uncle's street was quiet, as usual. Nothing looked out of place.

The house was quiet, too.

"Hello?" Dooley called.

"Up here," came his uncle's voice.

Dooley climbed the stairs cautiously. He peeked into his uncle's study. He wasn't there. Then into his bedroom. He wasn't there, either, but, boy, the place was a mess.

"I'm in the bathroom," his uncle called.

Dooley's stomach clenched. What was he doing in there?

Straightening out the place, it turned out. Dooley's eyes went to the tub. There was blue stuff in it and on the tiles around it.

"What's going on?" Dooley said.

"The police were here. With a search warrant."

Jesus, Randall hadn't been kidding.

"What did they want?"

"They were looking for clothing," his uncle said. "They sprayed the place with Luminol."

Dooley knew what that was about. He was as up on his *CSI* as anyone. They were looking for traces of blood.

"Did they find anything?"

His uncle went still. His eyes drilled into Dooley's.

"Is there anything to find?"

"No," Dooley said quickly.

"Then why did you ask the question?"

"What I meant was—"

"They asked me about the night that kid was killed, Ryan."

Dooley went numb all over.

"They asked me when you got home. They asked me if I noticed anything unusual."

Jesus. He couldn't have moved if he'd wanted to. His whole body had turned to ice.

"I'm not going to lie to the police for you, Ryan. You understand that, right?"

Yeah, he understood. He wondered if the inside of the washing machine was blue. He wondered if he had got that little bit of blood off the jeans he had been wearing that night. He wished he'd thrown them out.

"Where were you that night, Ryan?"

Dooley looked down at the gleaming white of the bathroom tile. He was pretty sure his uncle had his best interests at heart. But his uncle had spent most of his life as a cop, and cops had a skewed view of best interests. They kept mixing them up with their own strait-jacketed notion of justice, as in, if you did something you shouldn't have, it was in *everyone*'s best interest, including your own, to come clean about it. If you had some reason you thought you couldn't or shouldn't come clean, well then, you were simply wrong. If you said you needed to buy time, they assumed you were talking about time to get out of town or time to figure out how to get out from under it. It never occurred to them that you might have a nobler cause in mind.

He met his uncle's steely eyes.

"I can't tell you," he said.

"Did you have anything to do with what happened to Parker Albright?"

Dooley couldn't blame his uncle for the question, but, still, the apprehension on his uncle's face stung more than he would have imagined.

"I already told you I didn't."

The answer didn't satisfy his uncle.

"Why did you wash your clothes in the middle of the night that night?"

"They're not going to find anything tying me to Parker, if that's what you're worried about."

His uncle seemed to have grown an inch.

"That is not what I'm worried about." His eyes burned into Dooley's. "Randall has you in on it. He's not going to let up until he's got you where he wants you. If you had anything to do with it, Ryan, it would be in your own best interests to step forward."

See?

"I didn't kill Parker Albright."

His uncle's fist slammed down onto the faux marble counter-top. "Jesus H. Christ!" he said. "Don't dick around with me, Ryan. I deserve better than that. He already has Beth. He has her confession. But he thinks you were involved. He can practically taste it. You think you're going to put one over on him, is that it?

You think you're going to outsmart a guy who's put away dozens of murderers? You think you're that smart, Ryan?"

His uncle had moved so close to him that every word sent a rush of hot air against Dooley's face.

"I'm going to ask you one more time. Did you have anything to do with the death of Parker Albright?"

"No."

His uncle searched Dooley's eyes, hunting for what he had been taught were signs of deceit. He didn't look satisfied.

"They took a couple of pairs of black jeans."

Not just jeans, but black jeans. How did they know Dooley had been wearing black jeans that night?

"They were looking for a blue sweatshirt."

That brought Dooley up short. They must have talked to people who were at Parker's party. How else would they have put together his outfit that night?

"They didn't find it, Ryan," his uncle said. "You know anything about that?"

Dooley was glad he'd ditched the sweatshirt. He wished he knew more about trace evidence, specifically, blood. If you ran a pair of jeans through the washing machine twice on the hottest possible cycle, would there be any way they could find blood— assuming, he reminded himself, that there had been any blood on his jeans in the first place?

"Do you, Ryan?" His uncle sounded tense, impatient.

"I don't know what sweatshirt you're talking about."

"They said they're going to your school. They're going to search your locker, see if it's there."

Dooley had to bite his tongue to stop from saying, *It isn't.*

"Where were you that night, Ryan?" his uncle said.

"I can't tell you." He almost wished he could. Despite everything that had happened since he'd come to live here, it mattered what his uncle thought. It mattered more and more what other people thought, too, even though he knew he had no control over that. He was tired of being the notorious fuck-up, the guy you steered a wide circle around, well, unless you were some dickhead who thought he was tough. Then, maybe, you might make a show of standing up to him—see, I'm not afraid.

But if he came clean to his uncle up here in his sparkling white bathroom, it wouldn't go the way he wanted it to go. He needed more time.

"You have to trust me," Dooley said.

His uncle kept staring at him. He was breathing hard, which told Dooley he was furious. He had got used to demanding answers from Dooley. He had also got used to getting them. But this was different. This was Beth.

"I need a favor," Dooley said.

His uncle laughed, a short, bitter explosion: *You've got to be kidding*.

"I need to talk to Beth, but I don't know if they'll let me."

"And you want me to find out?" His uncle's tone made it clear that he thought Dooley had some nerve.

"I wouldn't ask if it wasn't important."

"Right," his uncle said. "I can see that." He threw down the cleaning rag he'd been using. That, more than almost anything else, gave Dooley a measure of precisely how angry his uncle was. "I got called away from the store to deal with this. I have to get back. I'm assuming you can fix your own supper."

Dooley started to nod, but his uncle was already out of the bathroom. Dooley heard his heels hard on the stairs. He slammed the front door on the way out, something he was always yelling at Dooley for doing.

Dooley stood for a moment, looking at the blue in the bathtub and trying to put himself in his uncle's head. But all he saw was his uncle's rage and frustration, and he didn't have time for that. He pulled out his phone and punched in Cassie's number.

"Is there a phone number and address on your mom's list for Annicka Charles?" he said.

◆ ◆ ◆

Annicka didn't just dress Goth. She lived the life. Dooley found her at the second of a number of places that Cassie had suggested—a no-alcohol place that catered to under-age kids. In this case, kids who dressed in black, dyed their hair to match, and seemed addicted to piercings and tattoos. Dooley wondered what effect Annicka had on her parents, who, presumably, were shelling out big bucks for her private-school tuition.

She was hard to locate at first. The place was gloomy, which was a factor. But it was the relentless sameness of the kids in the place that was the real stumper. It was like trying to find Waldo in a room full of Waldo clones. Then he became aware of a kid looking at him. Staring at him.

Annicka.

She stood up. He started toward her. She headed for the exit at the back of the black-painted room. He quickened his pace. She disappeared through the door.

Shit.

He ran, grabbed the door, and yanked it open.

Annicka was leaning against a dumpster across the alley from the exit. She was lighting a cigarette.

"There's no way I'm going to talk to you in there," she said.

It was almost as if she had been expecting him.

"You know why I'm here?" he said.

"It's about Parker, right?" She drew in a lungful of smoke and then blew it out in two streams through her nostrils.

"Everyone I talk to says the same thing—that Beth and Parker were holding hands when she went into the house with him. But no one actually saw that. No one except you."

She sucked on her cigarette again.

"You saw them, right, Annicka?"

"Yeah. I saw them." She had sharp little eyes that held his.

"You saw the two of them holding hands?"

"Actually, Parker was holding her by the wrist."

By the wrist. That wasn't the same as holding hands. Dooley's pulse began to race.

"It's not what you're thinking," Annicka said. "He wasn't dragging her up there or anything. He just had her by the wrist and was ahead of her on the stairs. He was telling her about some pictures he had taken. She went up there with him because she wanted to."

Jesus, what the hell was going on? Had Beth wanted to be with Parker or not? Had she known what was going to happen or not? Had she flirted with him all week or not?

"He's a pig," Annicka said. "But she didn't know it. Not when I saw her, anyway." She drew on the cigarette again, as greedily as Dooley used to knock back the beers or pull on a joint. "Some of the girls I know talk about her. Rachel is the worst. She's a total skank herself, but she makes Beth out to be some kind of psycho freak on account of something that happened to her when she was a kid. Something about her dad."

Dooley knew all about that.

"But she seemed nice enough to me. She never gave me a hard time or anything, you know, on account of all this." She waved her free hand at the stud in her nose and the rings in her eyebrows. "I don't think Parker was even interested in her, at first. I mean, she's pretty and all, but it's not like Parker has to go chasing girls, you know what I mean?"

Dooley could imagine.

"Ellie asked Parker if she and Beth could switch teams. She made out that it was all about helping Beth, but everyone knows she has this thing for Nevin. I guess she thought if she could spend the whole week working with him, he might notice her. Parker wasn't going to do it for her, though. It's not like he ever feels he has to do a favor for anyone, especially some girl he thinks is pathetic. You've met Ellie?" Dooley nodded. "She's kind of mousey. She hangs out with Rachel, who basically gets off on ordering her around."

"But he agreed to the switch," Dooley said.

"Yeah. After Monique—you know her?" Dooley nodded again. "After Monique told him that you were the guy who was involved in that whole thing with Win."

Winston Rhodes again. Dooley hadn't seen him since last fall, but all these kids knew Rhodes and knew what had happened to him.

"That made you famous all over my school," Annicka said. "Right after it happened, everyone was asking Beth about it. And about you."

Dooley wondered if that had anything to do with why she had never introduced him to any of her school friends.

"Monique's dad and Win's dad went to the same school.

They lived two blocks from each other their whole lives. That's how Monique knows so much about you." She crushed her cigarette butt under the heel of one knee-high-laced boot. "Is it true what you did to that woman?"

Dooley didn't answer.

"Monique told him about you because she didn't want him to let Beth on his team. She hates Beth. She can't believe Beth's boyfriend is the guy who ... She's known Win her whole life. They're friends. She thought if Parker knew Beth was seeing you, he'd say no, for sure. He wouldn't want the hassle."

"But he didn't say no."

"You should have seen Monique the next morning when Parker stopped by the table where she and Ellie and some of the other girls were sitting, and told Ellie that he'd spoken to Mr. DeLisle and it was okay, she and Beth could switch. For the rest of the week, he poured on the charm with Beth. It was so obvious what he was doing."

"Which was?"

"He wanted to do her," Annicka said. "It was like he made up his mind as soon as he heard about you. He was interested, you know. It made her something different. And you know what? Parker can be really charming when he wants to be. Believe me, I know."

Dooley had to think about that for a moment.

"He wanted to be with her because of me?"

"It was a kick, you know? You're supposedly this dangerous guy with a major rep, and he does your girl. Yeah, that was Parker."

Son of a bitch.

"What do you think happened?" Dooley said. "After they

went upstairs together, I mean?"

"What do I think? Or what do I *know*?" she said.

Dooley was confused. "Is there a difference? Because the last time I talked to you, you said they were holding hands when they went upstairs together. You said she looked upset the next day and that was because Parker was ignoring her."

"I know what I said." She pulled another cigarette from the pack in her bag. "My mother died last year. She was sick for a long time. She went through chemo three times." Her lower lip trembled just a little. Then she jutted out her chin and plunged on. "She used to be a teacher. She was very big on school. She always told me that I could do anything I wanted to. My parents did okay—my dad's an engineer and my mom taught up until she got too sick. But they're not like Parker's parents. Or Rachel's. Or Monique's. They gave up stuff to pay my tuition. My mom would have been crushed if I'd got expelled."

She looked down at the ground and fiddled with the cigarette in her hand. Then she looked up at Dooley again.

"I used to hang out with those girls—Rachel and Monique and Ellie. I thought it was a big deal. I'd go with them to their houses and I'd think, one day I want to live in a place like this and have a swimming pool and a closet jammed full of clothes, just like they do. I wanted everything they had. I wanted to be just like them. I wanted to go to all the same parties and meet all the same guys, rich guys, you know. That's how I met Parker. I was as bowled over by him as everyone else. I thought he was sweet and cool and witty. I thought anyone who got put down by him deserved to get put down. I laughed at all the dumb names he gave people behind their backs, like Silks and Casper—"

Casper? He had mentioned that name to Dooley.

"Who's Casper?"

"Nevin."

"Why Casper?"

"It's some kind of joke. You know, Casper, the friendly ghost, a ghost who doesn't scare anyone. Or a guy who's invisible."

Dooley didn't get it.

"I said it was dumb. Anyway, I liked Parker, but I didn't want to sleep with him. I—I'm not into that.

Dooley took in the piercings, the dyed black hair, the all-black Goth clothes. He couldn't believe that she had looked like that when she'd been hanging around with Rachel and Monique.

"He forced me." She looked Dooley straight in the eyes as if daring him to contradict her. "He took me hiking, just the two of us. I was so flattered—Parker Albright wanted to spend some alone time with me. Except we never got out of the car. He drove me up north of the city, pulled off onto this deserted country road, pinned me down and, basically, ripped my clothes off. You should have seen the look on his face. He really got off on it. He said if I did what he wanted, he'd wear a condom. Otherwise ..." Jesus. "He meant it, too. He said if I struggled and made him hurt me, I'd be sorry." The bitterness in her voice was fresh and raw. "If I *made* him hurt me. What an asshole."

Everything went black at the periphery of Dooley's vision. He remembered what Beth had said: *He scared me.*

"He was fucked up," Annicka said. "And he was strong. He scared the shit out of me. I told myself it was no big deal. If I did what he said, it would be over in, like, two minutes and I could get out of there, I could go home. But it wasn't over in two minutes. He just kept going and going. I thought maybe he'd taken Viagra or something. He was like the Energizer fucking bunny."

Dooley thought of him threatening Beth. Scaring her. And then being on her like that, for a long time, with her praying, like Annicka had, that it would just end. He wanted to kill Parker Albright all over again.

"When it was over, he told me to keep my mouth shut. He said if I made any trouble for him, he would make worse trouble for me. He said he'd tell—" She broke off abruptly. "He had a million ways to get to people. He knew stuff. A lot of stuff. He could have got me expelled from school if he wanted to." Her eyes shifted down to the ground again. What do you know? Tough little Annicka had a lot of secrets. "I—I did something I shouldn't have. I got involved with someone for a while and I kinda let things slide. So I paid someone to write a couple of papers for me. Parker knew about it. He knew who'd done it. He must have something on that person, too, because he said he had all the proof he needed to expose me. And at my school, they nail you for cheating, that's it, you're out. By then my mom was ... she was really sick. There was no way I was going to break her heart over some stupid move I'd made with an asshole like Parker Albright."

"So Beth ..."

"Don't get me wrong. A lot of girls went with Parker willingly. They'd do anything for him." She paused. "But if Beth says she was forced, then I believe her."

"So why didn't you say so to the cops?" What he meant was, now that her mother was dead.

Her eyes remained focused on the ground for a few moments. Then she drew in a deep breath and looked up, defiance in her eyes.

"If I tell you—"

"It'll stay between you and me," Dooley said. "I won't breathe a word to anyone without your say-so."

She studied him for a long moment.

"Rachel and Monique gave Beth a hard time in the cafeteria one time," she said. "Monique knew a lot about you, and she didn't hold back. Everyone was listening."

Well, it wasn't the first time something like that had happened.

"Beth just sat there. She didn't look embarrassed or anything like that. She sat there and listened and when Monique had finished, she said that you were the purest person she ever met."

"Purest?" What did that mean?

"That's what she said. I thought she was out of her mind. I thought, how could someone who'd done what you'd done be pure? But you know what? I kind of get it now. You're a pretty straight-ahead guy." Dooley wondered what his uncle would say about that. "Monique and Rachel and the rest of them, when they tell you they'll keep something to themselves, you don't believe it. Not after the first time they say it, anyway."

Dooley wasn't sure he was following.

"Parker told me what to say to everyone. He said that if it came to it, it's what I should tell the cops, too." She shook her head. "I don't think he believed it would come to that, though. I mean, Beth was thrilled when Ellie got her switched to Parker's team. Then she was around Parker all week, being nice to him and all, mostly because she was grateful to him. But people could read a lot more into that, you know?"

He did. He'd read more into it.

"He said if I didn't ..." She drew herself up tall, proud. "He said he would out me."

It took Dooley a few beats to understand.

"I keep telling myself I don't care," she said. "I tell myself I shouldn't care. The people who matter, the ones who care about me, they know. But my dad ..."

Oh.

"I don't think he's spoken more than two words to me since my mom died. He has this look in his eyes, like it takes everything he's got to get out of bed in the morning and drag himself to the office. And I know the only reason he's doing it is that he thinks it's what my mother would have wanted. He wants me to get through school. He wants me to graduate and go to university. He wants me to be just like my mother, only I'm not. But how am I going to tell him that? Everything with him is about her. How am I supposed to let Parker screw it all up by telling my dad that I'm nothing at all like what he thinks?"

"You could talk to him," Dooley said. "*You* could tell him."

She gave a little laugh filled with anger and bitterness.

"You don't know my dad. Besides, there's someone else involved and sh—that person doesn't want anyone to know. It's no one's business."

Dooley supposed that was true.

"It just seemed easier, you know? I mean, I got through it. I felt pretty bad when I heard Beth was in the hospital. And then I heard what happened to Parker ... I kind of wished I'd done it myself."

So did Dooley.

"You can tell the cops now, Annicka. You have to tell them."

She shook her head.

"If you don't, I will."

"I'll deny it."

"Parker's dead."

"But my dad isn't. I boxed myself in. I admit it. Suppose I tell him what Parker did to me? Suppose I tell him that I lied to the police because of it? What if Parker told someone else about me? Or what if someone else who knows decides to get even with me? Then what? What's my dad going to think of me then? Besides, if I tell the cops, it'll only make things worse for Beth. They're going to want to get her for first degree because, believe me, when a guy does that to you, sometimes all you can think about is different ways you'd like to see him die."

"You think that's what Beth did?"

"She said she killed him, didn't she? She has way more guts than I do. The guy totally deserved it. But she's a good person. She killed him and then she couldn't live with herself. That's why she ended up in the hospital, isn't it? She's a decent person that something indecent happened to. She did what I wanted to do, even though she knew it was wrong, and then she decided to punish herself for it."

Dooley stared at her. She looked like a freak, but there was a lot going on under the blackness, the tattoos, and the piercings.

"You were at Parker's party the night he died. How come?"

"I was invited."

"By Parker?" The guy must have been even more fucked up than Annicka had described.

"By someone else." There was something in her voice that made Dooley look at her again. He thought back to the party. He'd seen Annicka. He'd seen the warm greeting Parker's sister had given her. He decided to let it lie.

"Did you see Beth there that night?"

She shook her head.

"Someone I talked to said she saw Parker leave the party with some champagne and a girl with long dark hair." Just like Beth's.

"That must have been Pam," Annicka said.

"Pam?"

"She's new at our school. She's drop-dead gorgeous. Parker couldn't keep his eyes off her. Deecee—Parker's sister—said that Parker really liked her. And you know what? I think he really did. But her parents wouldn't let her go out with him. They're from India, really traditional. Her real name is Parmjit, but she calls herself Pam, you know, to fit in. Her parents don't want her dating a white boy; they don't care how loaded his parents are. They don't want her dating at all. She had to sneak out of the house and tell her parents all kinds of lies to see Parker. Even then, she was always nervous the whole time she was with him."

"Did you see her at the party?"

"No. But if she'd come, Parker would have snuck her in. She has this brother whose main job seems to be to keep tabs on her when her parents can't."

Dooley remembered a guy he'd seen on the street that night, a guy with dark hair and brown skin who seemed to be looking for something—or someone. The brother, maybe, trying to locate his MIA sister.

"Do you know how I can get hold of this Pam?"

"Honestly, I don't. She wasn't allowed to go on that school trip. She's not allowed to go to parties or anything like that. Her parents send her brother to pick her up after school every day and take her home. And any guy who calls her house and asks for her gets the third degree before being told she can't come to the phone."

"So how did she and Parker even meet?"

"I heard it was at the food bank, during the Easter food drive."

"How did Parker get in touch with her?"

"When they saw each other, they always arranged their next get-together. Pam's parents check her cell phone to see who she's been talking to or texting."

"You have her cell number?"

Annicka shook her head.

"Do you know who does?"

"Sorry."

There had to be a way. There just had to be.

"Do you know where she lives?"

Another shake of the head.

"What about the guy who showed up, Brad?"

"What about him?"

"He seemed pretty pissed off with Parker."

"He was. He was going with a girl who dumped him for Parker. Then Parker dumped her."

"You think he could have done it?"

"Killed Parker, you mean?"

Dooley nodded.

"I heard the cops talked to him. I heard they talked to Ashley, too."

"Ashley?"

"Yet another one of Parker's fuckees. She was at the party, too. She was like a freak, the way she just stood there and stared at him."

"She's a skinny girl?"

"You saw her?"

"Yeah." He wondered how much they had hated Parker. He wondered about their alibis, too.

FIFTEEN

Cassie had Parmjit's home phone number, but not her cell. She told Dooley the same thing Annicka had.

"There's no way you're going to get through to her. Her parents are really strict. That's why they sent her to a girls' school. Her brother—"

"I know," Dooley said. "But they have to let her out *some-time.*" Didn't they?

"I've seen her at the mall a couple of times, but she's usually with her mother or her brother."

"What about hanging out with girlfriends?"

"Her girlfriends are all her cousins. She doesn't socialize outside of school with anyone except her family."

And Parker. She'd found a way to socialize with Parker.

"So you're telling me there's no way I can get her alone long enough to talk to her?"

"Talk to her about what?"

He hesitated.

"I don't even know you," Cassie said, annoyed. "But I've been helping you out. And you don't want to tell me what's going on?"

"It's about Beth—and what happened to Parker. I think Pam might know something."

There was a long silence on the other end of the line.

"She trains with me."

217

"She does?"

"She hates being cooped up all the time. She's really independent. She told me she was excited when her parents told her they were going to move here. She thought her life was going to change. But so far it hasn't. Her father is super-strict. He has traditional ideas about women. So does her brother. Either he or Pam's dad take her everywhere. It drives her crazy. She said it took her forever to convince her parents to let her try out for gymnastics. She used to do it back home. And she's good. Amazingly graceful. You should see her. She really puts herself into it. That's one of the reasons we get along. She doesn't fool around. She wants to succeed. I think she thinks maybe it could be her ticket out."

"That's how you got your scholarship, huh? Gymnastics." Dooley said.

There was another long pause.

"It's a good school. It'll get me into a good university. Maybe some people care how I get there, but I don't. Once I'm out of there, those people are out of my life." She didn't seem at all embarrassed. She was matter-of-fact, and that reminded him of Beth.

"Where do you train?"

"At the athletic center. Her brother is always there watching her. But she has to hit the change room before and after practice, and there are usually a lot of people around, so ..."

He was getting the picture.

"When's your next training session?"

"Day after tomorrow. Five PM."

◆ ◆ ◆

Dooley's uncle got home a little after Dooley, which is to say, he was late. He had a couple of bags from the grocery store with him. Inside were a barbecued chicken, a side of potatoes, and another side of salad. Take-out food. His uncle never brought home take-out food.

He set out everything, and they sat down to eat. Only when Dooley got up to clear away the plates did his uncle finally speak.

He said, "You can see her tomorrow after school."

See her?

"Beth?"

His uncle nodded.

"You spoke to her mother?"

Another nod.

"She didn't give me an argument. She just said yes," his uncle said. "She didn't apologize for the other night, though."

Dooley wouldn't have expected her to.

"She didn't sound surprised, either. It was as if she'd been waiting for the call." Dooley's uncle looked directly at him for the first time since he'd walked through the door. "Randall might have talked to her, Ryan. He might have told her that if you wanted to talk to Beth, she should go along with it."

Dooley was alarmed but tried not to show it.

"Do you think they're going to listen in on what I say to her?"

His uncle didn't ask him why he would worry about that. He just said, "No. They can't. But they could ask you about it afterwards. Or her."

Dooley decided not to worry about that.

◆ ◆ ◆

Dooley was surprised by the wave of emotion that struck him

when he walked through the main door of the juvenile detention facility with his uncle. He had spent time in the same place.
It had been his home for longer than he liked to remember. It
was hard to imagine Beth in there.

He and his uncle had to sign in. His uncle took a seat in
the reception area. Dooley was directed to the room where his
uncle used to show up once a week. He sat down and waited. A
few minutes later, someone opened a different door and Beth
appeared. She was so thin, so pale. But she smiled when she saw
him, and his heart felt as if it were shattering in his chest and
each jagged shard was embedding itself into his flesh, ripping
him, tearing him, filling him with screaming pain.

He stood up and automatically opened his arms to her. The
guard at the door stepped forward, shaking his head, motioning
to him to sit again. He dropped back onto the hard chair.

Beth sat across from him.

"How are you?" she said.

She was the one who'd been in the hospital. She had been
arrested. Now she was in here. And she was asking him how *he*
was?

"I'm good."

"My mother said your uncle called. He said you wanted to
see me, and she said yes."

"That took me by surprise," Dooley said—a lie, but an insig-
nificant one.

She smiled again, a sad smile this time.

"She's not what you think, Dooley. She stuck up for me.
When Nevin's dad came over with Parker's dad, she stood up
for me."

"Parker's dad came to your place with Nevin's dad? When?"

"After my mom talked to Nevin's dad that first time. They both came over and Nevin's dad told her it would be best for me to drop the charges against Parker. You know what my mom said? She said, 'Best for whom?' I heard them talking. Parker's dad was all understanding and smooth. He said that he believed his son implicitly. He said there was a witness who saw me go up to his room willingly. And Nevin's dad jumped right in and went through all the facts—the witness, the fact that I didn't say anything to anyone for days, I didn't even tell my mother, and by then there was no physical evidence. All that. And then what Parker had said. He said the whole trial would be expensive and that it would be difficult for me." Her eyes were on him the whole time, just like Dooley's were on her. He couldn't get enough of her.

"Tell me why I'm not surprised," Dooley said. "Nevin's dad sounds a lot like Nevin—and vice versa."

"No," Beth said, shaking her head. "Nevin never brought up what happened. He never asked me about it and I never told him. It was hard enough telling you about it, and the cops were worse. They wanted to know all the details. They wanted to know exactly what he did. I had to tell them stuff I didn't even tell you." She looked up at him, her eyes wide and teary. "It's not that I didn't want to tell you—that I don't want to tell you. I didn't want to tell anyone. It's like, I'm afraid if I keep talking about it, it'll burn itself into my brain and I'll never be able to forget it. So I'm glad he didn't ask me. And I don't think Nevin's dad really wanted to get involved, either. I think he was doing it because Parker's dad asked him to or maybe pressured him to. My mom told me afterwards that Nevin's dad looked kind of embarrassed when he was trying to convince her that I should withdraw the charges against Parker."

"Yeah, but he did it anyway, right?"

She nodded. "And my mom stuck by me. She told them she believed me. She didn't question a single thing I said."

For some reason that he couldn't put his finger on, Dooley had trouble imagining that. When he'd thought about it, which had only been for an instant, he had pictured her mother being annoyed by the whole mess. He'd imagined her worrying that it would upset her relations with people like Nevin's parents.

"Beth, what were you doing in the ravine that night?"

She bowed her head, but only for a moment.

"I wanted to talk to Parker. I wanted to tell him that I wasn't going to back down and that there was nothing he could do about it. But when I tried to go to his house ..." She bit her lip. "I don't know. I just froze up. I couldn't make myself go in there, not when I knew what everyone had been saying about me. I know I shouldn't have cared, but ... Everyone believed him, Dooley. No one believed me. I thought even you didn't believe me. Until I saw you."

There it was again, those words—*I saw you*. He felt himself tremble all over when he asked the next question. She'd seen him. But she said the words so casually, as if what she'd seen was nothing special. His mouth was dry when he finally asked her.

"What exactly did you see, Beth?"

She looked around the room. Apart from a middle-aged woman talking in one corner to a guy who looked younger than Dooley, they were alone.

"You know," she said.

"I need you to tell me, Beth. I need you to tell me what you saw."

She glanced around again.

"It's okay." Dooley reached across the table and touched her hand. A jolt ran up his arm. That one touch, his hand lying lightly on tops of hers, sent the memory of a thousand other touches cascading through his mind. Her arms around his waist. The feel of her breasts, muffled by a sweater, a sweatshirt, a jacket, whatever she had on, pressing against his chest, insisting on their presence even through his T-shirt, his sweater, his sweatshirt, his jacket. The angle of her hip, naked beneath the flimsy crispness of a white sheet. Her lips, always soft, always full and lush, pressing against his.

The guard at the door zeroed in on Dooley's hand and started toward him.

Dooley slid his hand into his lap again.

"Sorry," he said to the guard, who stopped and watched for another few seconds before returning to his post.

It took her a moment to begin, and then the words came out slowly, fitfully. She refused to look at him, and he didn't force her. It was important that he heard everything she had to say, and if that was the way the story had to come out, so be it.

"I told myself I should just go home," she said in a whispery voice. "But I couldn't make myself do that, either. Out there on the street, looking at his house, I heard people laughing. I guess I knew it was because it was a party. People have a good time at parties. At least, that's the way it's supposed to be."

She fell silent. Dooley imagined that she was thinking about the last party she had attended.

She peeked up at him, her head still bowed.

"I'm not crazy," she said. "I'm not."

He would have given anything to be able to touch her again. "You're not crazy."

"But when I think about it, it feels like I was crazy. I was standing there on the street, and I heard all that laughing, and all I could think was that they were laughing at me. Everyone was laughing at stupid little Beth for being dumb enough to believe Parker, for going up to his room with him. And Parker was laughing louder than anyone. I kept seeing his face. Even with my eyes closed, I could see it."

She looked down again, and Dooley saw her chest heaving. Of all the places to be having this conversation. Of all the times. He should have held onto her that time in the coffee shop. He should have put his arm around her shoulder and taken her someplace private. He should have held her then, for as long as it took, and listened to every word she had to say.

"I tried to leave, but I ended up in the ravine behind Parker's house."

Here it was now—he was going to have to face it.

"I don't remember thinking that's where I wanted to go. I don't even remember going down there. But there I was, in the ravine, looking up at the back of Parker's property, still hearing all that laughing. I wished I could do something, you know? I wished ..." Her hands knotted together on the tabletop. Yeah, Dooley knew. He knew all too well. "And then I saw you." She raised her head now. Her eyes were filled with tears. "You were wearing a blue shirt." Dooley frowned. This wasn't going where he thought it would go, and she was speaking so fondly of him, almost reverentially. "I remember thinking about the last time I'd seen you in blue. Blue brings out your eyes." He remembered her telling him that. Dooley favored black. He used to like it because it didn't show up the dirt like other colors. Then he liked it for the way it made him feel—dangerous—and how it matched everything he felt. Now he was just used to it.

"I saw you shove him," she said. "Then you were fighting. And I—" Her head ducked down again. "I was glad. I even ... I wanted you to ..."

She couldn't say it. Jesus, didn't Randall see what kind of person she was? She couldn't even say it.

"Then I saw you pick up a rock. I saw ..." Her head was still bowed. She raised a hand and wiped away a tear. "I saw it all. I saw him fall. I saw where the rock landed. I ... I went to where he was lying." She looked at him, tears streaming down her cheeks now. "I saw him. His eyes were open. It was like he was looking straight at me."

He sat there helplessly, watching her cry, listening to the softness of the sobs she worked at stifling. No wonder she'd sounded so convincing to Randall. His uncle had said she'd given the cops the how and all the details, and what she had said obviously jibed with whatever they had found at the crime scene. Randall wouldn't have bought her confession, otherwise. He wouldn't have arrested her. Plus she had a motive, a damned good one. And some solid citizen—he'd heard on the news that the guy was a cardiac surgeon—had seen her near the scene. Put it all together, especially her telling the how of it, and it seemed like she'd given the cops a slam-dunk, because the only way she could know what she knew was if she'd done the deed, right?

Wrong.

There was another way.

She could have witnessed it. She could have seen it all and decided to take it all on herself.

After Dooley had left Randall, he'd thought about calling him and telling him to talk to Beth again, ask her more questions, grill her if he had to, because he was sure that if Randall asked enough questions he'd find the hole in Beth's story, the one that would make him doubt her confession, doubt that she'd had anything to do with it. But now he wasn't sure that was such a good idea, not after what Beth had just said. Not with Randall's agenda. He had it in his mind that Beth couldn't have pulled it off all by herself. She didn't have the physical strength. He thought Dooley must have been in on it with her. That explained his latest round of questions. And Randall could be smart with his questions. What if he tripped Beth up? What if she let something slip, even though she'd promised not to? What if she said something that didn't add up in Randall's mind? What if ...

He waited.

Eventually the tears subsided.

"Beth?"

She ventured a glance.

"Beth, why didn't you say anything?"

She looked blankly at him.

"Why didn't you make yourself known?"

"I couldn't take my eyes off him. I wanted to, but I couldn't. When I finally looked up again, you were gone."

When she'd finally looked up again.

"Dooley?"

He looked across the table and waited.

"I was glad." She sounded hesitant, as if the words were being dragged out of her on pain of death. "I was glad." As if she couldn't believe she would think such a thing, let alone say it out loud. "And then ..." Her voice broke. She wiped away a few more tears. "I was so ashamed of myself."

"Beth ..." He wanted to tell her she shouldn't have confessed to something she hadn't done. He wanted to tell her to come clean, to tell Randall everything. But if she did that, if she told him everything she'd seen and somehow managed to convince Randall that she'd had nothing to do with it, Randall would come after Dooley, and then what? He wasn't ready for that. He wasn't sure he would ever be ready. "What happened wasn't your fault. None of it was. What he did to you, he did it to other girls."

"I was glad he was dead."

"You were in shock after everything that happened, after what you saw."

"I was glad you did it, Dooley."

Shame swallowed him every time she said that. There was no way could he tell her to talk to Randall again. Not now. Not when she was so sure about what she had seen.

"Everything's going to be okay, Beth. I promise you." He wasn't going to let her take the fall for this—no matter what. "Nothing's going to happen to you."

"Nothing's going to happen to *you*, Dooley. When Warren told me the police had taken you in for questioning—"

"Warren?"

"I asked him how you were, and he said he'd seen the cops take you in. I knew I had to do something, Dooley. After what you did for me, because I was so stupid ..." She started to reach for his hand. He had to tell her it wasn't allowed. "I won't let anything happen to you, Dooley. I promise."

The guard at the door cleared his throat and looked pointedly at Dooley.

"I have to go," he said. He didn't want to take his eyes off her. How could he possibly make himself get up and leave when she had to stay? "I'll be back, okay? I'll be back to see you." He started to get up, then sank down again. "Beth, you're not going to do anything crazy, right? You're not going to try to hurt yourself." Telling her, not asking her. "It's going to be okay."

She nodded. "Okay."

Dooley's uncle had been nursing some residual pissed-off-ness when he'd pulled up in front of Dooley's school that afternoon to take him to see Beth. But by the time Dooley pushed through the door into the reception area after seeing Beth, his face had softened. His voice, too.

"How is she?" he asked Dooley.

I'm so ashamed.

"Okay, I guess. A little scared. A little nervous."

"She's a good person," his uncle said with surprising conviction. Sure, Dooley knew that his uncle liked Beth—a lot. But she was a confessed murderer. "She might get lucky on sentencing. A smart lawyer could play up extenuating circumstances."

Dooley wanted to tell him: She didn't do it. It wasn't her. But then he thought about the conversation that would follow: How do you know? Did she tell you that? If she didn't do it, why did she say she did? And Dooley would find himself lying to his uncle—again.

"Let's get out of here," he said instead. He started for the door.

His uncle grabbed him by the arm. "We have to sign out."

As Dooley scrawled his signature on Beth's visitor log for the second time, he scanned the rest of the names. There were hardly any: just her mother and Detective Randall, and, now, Dooley.

◆ SIXTEEN ◆

Dooley pictured it happening this way: his uncle, sitting in his cramped little office at the back of the first of two dry-cleaning stores he owned, his watch off his wrist and propped up in front of him like a little clock, staring at the minute hand and then the second hand until he calculated that Dooley had had enough time after the final bell to go to his locker, fill his backpack with homework, and make his way down the stairs and out the front door of the school to the sidewalk. Then, at the precise moment when he calculated—correctly, it turned out—that Dooley's foot had hit the sidewalk, he pressed the speed dial number for Dooley's cell phone.

Dooley groaned when he read the display. What now?

"Get over here right now," that's what.

"Why?" Dooley said.

A gusty, irritated sigh blew into his ear.

"Randall called."

Shit.

"What did he want?"

"He wants you."

That didn't sound good.

"Did he say why?"

"He said he wants you to go downtown and talk to him, so I can only assume he has more questions for you. I put in a call to

Annette. She's tied up in court. We're going in first thing in the morning. Randall's okay with that. But we need to talk, Ryan. Now."

Double shit.

"I have some stuff I have to do. Can we talk when you get home?"

There was another long pause.

"Do you have any idea how serious this is?" his uncle said at last. "He's a Homicide detective. He was at the house a couple of days ago with a search warrant. He took some of your clothes. And now he wants to talk to you—again. That doesn't tell you something?"

What it told Dooley was that Randall was still on him as a possible second suspect, but that right now he didn't have enough to arrest him. But he didn't say that to his uncle. He might jump to the wrong conclusion.

"I know it's serious," Dooley said. "But there's this stuff I have to do. I'll be home at supper. We can talk all you want. I promise."

He hit the END button, knowing, even as he did it, that he would regret it. His uncle had probably blown a gasket once he realized that Dooley had hung up on him.

He checked his watch. He didn't have to be at the athletic center until five o'clock. That gave him a little time. He headed down to the public park.

◆ ◆ ◆

The baseball diamond was swarming with little kids and parents. Dooley scanned the adult faces, but didn't see the one he was looking for. He loped down the hill to the diamond and approached one of the moms. She was standing alone behind the backstop.

"Excuse me," he said. "Do you know when Mr. Ralston will be here?"

She shook her head and opened her mouth to answer, but a man in a windbreaker beat her to it.

"He hasn't been around in over a week," he said. "Hasn't bothered to let anyone know, either. I left him some messages, but he didn't get back to me."

Dooley had a pretty good idea why.

"I heard he was coaching here," Dooley said to the man. "He used to coach me. I thought it would be nice to catch up with him."

"Yeah, well, good luck." The man turned and yelled something at the kid who had just gone up to bat.

Dooley looked at the woman again.

"Do you have any idea how I could get hold of him?"

She shook her head.

Terrific.

He glanced around and wondered if he would have any luck with any of the other parents. Little League coaches probably gave out their phone numbers to parents. But how many gave out their addresses? What was the point in that?

He saw a kid standing by himself to one side of the bleachers and headed for him instead. He stood beside the kid for a while, watching the game.

"You're not playing?" Dooley said finally.

"Can't," the kid said. "I sprained my wrist, so my mom won't let me. She says I need to let it rest at least another week." He nodded at a woman sitting in the bleachers with a couple of other moms. The woman's eyes were sharp on Dooley. He could read the expression on her face: I'm watching you.

"Tough break," Dooley said. "You have a good coach?"

"He's okay." There was a distinct lack of enthusiasm in the kid's voice.

"It's Mr. Ralston, right?" Dooley said.

The kid nodded.

"He was my coach when I was in Little League."

The kid didn't react.

"He was a lot of fun," Dooley said.

"He likes to buy stuff for us," the kid said. "Pop and chips and stuff."

"Yeah. He used to do that when I was a kid, too."

"But he plays favorites."

A chill of memory ran through Dooley. "What do you mean?"

"He takes some kids out for pizza. He invites some kids over to his house."

Dooley just bet he did.

"He never invited you, huh?"

The boy shook his head. Dooley glanced up at his mother again. She was staring at him. Dooley bet she hadn't taken her eyes off him even once.

"Do you know if he lives around here?" Dooley asked the kid.

The kid shook his head again. "You have to drive to get there."

"You know where it is?"

"You know that big white apartment building across from the plaza at Victoria Park?"

"Yeah. Sure."

"Right next to it, there's this house. My mom calls it a tri-plex. He lives there, on the ground floor. He has the whole back-yard to himself. He had a sleepover one night, but that was right after I sprained my arm. My mom wouldn't let me go."

Lucky kid, Dooley thought. To the kid he said, "I hope your arm gets better soon."

The kid nodded glumly.

◆ ◆ ◆

Dooley checked his watch again. He didn't have the time to stop by Ralston's and still get to the athletic center by five. As it was, the bus got hung up in a maze of roadwork. Dooley's guts started to roil as the minutes ticked by. He sprang off the bus the minute it reached his stop, sprinted the four blocks to the athletic center, and burst through the front doors, panting with nerves and exertion. There, right in front of him, was a glass wall that looked in on one of the center's smaller gymnasiums. Inside, dozens of girls in leotards were warming up for their ses-sion. He was late.

He hung around at the window until he caught Cassie's eye. She nodded to him just before she mounted the balance beam. Jesus, she was graceful. Dooley wondered if Kate and the rest of them were anywhere near as accomplished as Cassie was. He applauded when she leapt down after what was to him a flawless performance. After a brief chat with her coach, she headed for the exit. Dooley circled around to meet her.

"The bus was slow," he offered by way of explanation. "Is she here?"

"She's the one in maroon with the black stripe," Cassie

said. "Her brother's in there. He's on the chair under the clock. He usually stays there and waits for her when she goes to the locker room after training. The locker room is down that hall." She pointed. "We finish at seven." Seven. Shit. That meant he wouldn't be home until nearly eight. His uncle would freak out. "Down that hall, just past the door for the girls' dressing room, there's another hall. It leads to an emergency exit. Meet me there. I'll make sure she's with me."

"I really appreciate this, Cassie."

Her face was expressionless.

"I have to get back." She turned and ran back into the gym. She was something else in her leotard—confident, self-assured, astonishingly poised.

Dooley went back to the window to watch. He spotted Pam, no problem. She looked tiny beside Cassie, and Cassie was, like most female gymnasts, lithe, muscular, but petite. Pam's long, thick black hair was pulled back into a ponytail. She had large brown eyes and a heart-shaped face that was pulled into tight concentration. There was no mystery about why she had caught Parker's eye.

Dooley looked to the other side of the gym. A heavyset young man was sitting on a plastic chair under the clock, just as Cassie had said. He was the same guy Dooley had seen in Parker's neighborhood the night Parker had died. He'd been looking for something—for his sister, Dooley realized. Had he caught her with Parker? Had he gone back to Parker's later to teach Parker a few things about what happened to guys who fooled around with his sister? He looked like he could go a few rounds, no sweat. He had what looked like a Blackberry in his hands. His fingers flew over the keys. He didn't look at his sister even once.

But Dooley did. She wasn't as proficient as Cassie, but she was good. And her small taut body was a pleasure to watch.

Dooley's cell phone rang at six o'clock. He checked the display. It was his uncle, calling from home. Dooley hesitated. Then he switched off the phone. If his uncle was going to explode at him, Dooley would rather he did it all at once.

At ten minutes to seven, Dooley left the window and went to wait near the emergency exit that Cassie had told him about. He wondered what Cassie was going to say to Pam to get her to make a detour away from the locker room.

At exactly one minute after seven, he heard girls' voices. A lot of girls. Then, closer, another voice, "Where are we going?"

"Just trust me, Pam," Cassie said. "It's important."

Then there they were, still in their leotards, Pam's eyes wide with surprise. She looked to Cassie for an answer.

"He's Beth's boyfriend," Cassie said.

Pam froze.

"She killed Parker. Why have you brought me here, Cassie?" Dooley read accusation and betrayal in her voice. She spun around to leave.

Dooley grabbed her arm.

Pam whirled back, alarmed but furious and full of fight.

"I'm sorry." Dooley murmured. He dropped his hand. "But I need to talk to you. Cassie's right. It's important."

Pam glowered at Cassie.

"Beth didn't do anything," Dooley said.

"But she said—"

"She didn't do it." Dooley kept his voice calm, spiking it with as much gentleness as he could manage.

"Then why did she tell the police she did?"

"It's complicated. A couple of minutes. That's all I ask."

Pam looked at Cassie again. Cassie nodded encouragement.

"Kuldip will come looking for me."

"I'll watch for him," Cassie said. "Beth is a good person, Pam. Please?"

Pam hesitated, then relented. Cassie slipped around the corner.

"What do you want from me?" Pam said.

"You were at the party at Parker's house the night he died."

She fixed him with defiant eyes.

"Says who?"

"There were dozens of kids there, Pam."

Her answer came fast—too fast.

"No one saw me."

Dooley looked evenly at her until she realized she had given herself away.

"Yeah," he said. "Someone did."

"I don't believe you. If you tell anyone I was there, I'll deny it."

"I just want you to tell me about it, that's all."

"If my brother or my parents—"

"We can keep it between you and me," he said. "If you want." A veiled threat. He hated to have to resort to it.

She looked uncertain, but she didn't walk away. Finally her shoulders sagged, robbing her posture of grace.

"What time did you get there, Pam?"

"A little before ten. I was supposed to be there earlier, but I couldn't get away. I had to wait until my parents had gone to bed and Kuldip was out. Then I snuck out of the house. I called Parker and he met me out in front of his house. He got me in—I was so sure no one saw me. There's a hedge along one of the walls.

He stayed behind it. If my parents ever found out—"

"They won't. Not from me. What happened after that?"

"Parker had some champagne." She ventured a tiny smile. "It was expensive. We snuck to the back of the yard and sat under the stars, just the two of us. We drank the champagne and we talked. I know what Beth said about him. But I don't believe it. Parker is nice. He's sweet. He kisses me so softly." Her fingers went to her cheek, as if a kiss still lingered there. "We talked, that's all."

Dooley found that hard to believe, but she looked and sounded sincere. Maybe it was all the lying and sneaking around she had to do to live the life she wanted.

"How long were you with him?"

"Not long." Her voice broke a little. "Not long at all. I heard someone coming and I got nervous. My brother saw Parker talk to me one time. The next day, Parker told me he saw Kuldip sitting in his car outside his house. I was afraid he'd found out I snuck out of the house. I was afraid he might have seen Parker sneak me onto the property. If he found me at Parker's house, he'd—"

"Kill Parker?" Dooley said. A guy could hope, after all.

"Tell my parents," Pam said. "And they'd send me back home to get married. I don't want to go back there. I don't want to marry someone my parents choose. I want to make my own decisions."

Dooley thought through everything he knew about Parker and decided that, in this case, Pam's parents had the better idea.

"So what happened?"

"I told Parker I had to go. He said he'd stay there and head off whoever it was. He told me to stick close to the hedge along the wall where there are no lights. It was dark there. He said no one would see me."

Dooley wondered if Randall had noticed the lighting—or lack of it—along the wall. He probably had. He was pretty sharp. Maybe that's why he was sold on the idea it was Beth. She didn't have to scale the ravine face to get at Parker. She could have just stuck to the shadows. He probably thought Dooley had done the same thing.

"What happened then?" Dooley said.

"I did what Parker told me. I went home."

"Do you have any idea who you heard coming? Was it your brother?"

"I don't know. I don't think so. He was sitting out in front of the house with a bunch of his friends when I got home. It looked like they'd been there for a while."

"Did they stay there?"

"It got pretty quiet, but I didn't check on them or anything."

"So he could have left," Dooley said, mostly to himself. "Did you talk to him at all that night or the next morning?"

"He came into my room late—after midnight. He burst in, you know, without knocking. I think he was checking on me."

"And?"

"And nothing. When he barged in, I woke up. But he just stood in the doorway. He didn't say anything." She thought for a moment. "He was grinning, you know, like he had some big secret."

"He didn't say anything about the party?"

"He didn't know about the party."

"Are you sure about that?" Dooley said.

"If he knew, I wouldn't be here now. I think that's why they let me compete—so they have something to take away from me if I don't do what they say. I have to do what they say all the time. Kuldip ... with sons, it's different, that's all my dad ever says." The words were clearly bitter on her tongue.

Dooley hesitated.

"Where do you live, Pam? In Parker's neighborhood?"

"No."

"Does your brother have friends in Parker's neighborhood, maybe on his street?"

"No." Her voice was sharp again. "Why are you asking that?"

"Because I saw him the night of the party. Your brother and, I think, some of his friends. They were on Parker's street."

Pam's eyes widened. She glanced over her shoulder. When she spoke again, her voice was a whisper.

"Are you sure?"

"Positive." He let it sink in. It took a moment, but then she was shaking her head.

"No," she said. "No."

"He was there," Dooley said. "What was he doing there if he didn't have any friends on the street? It's not the kind of street where you go just to hang out. For a moment there, just after I left through Parker's gate, it looked like he was going to say something to me."

She was still shaking her head.

"Maybe he was going to ask me if I'd seen you," Dooley said. "Maybe he was there because he got wind of the party. Maybe he thought you were going to be there and that's why he was hanging around there with his friends."

"No."

"Maybe that's why he burst into your room after you got home and asked you that question. He knew where you were, Pam."

"I already told you, if he'd known, I wouldn't be here to-night."

"Maybe he found a different way to deal with it." Like, elimi-nate Parker. Maybe have a bunch of friends good and ready to alibi you, too. Dooley thought back to his first encounter with Kuldip, before he knew who he was. He'd been wearing dark pants, Dooley was sure of that. And some kind of shirt. But, really, Dooley hadn't paid him much attention. Why would he?

"Do you remember what he was wearing when you saw him, Pam?"

"Why are you asking me that?"

"Do you?"

"Clothes."

"A shirt?"

"Of course, a shirt."

"Long-sleeved?"

Her eyes drilled into his. There was a lot of spunk behind that sweet face and, he bet, a lot of strength in that tiny body.

"Yes," she said finally.

"You remember the color?"

"No."

"Was it blue?"

"I just told you, I don't remember." Her tone made it clear that was the end of that particular line of questioning. Dooley shifted gears.

"Who do you think it was who interrupted you and Parker that night, Pam?"

"I don't know. I didn't look. I kept my head down and got out of there as fast as I could."

"So you don't know if it was a guy or a girl?"

She hesitated.

"It was a guy." The words came out reluctantly, as if she wished she could answer differently, as if she wanted it to be a girl—to be Beth—and not a guy, for sure not her brother, no matter how strict a keeper he was.

"Did you hear his voice?"

"No. But I heard Parker. He was angry, I think because if the person hadn't shown up, we would ..." She blushed and looked down for a moment. "I know it was a guy because Parker said, 'What the F are you doing here, man?'"

"But you didn't see who it was?"

"No."

Well, that was something—although not necessarily something he wanted her to tell the cops. Not yet, anyway.

"You didn't notice anything else, anything at all?"

She shook her head again and glanced nervously over her shoulder.

"My brother—" she began.

He nodded and she scurried back around the corner to the change room. Cassie was leaning against the wall, her arms crossed over her chest, studying him.

"You don't believe her, do you?" she said.

"Pam? Yeah, I do." Unfortunately.

"I mean Beth. She said she killed Parker, but you don't believe her."

He didn't want to get into what Beth had said to him, so he shrugged.

"You think it was Kuldip?" Cassie said.

"I wouldn't mind knowing more about him and where he was that night."

Cassie stared at him in silence for a few moments.

"He works out," she said finally. "There's a gym near his place. He's there every morning, six-thirty to seven-thirty."

He wondered how she knew that.

"There's this guy I know who hangs out with him," she said, answering the question he hadn't asked. "He's fun to talk to. We went out a couple of times. Then his parents brought over this girl from India—they're getting married in the summer."

Dooley didn't know what to say.

Cassie told him where the gym was.

"But good luck," she added. "The guy I knew, he was okay. But Kuldip? He's a first-class asshole. I'm not kidding."

◆ ◆ ◆

On his way out of the athletic center, Dooley pulled his cell phone out of his pocket. He wondered how many times his uncle had called him in the past hour. He was probably foaming at the mouth by now. But Dooley had one more stop to make before he went home.

As he rode the bus, a thousand thoughts jangled in his brain: Beth's confession, Randall's questions, what Beth had seen, what Pam had heard ... what he himself had seen and heard and done.

One thing for sure: he and Beth weren't the only people who had a hate on for Parker.

Annicka was no friend of Parker's.

Neither was Ashley. He wondered about her, about what she might have seen that night as she stood sullenly watching Parker. Had she tracked him when he'd gone to meet Pam? Had she seen them together? Had she decided on revenge?

No, it didn't fit. Beth had seen the whole thing. She said

she'd seen a guy—Dooley—not a girl. Not Ashley.

What about Brad? Mr. Wrestler, who'd shown up itching for a fight with Parker and had to be escorted off the property? He could have snuck back later. And he was built. Dooley bet he could have smashed Parker over the head with as little effort as it might take him to skip stones on a lake. It was possible. It was possible, too, from down where she was, that Beth hadn't got the best look. Well, except for the blue shirt. She'd been pretty definite about that. Brad had been wearing a white T-shirt. Dooley remembered it clearly. It was what had made him pay special attention. The T-shirt was so taut across Brad's chest that you didn't need any imagination at all to know what his pecs looked like or to be sure he had a six-pack, hell, an eight-pack.

But he could have changed. Or thrown a blue shirt over his T-shirt later that night when he snuck back into the party and made his way to the back of the yard where Parker was.

Had anyone told the cops about Brad and his grievance? Had Randall or some other cop talked to him? Had they given him a serious look? Or had Beth's confession thrown them off? Had it shut down the investigation before they considered all the possibilities? Or had the cops had tunnel vision from the get-go? It happened. It was one of the main reasons, right up there with incompetent defense attorneys and faulty eyewitness identification, that innocent people ended up doing time. And yes, Virginia, despite what a lot of cops will tell you, there actually are innocent people in prison.

So what about Brad? Where had he been later that night when Parker was killed?

And where had Kuldip been?

He bet the cops hadn't looked into that because (A) Kuldip hadn't been at the party, and (B) the cops probably didn't know that Pam had been there. But from what Dooley could see, Kuldip had as good a motive as Beth, maybe an even better one, given how his family was determined to keep a short leash on Pam. The family wanted Pam to be a good girl. They wanted her to marry someone not just approved by, but chosen by, her parents. They didn't want her hanging out with some white boy; it didn't seem to matter how wealthy his family was. Kuldip knew about Parker. He knew where Parker lived; Parker had seen him sitting out front once. Kuldip was in the neighborhood the night Parker died. Dooley was willing to bet he knew Pam had been out of the house; he probably knew exactly where she had been. He had dark hair, too, just like Dooley. Looking up from a dark ravine, Beth could have made a mistake, especially if he was turned partly away from her. But what had Kuldip been wearing that night?

And how could Dooley find out? He knew where to find him. But what were the chances he would tell Dooley anything? Maybe he should just go to Randall and spell out his theory.

But before he did that, he wanted to make sure that he was in the clear himself, in case Randall decided to follow up on his own theory and try to get Beth to come clean about her accomplice. Boy, Dooley could picture him at work: *Ryan must have gone crazy when he found out what happened. He's a hard case, that one, but you know what, Beth? I believe he loves you. I believe he'd do anything for you. Is that what happened, Beth? Did he help you?* All the time probably sitting there with Dooley's file in front of him, reading and re-reading about baseball bats and the woman in the wheelchair, thinking not only wasn't it a stretch but it was a pattern; anyone could have seen this coming a million miles away. So, job one (and he couldn't believe he had put himself in the situation where he actually had to do this): find Ralston.

He got off the bus at Victoria Park and walked south one block until he was standing in front of the new white apartment building there. Sure enough, just as the kid at the park had told him, there was a sand-colored brick triplex next to it, the place further subdivided into six apartments. Dooley read the names beside the buzzers to the left of the main door. There it was: Ralston, 1A. He pressed the corresponding buzzer.

No answer.

He pressed again.

Still nothing.

He read the other names and pressed the buzzer for the basement apartment.

"Yes?" came a tinny voice.

"Are you the super?"

"Yes."

"I'm looking for one of your tenants—Ralston, 1A."

"Just a minute."

A man in work pants and a plaid shirt appeared. He looked gruffly at Dooley as he pushed open the door.

"You a friend of his?"

"I'm looking for him," Dooley said.

"He didn't send you here?"

Send me here? Why would Dooley be asking for Ralston if Ralston had sent him here? More to the point, why would Ralston send him here?

"He skipped out of here a week ago," the man said. "The rent was covered—he paid first and last when he moved in. But he left all his stuff here. I need the place cleared if I'm going to rent it."

"He didn't leave a forwarding address?"

"Would I be talking to you if he did?"

"And you haven't heard from him?"

The man stared at him, probably wondering how a guy who obviously spoke English didn't understand when it was spoken to him.

"Did you notice a kid hanging around with him, maybe thirteen or fourteen, say, this tall?" Dooley held his hand at shoulder height.

"I'm not that kind of super," he said. "People don't pay their rent, I talk to them. Someone complains about noise or whatever, I talk to them. Otherwise, they got their privacy. It's what they pay for. It's what we all pay for." He turned to go back inside.

"Hey!" Dooley said.

The man turned, but the look on his face made it clear that he had better things to do.

"Did you notice anything about him before he left?"

"Like what?"

"I don't know. Anything different.?"

"All I know is, I heard him come in a week ago Saturday night, and a couple of days later when I saw the mail piling up in his mailbox and went to knock on his door to see if everything was okay, there was no answer. I never saw him again."

Terrific.

SEVENTEEN

Dooley's uncle flew out the front door and down the steps before Dooley had even set foot on the front walk.

"What the hell is the matter with you?" he roared, which told Dooley exactly how angry he was. Normally Dooley's uncle kept his business indoors, away from the neighbors. "You told me you'd be home for supper. That was two hours ago."

"I told you I had a few stops to make."

"Do you have any idea how serious this is?"

Jesus, that again.

Dooley glanced around. There were a couple of junior high kids a few houses down, skateboarding in the street. They stared in awe at Dooley's uncle. Old Mrs. Tanley across the street was looking at him, too.

"Let's go inside," Dooley said. "We can talk."

His uncle glanced around. He waved brusquely at Mrs. Tanley and then stomped up onto the porch and held the door for Dooley.

"Where were you?" he demanded as soon as they were both inside. "I called you. I couldn't get through."

"Did Randall call again? Is that what this is all about? Did he find something?"

"Find something?" his uncle thundered. Okay, bad question. "I thought you said he wouldn't find anything." He'd been pissed off when Dooley had said that, too. Dooley had the impression he would blow his top no matter what, so he kept his mouth shut and counted silently to ten. His uncle's breathing gradually slowed. "He wouldn't be calling you in again unless he had something he wanted to ask you about—or unless he found something. What's going on, Ryan?"

It was a question Dooley could answer honestly: "I don't know." He truly didn't, although he had a few theories. "You said you left a message with Annette. Did she call you back?"

"Half an hour ago. She's going to see what she can find out, but—" His shoulders heaved helplessly. "Is there anything I should know about this Albright kid that you haven't told me?"

"Only that what he did to Beth he did to at least one other girl that I know of," Dooley said. "And that I didn't find that out until after he was dead. And the so-called witness, the one who said she saw Beth and Parker holding hands the night he raped her, she was lying, not that that's going to help Beth. It's not about that anymore."

His uncle considered this.

"Anything else I should know?"

Dooley thought the question over. *Should know?* Not really. Not now. Would be nice to know? Well, maybe. But not until he had a little more information.

"No," he said.

"You hungry?" his uncle said.

"Yeah."

"Come on."

His uncle had made spaghetti with meat sauce with a side of garlic bread. It was sitting on the stove. Two clean plates were on the kitchen table. His uncle pulled a green salad out of the

fridge and dressed it while he reheated the rest of the food. Then
they sat down to eat. The meal passed in silence, but not an angry silence. Dooley felt the tension of anticipation, but it didn't
feel like it was directed at him. He didn't get it. If he were his
uncle, looking after some screwup of a kid, he'd be blowing a
gasket every other week. And, sure, his uncle did that sometimes. But mostly he seemed worried about what was going to
happen. Mostly he seemed to care.

Dooley was on seconds when the phone rang. His uncle answered it before Dooley could even think about getting up. After hello, he said yes and okay. That was it, until he said goodbye.
He sank back down on his chair.

"That was Annette. She's on her way over. She wants to talk
to you."

Somehow Dooley didn't take that as a good sign

◆ ◆ ◆

Annette Girondin came up the walk thirty minutes later, looking lawyerly and efficient in a navy business suit with a silk
blouse underneath and a large but feminine briefcase in her
hand. Dooley's uncle invited her in.

"Thanks," she said. "But I can't stay. I just wanted to impress
on Ryan"—she turned and looked directly at him—"that I have
it on good authority that Randall has you in his sights for the
Albright murder."

"Did you talk to him?" Dooley's uncle said.

"We had words."

"And?"

"And the only thing he told me was that if Ryan doesn't show
up tomorrow, he'll get a warrant."

Dooley's uncle didn't say a word.

Neither did Dooley.

"So you're going to be here when I come by tomorrow at nine-thirty sharp, right, Ryan?" Annette stared at him as if trying to divine the answer for herself.

"He'll be here," Dooley's uncle said.

It wasn't good enough for Annette.

"Ryan?"

"Yeah," he said. "I'll be here."

Annette looked at him for another few seconds.

"Okay, then." She nodded at his uncle and let herself out.

Dooley and his uncle stood in the front hall. Dooley wondered if Randall had said what he had because of something he'd found on the clothes he'd seized. Or was it something else? He thought back to that night. Maybe there had been someone else down in that ravine, someone he hadn't seen but who had seen him. Someone besides Beth. He knew how the cops worked, especially when they thought they were on to something. He knew Randall, too. He had Dooley as being part of it, and Dooley bet he wouldn't give up until he could make his case. He probably had other cops out there, talking to everyone who'd ever gone into the ravine—dog walkers, runners, ramblers, kids. Maybe he was out there himself, asking everyone he could find if they had been in the ravine that Saturday night and, if so, had they seen anyone. Maybe he even had a photo array with him: *Any of these people look familiar?* Once Randall had Dooley in the ravine, he had opportunity. He already had motive: revenge for what Parker had done to Beth. He had method, too. He probably even had it as Dooley's M.O.—*Nothing like a solid blow to the head to get the job done, right, Ryan?*

His uncle spoke first: "You have some kind of alibi for that night, don't you, Ryan?"

There was only one way Dooley could answer.

"No," he said.

One thing that always shook Dooley was seeing his uncle look worried. The man was a rock, after all. He was tough and solid and dished out more than he took in. So when he started to look like he was expecting the roof to cave in, Dooley thought, *Aw shit.*

"I'm going up to my room," Dooley said.

His uncle didn't try to stop him; well, except for the question he asked when Dooley was halfway up the stairs: "You *are* going to be here tomorrow morning, Ryan, aren't you?"

"Yeah."

He felt his uncle watching him climb the rest of the way. Watching and probably wondering what the chances were that he'd be knocking on the door to an empty room in twelve hours' time.

Dooley sat on his bed and thought about Beth. Had Randall been at her again? Boy, he wished he knew. If he went in tomorrow and if it turned out that Randall had spoken to her and he had something on Dooley, something that Beth had maybe let slip, Randall wouldn't likely be in a mood to hear Dooley try to finger someone else. But worse than that—far worse—Dooley wouldn't be able to see Beth again. He wouldn't be able to talk to her. Even if they didn't end up hanging the murder on him—and he wasn't altogether sure that they wouldn't; after all, shit happened—there was an excellent chance they'd get him on a lesser charge. And that would be enough to land him in a whole new round of trouble.

But he had to talk to Beth.

He had to talk to her right away, before anything else happened.

He dialed the number for the facility where she was being held and was told that a call could not be put through to her. He was told, because he asked, even though he knew better, that, no, she couldn't call him back, either. It didn't do any good to say it was an emergency.

"Are you on her approved list?" the woman on the other end of the phone said.

"No." Of course not.

"Well, then, I'm sorry."

Sure she was.

He thought of calling Beth's mother, but what were the chances that she would even talk to him again, much less arrange for him to speak to Beth?

There was only one person he could think of who could help him.

He listened at his bedroom door for a moment. His uncle was still downstairs. Dooley crept into his uncle's upstairs office, grabbed the telephone directory he kept on the bottom of one of his bookshelves, and went back to his room. He looked up the number he needed and made the call, only to be told by the man who answered, "I'm sorry, he isn't here."

"I'm a friend of his," Dooley said. "Maybe ... do you think you could give me his cell phone number?"

"You can't be much of a friend if you don't have his cell number." There was a superior finality to the man's voice.

"Could you give him my number, then?" Dooley said. He said it slowly and hoped the man was writing it down.

"And to whom should I tell him this number belongs?" the man said.

"Ryan. Tell him it's Ryan."

He waited an hour, but his phone didn't ring.

It didn't ring all night.

◆ ◆ ◆

He woke up at six the next morning and checked his cell. No messages. Goddammit.

He sat up, rolled onto his side, and swung his legs over the side of the bed. He padded over to his desk and dug through the books and papers that littered it until he found the torn sheet where he had scribbled down the numbers that Cassie had given him. He dialed one of them, praying the right person would answer and would be both able and willing to help him.

She did.

And she was. Well, sort of. She was also pissed that he'd woken her up so early.

"Anything else I can do, don't hesitate to call," she said, the dry sarcasm in her voice making her the verbal twin of Linelle.

The hardest part was sneaking out of the house. He left a note that said he'd be back as soon as he could. He said he had his cell phone with him. But he had the feeling that all of this would be small comfort to his uncle.

Twenty minutes later he was standing in front of the gym Cassie had told him about. Good news: he caught Kuldip on his way in. Not-so-good news: he had three of his buddies with him, all muscle guys, all of them breaking into scowls and tightening their formation when Dooley stepped in front of them and said, "Hey, you got a minute?"

Kuldip was shorter than Dooley but hard, with an erect posture. He met Dooley's eyes with the intense confidence of a guy who knew how to handle himself. He ran his eyes over Dooley in his jeans and beat-up sneakers.

"Get a job," he said, moving forward right at Dooley, the kind of guy who expected obstacles to get out of his way. Dooley stood his ground and wasn't surprised to see Kuldip keep on coming until their two chests were almost touching. His buddies flanked him and Dooley saw in their eyes an itchiness to get into it.

"It's about your sister Pam," Dooley said.

That took Kuldip by surprise.

"You know my sister?"

"I saw you on the street in front of Parker Albright's house," Dooley said. "You remember Parker, right?"

Kuldip said nothing. His buddies tightened their formation.

"Somebody killed Parker," Dooley said. "The cops talked to you about that?"

"Why would they?" Dooley had to hand it to him, his puzzlement was convincing. Maybe he was a good actor.

"Why wouldn't they?" Dooley put an arm around Kuldip's shoulders. "How about we have a private conversation."

Kuldip didn't resist when Dooley eased him away from his friends and walked him a few paces away from the front door of the gym.

"You were at Parker's house the night he died. You want to tell me about that?"

Kuldip's face hardened again.

"I can tell the cops you were there," Dooley said. "I can steer them to your sister."

No, Dooley decided, old Kuldip wasn't much of an actor after all. If he'd been a cartoon character, smoke would have been streaming out of his ears, he was that burned up.

"I know you know Parker. I know you know your sister was seeing him. You know what I'm saying, Kuldip? I know you went into her room late at night. She said you were grinning at her, like you had some kind of secret. You knew he was dead, didn't you, Kuldip? That's why you didn't rat her out to your parents. You knew Parker was dead and that she wouldn't be seeing him anymore."

Kuldip didn't say a word.

"Fine. Whatever," Dooley said. "Like I said, I'm sure the cops will be interested."

Kuldip stared at Dooley. Jesus, what a hard case. Dooley turned to leave.

"There was this girl," Kuldip said, his voice calm, like he didn't care whether Dooley waited to listen to what he had to say or not. "She came out of the party after you. A long time after you. Blonde girl." Dooley thought maybe it might be Ashley. "I asked her if she knew my sister."

Dooley didn't get why Kuldip was telling him that. He must have had muscle for brains. The cops could check. It would just make things look worse for Kuldip.

"I asked her if she'd seen my sister at the party. She said no."

Pam was like a ghost. She'd been there, but no one had seen her, at least, not clearly enough to identify her.

"She said Parker had disappeared from the party and that he was probably fucking some girl in the bushes at the back of the yard, overlooking the ravine." He was peering evenly at Dooley. "We didn't go on the property. But we did go down into the ravine. All of us." He nodded over his shoulder at his friends. "I wanted to see if I could see who he was with. I wanted to see if it was Parmjit." His eyes were boring into Dooley's now. "When we got there, we got a good look at him. He was lying on some rocks at the bottom of the ravine. His eyes were open, like he was looking up at the stars, only he couldn't see them, you know what I mean? He was already dead."

"Well," Dooley said, "that's *your* story."

Kuldip looked over his shoulder. "Parv," he said, nodding. One of the muscle boys trotted over to him. "Tell him what you saw when we were in the ravine, you know, when we found the dead guy." Parv looked confused. "You said you saw someone. Tell him."

Parv said something in a language Dooley didn't understand.

"Yeah," Kuldip said. "Tell him."

"My laces came undone. I stopped to tie them and this girl almost slammed into me."

"Tell him what she looked like."

"Long dark hair. Thin but not skinny. Nice-looking. Wearing jeans, a dark-colored T-shirt, and a light-colored jacket. Pink. She was running, and she looked freaked out, like something had scared her."

"Direction," Kuldip said.

"The opposite direction from us."

"What else?"

"I don't think she saw me, but I saw her real good. I seen her at your sister's school one time, too, when we went to that gymnastics thing. Your sister told me her name."

Dooley waited.

"Beth," Parv said.

"You want me to," Kuldip said, "I could make sure Parv tells the cops that, too. I bet they could check what she was wearing when she left home that night. I bet someone saw her, even if her mother didn't. There's always people who see things."

Kuldip waited a few beats, then swung away from Dooley. His buddies closed around him, and they disappeared into the gym.

◆ ◆ ◆

From the gym, he headed east to the street that ran along the southern boundary of the swank neighborhood where Parker and all his friends lived. He pulled out his cell phone and punched in the number he had been given. A groggy voice answered.

"Nevin?" Dooley said.

"Yeah?" The voice suddenly sounded a little more alert—and a lot more cautious. His eyes had probably focused. He was probably checking call display. Even so:

"It's me. Dooley."

Silence. Then: "I heard you called."

It figured he hadn't called back.

"I need a favor," Dooley said.

"A favor?" As if a switch had been flicked, Nevin's voice was now flooded with condescension. "You want *me* to do *you* a favor?"

"I want you to do Beth a favor."

That got his attention.

"What favor?"

"I need to talk to you in person, Nevin. I need you to meet me."

"Where are you?" He was back to being cautious, suspicious.

"At a pizza place at the end of your street. Tino's. You know it?"

"I know where it is." His tone suggested that he would never eat the food there, much less set foot in the place.

"I'll wait for you," Dooley said. He hit the END button. Would Nevin show up? Had Dooley given him enough reason to? He hated that it all came down to this, that everything between him and Beth depended on Nevin dragging his ass down the street.

Five minutes passed. Jesus, how long could it take? He looked out through Tino's plate-glass window. Trucks lumbered by, their heavy bodies clattering over some thick metal sheets that had been set across the road in places. A construction crew arrived and started to block off a lane in either direction. Things would get hairy when rush hour started. It was hard to believe that just north of this busy street was a peaceful enclave of lavish mansions on large estates.

Another five minutes went by. Dooley started to get antsy. Then he spotted Nevin across the street, turning his head first left and then right before jogging across to the pizza joint, where Dooley was nursing a coffee while the guy behind the counter prepped some tomato sauce.

Nevin stood in front of Dooley, his hands shoved in the pocket of what looked like a brand-new jacket.

"What do you want?"

"Have a seat." Dooley used his foot to push out the chair closest to Nevin.

Nevin hesitated a moment before sitting.

"Coffee?" Dooley said.

Nevin wrinkled up his nose.

"You know a guy named Kuldip?" Dooley said.

Nevin's eyebrows knit together in irritation.

"Should I?"

"So you don't?"

"I thought you said you wanted a favor. If it's about some guy I don't even know—"

"It's not about that."

"What is it about? You've got five minutes, and then I'm going back to bed."

Not for the first time, Dooley wondered just what it was that Beth's mother saw in Nevin. Or what Ellie saw. She had it bad for him. A little voice inside Dooley said, Kick him in the nuts. Dooley ignored it. The fact was, he needed Nevin. And when you need someone, you sometimes have to swallow a lot of shit.

"I'm going to level with you, Nevin." He kept his voice calm, even pleasant. It wasn't easy. "The cops want to see me. I have to go in and talk with them. If I do, I probably won't get out again real soon."

Suddenly Nevin looked interested.

"I can't get hold of Beth," Dooley said. "They won't let me talk to her unless I'm on her approved list, and that totally depends on her mother. But you—" He'd rather bite his tongue off and swallow it than have to be doing this. "Her mom likes you. You were able to see her in the hospital. I bet you're on her approved list. You could get through to her, right?"

"Is *that* why you dragged me out of bed? You want me to talk to Beth for you?" He started to get up, shaking his head in disgust.

"Nevin, whoa." Dooley stood up. He hated the whole set-up, hated that he had to talk to Nevin, worse, that he had to ask for his help. "I need to talk to her. As soon as possible."

"Why?"

Dooley said nothing.

"Right," Nevin said. "Drag me out of bed, ask me to do something for you, and then treat me like shit. Perfect."

"Come on. Sit down."

Nevin crossed his arms over his chest.

"I know you don't like me, Nevin. But you do care about Beth. You were right there in the hospital with her. You didn't give her a hard time about what happened." Nevin seemed to like that. A smug little smile appeared on his face. Well, Beth appreciated the way Nevin had reacted. She didn't know that he had rubbed Dooley's face in it, or the way he'd presented it—Beth had done the deed with Parker and then had been dumped—or that Nevin had delighted in conveying that to Dooley. He probably thought he could benefit from the situation. After all, he'd had no problem getting into the hospital to see Beth, to comfort her. "She said your dad seemed embarrassed when he went to see her," Dooley added. He needed that phone call and was determined to get it, no matter how much ass-licking he had to do.

"My dad went to see her?" Nevin dropped back down into his chair. "What for?"

"Reinforcement. He didn't tell you?"

"Tell me what? What are you talking about?"

"Your dad went over to Beth's with Parker's dad and tried to pressure her into dropping the charges against Parker."

"Who told you that?"

"Beth." Dooley looked at the surprise on Nevin's face. "You didn't know?"

"You're saying my father talked to Beth about what happened?"

"Your dad and Parker's dad, both," Dooley said. "They went over to her place. They talked to Beth and her mom."

"When did this supposedly happen?"

"It didn't supposedly happen, Nevin. It happened. The two of them went over there as soon as they found out Beth had pressed charges. A couple of days before Parker died. She was really hurt by that, you know, because your dad is such a good friend of her mom's. But she said he looked embarrassed, like he didn't want to be doing it." It kind of reminded Dooley of the way Nevin had looked when he'd brought drinks for Parker and his friends. Nevin and his dad were a lot more alike than Beth realized.

"Jesus Christ," Nevin said.

The guy behind the counter turned and scowled at the profanity.

"Sorry," Dooley said. "He's upset."

"She talked to *him* about what happened, but she didn't talk to me?"

"Your dad and Parker's dad showing up at her place—that's part of the reason she did what she did, you know, to end up in the hospital. First Parker—" He couldn't make himself say it. He could barely stand to think about it. "First he does what he does, and she's afraid no one will believe her if she says anything. Then, when she finally decides to do something, her friends gossip about her. A witness lies to make her look bad. Your dad shows up to pressure her. And, just like she thought, no one believes her." He thought about his own reaction and was ashamed all over again, especially here, sitting across the table from Nevin. You had to give the guy some credit. "But you stood by her. You went to see her at the hospital."

Nevin was staring down at the Formica tabletop.

"Look, Nevin—"

"I've known Parker for a long time. He's an asshole," Nevin said. "I've seen how girls go for him, and how he treats them. But never in a million years did I think he would do what he did to Beth. To hold her down like that, to say those things to her, to fucking get off on it." He slammed a fist down. The man behind the counter gave him another sharp look.

"Sorry," Dooley said again.

"You finish your coffee, you go," the man said.

Dooley nodded. "In a minute. Promise." He turned to Nevin. "I need you to give her a message, Nevin. I need you to tell her to talk to Randall, to tell him she didn't do it."

"I told her not to talk to them in the first place," Nevin said. "I don't even know what happened. One day, she was just lying there. She wouldn't talk to anyone. She wouldn't eat. She just said she wanted to die. Then the next day, I go to see her and all she can talk about is that she wants to call the police and tell them what she did. I asked her what she was talking about, but she just kept saying it was all her fault; she wanted to call the cops. Next thing I know, she's confessed to them. She's told them she killed Parker."

Dooley knew exactly what had made her say it—Warren had told her that the cops had taken Dooley away. When she heard Dooley was in trouble, she decided to help him. Jesus, what a mess.

"I need you to tell her, from me, that she has to talk to them. She has to tell them she didn't do it. It's important, Nevin. Tell her I said to tell Randall the truth. Tell him everything she saw."

"What do you mean?"

"Just tell her, Nevin. Please?" The last word costing him more than it should have under the circumstances.

"Okay," Nevin said. "But what about you? You said the cops want to talk to you. What about?"

"What do you think? Parker."

Nevin shook his head slowly.

"You're going to do the same thing she did, aren't you?" he said. "You're going to tell them you did it."

Dooley didn't feel like arguing. Besides, it was getting late. He had to get home.

"Just give her the message, okay, Nevin?"

"You two are like that Christmas story, you know that one? 'The Gift of the Magi.' It's about this couple, they love each other but they're so poor they can't afford to buy Christmas presents for each other. So she goes out and gets all her hair cut off—she sells it—so she can buy him a fancy chain for the pocket watch he's so proud of. Meanwhile, he's selling the pocket watch to buy her some combs for her hair, which he thinks is so beautiful. They're so cross-eyed in love that neither of them stops to think maybe they shouldn't waste their money on stupid gifts, maybe they should focus on getting themselves on a good footing or, if you want to be realistic about it, they shouldn't have married each other in the first place. Instead, they act just plain stupid."

Dooley knew the story. They'd had to read it one year at Christmas. The guy who had written it referred to the young couple as foolish children. Dooley had more or less agreed.

"She told the cops she killed Parker because she wanted to take the fall for you, didn't she?" He shook his head in disgust. "That's what she meant when she said it was all her fault. She meant because she got close to Parker and then he did that to her. She knew you'd go crazy. She confessed to cover for you. Jesus, and now you're doing the same thing."

Dooley stared across the table at Nevin. You never knew what he was going to say. You never knew what kind of mood he was going to be in where Dooley was involved. But he obviously didn't think that Beth had done it. He didn't believe her confession. That was good. It meant maybe he could get her to do the right thing—he could get her to take back the lie she had told the police.

"You make a big deal about caring about Beth, Nevin. This is where you get to prove it. Just tell her what I said." He got up and went over to the counter and paid for his coffee. While he waited for his change, he glanced in the mirror. Nevin was standing up, pulling on his jacket. Dooley hated to admit it, but he looked good. He wondered what would have happened between him and Beth if Dooley hadn't showed up on the scene, and what would happen between them if it turned out Dooley was out of the picture for a while. It was like Linelle said, Beth definitely had a type.

Nevin held the door for him, and they stepped out into the street. The construction crew was hard at work now, digging up a whole section of street. Traffic had picked up, too. Cars, buses, and more trucks filled the two remaining lanes. They moved briskly, too.

"So you'll talk to her?" Dooley said.

Nevin nodded before turning to wait for a gap in the traffic. Dooley wondered what was going through his head. Maybe he thought it was his shot now, that he had a real crack at getting to Beth. Maybe he couldn't wait to get to the phone and throw her a lifeline so that he could watch Dooley drown instead. He thought about the story Nevin had told—two people, two fool-ish children acting foolishly because they loved each other. It was a funny story to pick. It wasn't even a good analogy.

Or was it?

Who cared, so long as Nevin talked to Beth, so long as he convinced her.

Jesus, Beth. He wanted her out of that place. He wanted her to maybe get some help, find a therapist, like Dr. Calvin, and pull it together after what Parker had done to her. Holding her down like that, saying those things to her.

He glanced at the back of Nevin's head as it swiveled back and forth, searching for an opening in the traffic.

Holding her down like that.

Saying those things to her.

"Nevin!"

Dooley's cell phone rang. His uncle.

"Ryan, where the hell—"

Holding her down like that.

Nevin finally caught a break. He darted through an opening between a truck and an SUV.

"I'll call you right back," Dooley said into the phone. He flipped it shut and jammed it into his pocket. "Nevin!" he called. "Yo, Nevin, wait up!"

Nevin was in the blocked-off part of the street. Dooley couldn't tell if he had heard him or not.

"Hey, Nevin!"

Nevin turned. Dooley zipped out into the street in front of a Smart Car whose driver leaned angrily on the horn.

"I'm sorry about that last crack," Dooley said. "You know, about you having to prove you care about Beth. I know you do. And I know this has been hard for you, too. I saw the way Parker treated you that night, Nevin, like a gofer—making you hop around, getting him and his friends drinks when they wanted them, probably getting them food, too. Whatever they wanted. Making fun of you behind your back. He called you a ghost, did you know that?" Nevin's face turned crimson. "Like you weren't really there," Dooley continued. "I saw those kids laugh. You said it yourself, he's an asshole. You've known him forever and he's an asshole. Jesus, this whole thing must have been hard on you, too, especially when Beth asked to get transferred off your team and onto his."

Dooley could see Nevin was thinking back over the whole miserable time.

"Then you heard she went upstairs with him," Dooley said. He laid a sympathetic hand on Nevin's arm. "They were holding hands. Isn't that what Annicka told you?" She must have. It was what she'd told everyone else. She'd lied for Parker because she'd been too afraid to tell the truth. Even now that Parker was dead, she didn't want to come forward. So Nevin had heard the same thing everyone else had heard. "She wouldn't go with you, but she went with me and then she went with Parker. I bet that didn't make you feel too good, huh?"

Nevin brushed him off.

"Did she tell you what I said?" Dooley asked quietly, so quietly that Nevin had to lean in a little to hear him above the rumble of the traffic. Jesus, it was hard enough to remember, let alone say out loud, let alone say out loud to Nevin. "Did she tell you she came to talk to me? Did she tell you what I said when she told me about Parker?"

"Yeah. She told me you were pissed off," Nevin said, puffing himself up again, back on sure ground. "She told me you were mad at her for going up there with him. But *I* wasn't," he added. "I saw them together all week. I saw them leave that party together. I was there. She said you were angry, but *I* forgave her."

Dooley hung his head a little. "You didn't know the whole story, but I did," he said. "She told me what Parker did to her." Nevin was the last person he wanted to admit this to. "She told me that he forced her, and you know what I said? I said, What were you doing with him in the first place? You get what I'm saying, Nevin? You thought she went with him in the first place because she wanted him, but I knew—*I knew*—what he'd done, and the way I acted, it was like I was blaming *her*."

"You made her cry," Nevin said, an accusation.

"Yeah." It had eaten at Dooley ever since. "Yeah, I made her cry. She went with Parker, and he did that to her. She told me about it, and I got mad at her. She tried to kill herself, and who was there for her? You were, Nevin. *You* were there for her."

Nevin didn't say anything.

"You want to know why she confessed?" Dooley said.

Still nothing from Nevin, but he was leaning even closer, his whole body tense. He wanted to know. He ached to know.

"It's just like you said," Dooley said. "She did it because she loves me." He leaned on the present tense of the word, sure of it. "She knows I'm not perfect, but she also knows I would do anything for her. Anything. That's why she confessed. Because she saw me kill Parker, and that was her way of thanking me."

Nevin stared at him.

"Did she tell you that? Did she tell you she saw me?"

Nevin shook his head.

"I don't know what's going to happen," Dooley said. "I don't know what kind of time they're going to give me. It could be ten, with three served in the community. That's not so long. And it won't be so hard, not with her waiting for me."

Nevin looked like he was going to say something, but in the end, all he did was turn to go. Dooley grabbed him by the arm again, harder this time, holding him back. Nevin shook him off easily. Dooley was almost impressed with the force behind it. He had Nevin down as an inflated ego, period. The guy was a debater. He was flashy. But he was also a lot stronger than Dooley had imagined.

"How did you know what Parker did to her, Nevin?"

"What?"

"What you said—the way he held her down, what he said to her. How did you know?"

"Beth told me."

"No, she didn't. She told the cops because she had to, but that's it. She didn't even tell me that stuff."

"Well, she told me."

But she hadn't. She'd specifically told Dooley that she hadn't discussed what happened with Nevin. But Nevin knew. Dooley bet what he'd just told him would match perfectly with what Beth had told the cops.

"What did you do with the shirt, Nevin?"

"What shirt?"

"The blue shirt. The one you were wearing at Parker's party."

"I have no idea what you're talking about," Nevin said.

"You probably dumped it in your hamper for the maid to wash, right? Well, I got news for you, Nevin. They can find blood traces on anything these days, and they don't need much for a DNA match. I should know, believe me."

Nevin met Dooley's eyes.

"I believe that shirt was donated to charity," he said. "My mother does that a couple of times a year—rounds up stuff we don't wear anymore and donates it somewhere. God knows where it is now."

"Too bad there were so many people at that party, huh?" Dooley said.

Nevin looked blankly at him, but Dooley saw the brain working behind his dull eyes.

"All those people—you think there aren't at least a few of them who are going to remember what you were wearing? Hey, I'd be surprised if someone didn't take pictures. Bet you anything pictures of the whole party are up there on the Web where everyone can see them. Where the cops can see them, Nevin. You think they aren't going to wonder about that shirt after Beth tells them what she saw—the shirt that got conveniently donated to charity right after Parker was killed?"

"Are you suggesting—"

Dooley had to hand it to him. He did indignation well.

"Parker told you, didn't he?" Dooley said.

Nothing.

"What happened?" Dooley said. "Did you see him slip back there with a girl? Did you think it was Beth? Is that it? Did you go to find out?" No answer. "He was pissed off, wasn't he? He asked you what the fuck you were doing there?"

The startled look in Nevin's eyes gave him away.

"He was back there with a girl, Nevin. Not Beth, another girl. And you barged in and messed it up for him. You pissed him off, and when Parker gets pissed off, I bet he gets mean. That's when he told you, isn't it?" Dooley could picture it. "I bet he told you all the details, every last one of them. You just can't catch a break, can you? She goes with him—that's what Annicka said, right? And you're such a good guy that you forgive her. Then Parker, the asshole, he wanted to get back at you for ruining it with the other girl. And he knew the reason she wanted on his team was to get away from you. He knew how you felt about her, didn't he? So he told you what he did. He told you what really happened. Jesus, if I'd been there and he'd said that stuff to me, I would have done the same thing you did. I would have beaten his brains in, too. But you can't be Beth's hero, can you? You can't tell her what you did. You can't tell anyone. So you do the next best thing. You stick right there by her side—you're in the hospital with her every day. You're true blue. And how does she repay you? *She* says *she* did it. She confesses. You know she didn't do it, Nevin. You must have been wondering, what the fuck? Why is *she* confessing? Did you figure it out? Or did she finally tell you? Did she tell you she was doing it for me? Jesus, what a kick to the head. Is that when you cut her off?"

Nevin stared stone-faced at him.

"You were at the hospital every day. But you haven't gone to see her even once since they transferred her out," Dooley said. "Did you decide she deserved whatever happened to her, is that it? If she was stupid enough to turn herself in to save me, that was her problem, right?"

Nevin turned abruptly to cross the street. A truck horn blared. Jesus. Dooley reached out with both hands and pulled Nevin back just in time. The truck thundered by, burnishing Dooley's face with the heat of its wake.

Dooley stood there, hands dug into Nevin's shoulder, heart pounding. He spun Nevin around and read the blank look on his face.

Dooley told him, "Call your dad." He said, "At least get a lawyer." But Nevin shook his head both times. Dooley didn't get it. Did he think his dad would cut him off? Or was he just tired of it all? Had it all become too much, weighing too heavily on him? Dooley knew the feeling. You did something. You didn't think about it, you just acted or, sometimes, reacted, and by the time you got a grip on yourself, it was too late. The deed was done. All you could do was wait. You could run and wait or stay put and wait, it was all the same. You still had to contemplate what you had done, and you had to come to grips with the fact of the law. You knew the odds were against you. Sure, some people get away with murder. But even those people are looking over their shoulders. The cops don't give up. They keep chipping at it. Yeah, they might have to let it go for a while. Maybe a long while. But eventually they get back at it. And a lot of times, they figure it out. They are tenacious little fuckers. And the whole time you were waiting and wondering. Wondering what they might find. Wondering what you might have overlooked. Wondering who might have seen something, who might finally come forward. Always wondering, no matter what you were doing.

Nevin walked back across the street with him to the restaurant. He ordered a slice of pizza and a can of pop, while Dooley made a couple of calls.

"You really should call a lawyer, Nevin," Dooley said. "You don't know what they're like."

Nevin chewed on his pizza. It was as if he hadn't heard a word Dooley had said.

Randall showed up first, along with a squad car and two uniformed officers. He looked skeptical until Nevin started talking. Randall glanced at Dooley, but didn't say anything to him.

He stood up and got Nevin to stand. He told Nevin he was under arrest, cuffed him, and read him his rights. Dooley's uncle walked into the pizza place just as Nevin was being led out.

"What's going on?" he said.

◆ EIGHTEEN ◆

Dooley sat on the bench-like swing on his uncle's porch, a near-empty cup of coffee in his hands. Eight o'clock in the morning, and it was pleasantly warm. There were some flowers coming up in the strip alongside his uncle's front walk. That was something he had never got used to, his uncle down on his hands and knees, fiddling around with flowers. He commented on them, too, sometimes, when he sat out there on the porch after work.

"Zinnias are looking good this year," he'd say. To which Dooley would think, what the hell is a zinnia? Or, "I think I'm going to pull out those Shastas, put in more Echinacea." Okay, sure, whatever.

And now here was Dooley, drinking his coffee outside, looking at the shoots of flowers poking through the earth, and thinking. How does that happen, year after year? How do they know when it's time?

He'd sat out here last night with Beth. He'd gone over to her place and pressed the buzzer, and when her mother answered, he'd given his name politely, respectfully, for once not thinking what a controlling, narrow-minded, pain-in-the-ass bitch she was. And she'd answered if not respectfully, then at least not disdainfully. She'd buzzed him up. She'd stood back out of the way when Beth came to the door. She hadn't argued when Beth reached for his hand and he took it. She hadn't warned Beth that she'd better be back at a certain time, or else. It was Dooley who had spoken up on that. He'd said, "I'll bring her back before midnight." Beth's mother had nodded. She'd held Dooley's eyes for a moment. Then she'd closed the door behind them, softly, letting the door speak for her like she always did, only this time, making it say something different.

They'd walked back to his uncle's house hand in hand. His uncle had come out to say hello, but otherwise had let them be. They'd sat out on the porch, just the two of them, watching the sun go down and then sitting in the dark, Beth's hand slipped through one of his arms, her body pressed up close against his, her head half of the time on his chest. They didn't say much, but Dooley knew it was okay. He walked her home and took her upstairs. She kissed him lightly on the lips. He accepted it and didn't press for any more. And then she clung to him. She wrapped her arms around his neck and held him and made his shirt wet with her tears.

"I'll call you tomorrow," he said when he finally got her to stop crying. "Okay?"

"Okay," she said.

She went inside. He stood out in the hall for a moment. Was she going to be okay? He knew it wasn't all over yet. Was she going to get through it? She wasn't going to do anything crazy, was she? It was going to be okay, wasn't it?

He'd barely slept for thinking about that, for wanting to call her and hear her voice and know for a certainty that she was okay.

He'd finally got up and made some coffee and had come outside to watch the sun get up. He was still there when his uncle stuck his head out the door.

"You okay?" he said.

Dooley nodded.

"And Beth?"

"I think so," Dooley said. "I hope so." He swallowed down the rest of his coffee. It was cold in the cup. "There's something I have to tell you."

His uncle came all the way out onto the porch.

"There's this kid I used to know," Dooley said. "His name was Tyler Brock."

His uncle sat down next to him.

"Was?"

"He died—killed himself."

His uncle waited.

"There was this guy at this group home I was in. Jeffie was in there one time, too."

He felt his uncle tense on the bench next to him. Neither of them had mentioned Jeffie in a long time.

"This guy, his name was Ralston." He still couldn't say the name without his gut clenching. "He's the reason Tyler offed himself." He was breathing hard now, even though he was willing himself to stay calm. "He was a predator, you know? He had all this power. All he had to do was report you for something and he could make your life a living hell. He had other ways to do it, too. He came at me." It was the best way he knew to say it without actually saying it. He couldn't, even now. He just couldn't.

His uncle looked at him.

"Did he—"

"No. He tried. But no. So then he went after Tyler."

"You didn't report it?" his uncle said.

Dooley looked at him. Didn't he get it? Then his uncle nodded, a curt little gesture. Yeah. He got it.

"I knew what was happening," Dooley said. "But I didn't do anything." Not a thing except, once in a while, tell himself: Better him than me. "I guess I thought—" But he couldn't say it, not that part, anyway. "I thought, I got him off me. Tyler could do the same thing if he wanted to." Because he'd thought that, too. He didn't think it anymore, had given up that notion a long time ago. But back then, seeing what a mouse Tyler was, yeah, he'd thought that. He'd thought, if the guy wasn't such a mouse, he could get Ralston gone.

His uncle didn't say anything.

"The thing is," Dooley said after a little while, "it wasn't all me. I didn't make him back off all by myself. And Jeffie was the one that finally got rid of him."

"We're talking about Jeffrey Eccles, right?" his uncle said.

Dooley nodded.

"He told Ralston he had pictures."

"And did he?"

"I don't know. Maybe. You could never tell with Jeffie. But, yeah, I guess maybe he did, because Ralston resigned. But by then Tyler ... Tyler had done it."

He hadn't shown up for breakfast one morning, and Dooley, for some reason, had been sent up to get him. He'd checked the john first. A lot of times when a guy was late for breakfast, it was because he was on the john. But Tyler wasn't there. So Dooley went to his room and found him hanging from one of the exposed pipes that ran through the building. He was cold to the touch. Dooley had pulled his hand away and stepped back. He stood there for a few moments, not believing what he was seeing.

"I haven't thought about it in a while," he said. "Then a couple of weeks ago, I was at work and I looked out and I saw him on the street."

"Ralston," his uncle said.

"Yeah. He was carrying a duffle bag. It said Little League on it."

His uncle was staring out at the street now.

Dooley wished he hadn't looked out the window that day. He wished he'd been in the back of the store, re-shelving product. That way, maybe right this second, he'd be blissfully unaware of Ralston's presence in town.

"I wasn't going to do anything."

His uncle's eyes came back to him.

"Then I went to Parker's place that night, the night he died. I talked to him." Jesus, if you're going to tell the story, tell it right. "I was pissed at him. I wanted to let him know. I wanted—" I wanted to kill him. "I talked to him and then I left. I went down into the ravine."

"The one behind his house?"

"Yeah. I looked up there, too. And then I headed home. That's when I ran into him."

"Parker?"

"Ralston. He was walking up the ravine. He had a kid with him. He'd looked a year or two older than Tyler had been."

"Anyway, when he saw me, he told the kid to go on ahead. Then he asked me how I was." His eyes raked over Dooley: *Well, well, Ryan Dooley. How are you? How's your friend Tyler?* Like he didn't know. "I hit him," Dooley said. "With a piece of tree branch I picked up." Swinging it like it was a Louisville Slugger.

"Jesus, Ryan."

"I hit him pretty hard," Dooley said. At the time, filled with rage and regret, he'd hit to hear the sound of the connection—bark on bone. "He was bleeding."

"That's why you came home and washed your clothes?" his uncle said. "It's probably why Randall wanted to see you. They probably found blood. They didn't have enough time for a DNA analysis—the request was probably in at the lab, though. This guy Ralston—you didn't—"

"He was on the ground when I left him," Dooley said. "He was bleeding but he was okay." Dooley knew that for a fact because Ralston had been laughing. Dooley hit him, as hard as he could, knocked him right off his feet, and the guy lay there laughing at him. Dooley knew why, too. Because he'd just been rash enough and dumb enough to hand his life over to Ralston. All the guy had to do was put in a call, and Dooley would be scooped up off the streets. "I thought he was going to turn me in."

"He still might," Dooley's uncle said.

"I don't think so," Dooley said. "He skipped out on his landlord. And the Little League team he was coaching."

They sat in silence for another few moments. Then his uncle said, "What do you want to do about it?"

What did he *want* to do? He wanted to forget it, that's what. But that wasn't really the question.

"I was thinking maybe I should talk to Randall," he said.

"You sure?"

He'd thought about it from the time he left Beth's place last night.

"Yeah, I'm sure."

"You want me to come with you?"

"Yeah." In fact, he'd been hoping his uncle would offer.

◆ ◆ ◆

Annette Girondin went with them because Dooley's uncle thought it would be smart for them to have a lawyer handy. The three of them, Dooley, his uncle, and Annette, sat on one side of the table, and Randall sat on the other. Dooley told Randall what he had already told his uncle. Randall didn't interrupt and remained silent for a few moments after Dooley had finished. Then he let out a long sigh, leaned back in his chair, and stared across the table at Dooley. Finally he pulled out a notebook and a pen.

"You have the address where Ralston lives?"

Dooley gave it to him. "But he's not there anymore. He's gone."

Randall wrote down the address anyway.

"And this kid he was allegedly with?" he said.

"I didn't get a good look at him. Ralston sent him up ahead."

"Would you recognize him again if you saw him?"

"Maybe. I doubt it."

"How old was he? You think he was a Little Leaguer?"

"Not the ones he was coaching. They're all ten or eleven. This kid was a lot bigger. He must have been fourteen or fifteen, something like that."

Randall stood up.

"Give me a few minutes," he said.

He left the room.

Dooley's uncle glanced at Annette Girondin. Annette's face was unreadable. Dooley stared at the tabletop. He'd told his uncle. He'd told Annette. Now he'd told Randall. Sooner or later he was going to have to tell Beth. Jesus, what would she think? That kind of stuff was supposed to be behind him now. He was supposed to be a solid citizen. And yet, when faced with Ralston, he'd forgotten everything he'd struggled so hard to learn over the past two years, and he'd lost it. He'd reverted back to what he thought of with disgust as his true self.

He'd have to tell Beth.

It was out there now. He had to face the consequences. And one of those consequences was Beth.

Maybe he should have kept his mouth shut. What had possessed him to come clean to his uncle? What had made him think it was a good idea to come down and bare it all for Randall?

Only everything he'd supposedly learned in the past two years.

His only hope: she would come to visit him.

Or—talk about clutching at straws—maybe they would take his recent past into consideration. Maybe they wouldn't lock him up. Maybe they'd put him under house arrest. He could deal with that. Or—if you're going to dream, dream big—maybe just a stricter supervision order.

It seemed like forever before the door opened and a somber-faced Randall walked back into the room. He dropped down onto the chair directly opposite Dooley.

"You're a piece of work, Ryan, I'll give you that," he said.

Out of the corner of his eye, Dooley saw his uncle straighten in his chair, bracing himself.

"You waltz in here and spin me some yarn about where you were the night Parker Albright was murdered—putting in batting practice on some guy's head, is that it?"

Annette glanced at Dooley.

"I go and check, and what do I find out? Nobody named Ralston has made a complaint against you."

"Yeah, but—"

"I talked to the guy last year," Randall said. "You remember?"

Dooley did. Randall had spoken to Ralston in relation to what had happened to Lorraine.

"The man does not have a high opinion of you. He made that perfectly clear. You'd think if you had done what you told me, he'd have been in here within ten minutes, pressing charges against you."

Randall looked like he always did—hard-nosed, business-like, no-nonsense, kind of like Dooley's uncle, only a decade and a half younger.

"If I were you, Ryan," he said, "I'd make a few changes in your life. The number one change I'd make would be to stop lying to the police. All it does is cause problems—for everyone. For you, for your uncle, everyone. From a police perspective, well, we don't like it when people aren't straight with us. And we sure as hell don't like it when they come in here with a bullshit story and waste our time."

Dooley's uncle shifted in his chair.

"Get out of here, Ryan," Randall said. "Stop spinning me. You got it?" He stood up.

Dooley stared at him. He looked at his uncle, whose face, like Randall's, wasn't giving anything away. But he stood up, too. Annette followed his lead. Dooley stumbled to his feet.

"Now, if you all will excuse me," Randall said brusquely, "I have real police work to do." He showed them to the door.

"Don't ask," Dooley's uncle said a few moments later when

Dooley opened his mouth to ask what the hell had just happened. "Just be grateful."

Dooley was that, for sure.

◆ ◆ ◆

When Dooley came out of school a week and a half later and saw Randall leaning against a nondescript car at the curb, he thought: Shit. The feeling of doom in the pit of his stomach intensified when Randall pushed himself off the car and came toward Dooley. He imagined that same look of smug satisfaction appeared on Randall's lips every time he was about to throw the cuffs on someone.

"Another couple of weeks and you're done here for the summer, am I right?" Randall said pleasantly. Dooley had to hand it to him—he enjoyed his work. "Step into my office a moment, Ryan," he said, gesturing toward his car.

Warren came down the steps. He stopped and watched as Dooley walked to the car with Randall. Dooley tensed a little more with every step he took.

"Get in," Randall said, opening—surprise!—the front door for him before circling around to get in behind the wheel.

Dooley glanced at Warren as he shut the car door behind him. Warren waited on the concrete walkway.

When Randall turned to Dooley, his face was somber.

"Ralston never showed up at his place to claim his stuff," he said. "Wherever he went, it looks like he went in a hurry."

Dooley waited.

"I checked out the team he was coaching. All the kids are ten and eleven, and not a single one looks like he could be mistaken for a fourteen or fifteen year old. I asked around. One of the Parks and Rec outdoor workers thinks maybe he saw Ralston with an older kid a couple of times. He described the kid as best he could. He didn't know the kid but was pretty sure he wasn't a park regular. Apart from that—" his shoulders heaved up in defeat—"maybe he'll surface again. Maybe I'm kidding myself, but I like to think that guys like that always float back into view, kind of like the crap people throw into a lake or an ocean. Sooner or later, it always washes up."

Maybe, Dooley thought. But if Ralston did come up high enough and for long enough to register on police radar, it would be because of something he had done. Something bad.

"Keep your nose clean, Ryan," Randall said. "And do me a favor—don't figure in any of my investigations ever again. You got it?"

Dooley nodded. No problem. He climbed out of the car and watched as Randall drove away. When he turned again, Warren was behind him.

"Is everything okay?" he said.

"So far, so good," Dooley said, smiling.

◆ ◆ ◆

Dooley stepped out of the elevator and, for once, bypassed Beth's door and walked to the window at the end of the hall. The building was on an elevation, and even though Beth's place was only on the tenth floor, still, it had a view of the city to the south, clear down to the water and, a little to the west, the downtown core.

Ralston was out there somewhere. Maybe not in the city. Maybe he was hundreds of miles away. Maybe thousands. Dooley wished he'd said something back when Ralston had tried for him. Or that he'd talked Tyler into saying something, maybe even gone with him to back him up. For sure, it would have stopped for Tyler. It might even have put an end to Ralston.

But he hadn't done that.

And now Ralston was out there again, trolling for another kid that no one else cared about. A kid like Tyler.

He heard the *ping* as the elevator doors opened behind him, but he didn't turn around until he heard someone say, "Ryan?"

It was Beth's mother, two plastic shopping bags hanging from each arm, a look of alarm on her face.

"Is something wrong? Isn't Beth—"

"She's fine," Dooley said. He took the shopping bags from her. "She texted me a couple of minutes ago."

Beth's mother relaxed.

"I was just ... just looking at the view."

Beth's mother unlocked and opened the apartment door.

"Hello?" she called.

"In here," came Beth's voice.

Dooley set the bags down and pulled off his boots. He picked up the bags again to carry them through to the kitchen.

Beth was where she always was when Dooley came over after school. She was in the dining room, her school books spread out around her, a laptop computer open in front of her. She'd quit going to school. It was too hard, she told him, being around all those people, knowing what they had thought. Her mother hadn't argued with her. She'd arranged for Beth to work from home for the last few weeks of school and for Beth's teachers to grade her work. Dooley smiled at her as he passed her with the bags of groceries. He set them down on the kitchen counter and then went back through to the dining room and wriggled out of his backpack.

"You're not working tonight?" Beth said.

"No. But I'm on tomorrow night and the night after that." He sat down beside her. "What are you working on?"

"English essay."

God, she was beautiful. She'd lost some weight and still looked fragile. And because she spent most of her time indoors, she was paler than usual. But all he had to do was look at her, and he could hardly breathe.

"I brought you something," he said. He dug in his backpack for the envelope he had wedged between the pages of his math book for safekeeping. He opened it and handed her the small photograph inside. He'd found himself thinking about Lorraine last night—he didn't even know why. The next thing he knew, he was thumbing through the old photo album he'd found in her apartment. Beth had never seen it. He'd paused when he came to a photograph—Lorraine, with Dooley on her lap, in one of those photo booths in the train station. He thought maybe ...

Beth frowned as she studied the photo. She glanced at him. "Is this—"

He nodded. "Age four. Doing my thing. Point a camera at me, and I made a face—it was automatic. It drove my mother—" It felt funny saying that word, even now. "It drove her crazy."

Beth looked down at it again, and a miracle happened. She laughed. It made his heart stop. It made her mother, busy putting groceries away, appear in the door to the kitchen. Her eyes went from Beth to Dooley, and she nodded.

"You were adorable," Beth said.

"I was a pain in the as—in the butt."

She ran a thumb lightly over the surface.

"Can I keep it?" she asked.

"Of course."

She set it into the corner of her computer screen.

"Are you staying for supper, Ryan?" her mother asked.

Beth looked expectantly at him.

"Sure," he said. "Thanks."

Beth pulled her chair closer to his and laid her head on his shoulder. One of her hands slipped under his arm, and he basked in her warmth. She'd had him from the very first time he'd set eyes on her. She'd had him every day since. Now he knew that, no matter what happened, no matter how much things changed, she would have him for the rest of his life.

Norah McClintock
Author Interview

Writing a mystery novel requires a very special kind of talent. Without giving up any secrets, can you tell us why you have been so attracted to this genre throughout your career as a published author?

Every since I was a kid, I have been drawn to mystery novels. When I was reading *Nancy Drew, the Hardy Boys, Brains Benton,* and mysteries involving countless other, mainly British, amateur sleuths, I always liked to imagine myself as clever, resourceful, and courageous, just like they were. I've never lost my love of mysteries and my (perhaps morbid?) fascination with crime and crime stories.

In many novels for teenagers, the stories are told in the first person, but not in the Dooley series. Why did you choose to tell his story in third person?

I'm not sure that this was an entirely conscious decision. It just seemed right. Most of the books I have written have, indeed, been in the first person, which, some would say, lends an immediacy to the story and a ready identification for the reader. But, although the

Dooley books are told in the third person, the viewpoint throughout all three books is very much Dooley's. We are in his head all of the time and see everything purely from his perspective.

Some writers of novels say they write to find out what will happen to their characters, that they don't use a plan when they start. When you're writing a mystery or crime novel, to what extent do you need to know how things will turn out before you begin?

Experience has taught me that it is wise to plan a mystery novel in advance of sitting down and beginning to write. I usually have a general idea of how it will end and, of course, I know who dunnit it and why and how, so far, they have gotten away with it. I have a plan. But it's inevitable that changes are made along the way as I get into the characters and understand the possibilities that they present.

In Canada we don't think we have a class system as is found in older, more established societies. But what Dooley is dealing with is a kind of class system, in which he's often placed at a disadvantage. Why does this aspect of his character appeal to you?

Dooley grew up very disadvantaged. His mother never had a steady job. Money was always an issue. Lack of it, and of a responsible parent, meant that Dooley never had the advantages that even middle-class kids have. When he finds himself associating with well-off kids like Rhodes and Beth, he suddenly becomes very aware that he is not at all like them. They take many things for granted and have a sense of themselves as worthy, even entitled, which is completely foreign to Dooley. His visceral reaction is that these kids don't have a grasp on what Dooley considers "the real world." He is somewhat envious of them, but resents their sense of superiority and entitlement and the way they throw him off balance and make him aware of the relative raggedness of his jeans, shoes, etc.

Dooley is a fascinating, many-layered character. He's courageous, sometimes dangerous, loyal, dogged in his determination to change his life. When you develop a character like Dooley, to what extent does he come out of your imagination, and to what extent do you model him on real people you have met?

Dooley is an imagined character based on a series of musings about a very real but very small boy who has a mother very much like Dooley's. I could not stop wondering what would happen to this boy—how would he turn out, what could he count on in life, what could he not count on? If he got into trouble—which I imagined he would at some point—what would become of him, especially if there was no responsible adult willing to go to bat for him? Or—big what if—what if such an adult were suddenly to appear? What if someone decided to give him a second chance? How would Dooley handle it? Would he recognize this as a second chance and welcome it? Would he blow it off? If he did decide to take it, what would he be up against? And so on and so on ...

What about other characters in this book?

Every character is, to one extent or another, a combination of people I know or am acquainted with, and make-believe. Dooley's uncle (whom I adore) is a tough guy with secrets of his own, but also with a strong sense of right and wrong, which he feels obliged to try to pass on to Dooley. Jeannie is a no-nonsense independent woman who seemed a perfect partner to such a man and who provides some invaluable aid and advice to Dooley along the way. Warren—well, he's the guy who seems least likely to end up as Dooley's friend, which only goes to show ... And Beth? Beth is far from perfect herself. But she's the one who, more than anyone else, inspires Dooley to become a better person.

What advice do you have for young writers?

Read. Read, read, read. Then read some more. Write. Write, write, write, and write some more. And don't listen to anyone—not that doubting little voice in your head, not friends, neighbors or relatives—who tells you it's impossible. Nothing is impossible if you want it badly enough, are prepared to work at it, and refuse to become discouraged.